PsychoActive

Transformative Horror Novellas

Ryan C. Thomas,
Anthony Trevino
Cody Goodfellow, Ed Kurtz

BOOK 16 IN CRYSTAL LAKE'S DARK TIDE SERIES

Let the world know:
#IGotMyCLPBook!

Crystal Lake Publishing
www.CrystalLakePub.com

**Follow us on
Amazon:**

WELCOME
TO ANOTHER

CRYSTAL LAKE PUBLISHING
CREATION

Love is a Monstrous Death

RYAN C. THOMAS &
ANTHONY TREVINO

"You fall in love and it completely consumes you."
—Selena Gomez

"I want to fuck you to death."
—Jill Janus, Huntress

1

Dishonorably discharged Private Theodore Treadway was working the handle of his double-sided axe—affectionately named Lucinda after one of his favorite songs—with the old polish rag he'd used to shine his boots in the army when the smell crept in from the air vents.

He stared up, wrinkling his nose, ignoring the distant party music still thumping the walls, trying to place this new stink.

Rank odors in his apartment weren't anything new. Sunshine Spires existed in a state of perpetual funk. Last time something foul had wormed its way into his dingy living space, it'd been the stench of summer-roasted corpse. After three tours in Afghanistan, he knew it well, but that hadn't been enough for their squat, power-tripping property manager, Jesus, to conduct a wellness check. It had taken several more complaints from other tenants and numerous collective threats of breaking his office door down to get his ass in motion.

They'd found Rodney Yribe melted to the old leather chair he'd dragged in from beside the dumpster. Poor bastard had choked on undercooked pork and sat there for days, fusing to the furniture, his skin gooping into the seams, becoming one with the chair. The EMTs had to cut his flesh away from the leather. He'd always made jokes about how the fabric was perfectly molded to his ass, so Theo liked to think the retired bus driver would've found a slice of humor in his posthumous situation.

Whatever was sneaking in through the ductwork now was different. It wasn't smashing his senses the way Rodney's baked-in-one-hundred-and-ten-degree-heat carcass had. It was more like the sting of lingering antiseptic, the type of smell prominent in recently cleaned public restrooms and old adult arcades where someone's actual job title was jizz mopper.

Theo's temples throbbed. The hairs of his massive, Viking-style beard felt as if they'd come alive to crawl over one another.

Maybe someone spiked the punch at the Valentine's Day party.

He wasn't sure what management's goal was hosting a get-together for the tenants, but he'd shown up anyway, thinking maybe it'd be an opportune time to get his junk wet and end the miserable drought he was stuck in.

Surprisingly, a good amount of people had come crawling out of their sad hovels to fail at communicating with one another, and true to the vibe, most had avoided him as he stood in the back, thinking about how pathetic they all looked fumbling around on the dance floor. The kitschy red-and-pink streamers dangling above them looked like strands of bloody diarrhea. Someone had tried to be funny by setting up a bachelorette-party-style cock piñata at the end of the room. Filled with candy or condoms? he wondered. Two folding tables pushed against a wall were packed with homemade desserts, overly frosted cookies, wines, and an assortment of cheap convenience store chocolates.

It became apparent thirty minutes in there'd be no happy ending for Theo tonight. He'd quietly excused himself from the party, grabbing one of the glossy red gift bags that sat on a circular table by the door on his way out.

Theo set Lucinda back onto the wall-mount he'd installed for her just above the TV, moved closer to the ducts, squinting as the smell became more ammonic, not unlike the chemical bombs he'd smelled in the desert. His eyes watered.

Mentally unfit for service was what they'd written on his paperwork—a label that continued to hang over him like a toxic cloud, keeping potential employers at bay and removing any chance he'd had of legally obtaining a firearm. Knowing he couldn't go out to the range to relieve some stress, Theo's brother, Johnny, had gifted him the axe, saying, "I used this for LARPing, but with the kids there's no time, and it's just sitting in the corner. Feels a little unsafe having it around, anyway. Maybe you can chop wood or go to one of those axe-throwing places."

It took Theo a few months to warm to the idea, but after lurking at the only bar in town night after night, desperately hoping for a reason to put fist to flesh, he figured burying the blade into something that couldn't call the cops would be a less problematic form of catharsis.

The next day he'd received an exasperated phone call from Jesus. "People see you coming and going with that axe, Mr. Treadway. You're making them uncomfortable and my life difficult. Please find a new hobby to replace whatever it is you're doing out in the woods."

"Some real crybaby bullshit," Theo barked, angrily swiping his thumb across the face of his cell to end the call.

Tears dribbling down his cheeks from the fresh chemical breeze blowing down on him, Theo grabbed a pair of foam ear plugs and slid them up his nose. It wasn't the best option, but it'd do. Satisfied with that, he popped the cap off a beer with his belt buckle, started cycling through the handful of satellite channels they managed to get in the ass end of their mountain town. Options were limited. Sitcoms, the occasional classic like *Patton* or *Black Hawk Down*, and another that seemed dedicated to getting veterans to re-enlist.

He felt a sudden intense pressure at the base of his skull. His eyes itched. The pulse in his temples grew angrier.

He settled on the Military Channel where a bunch of overweight preppers who'd probably never served were talking about retrofitting vans for domestic warfare. Fucking TV hosts, not soldiers. Most of these guys couldn't hack basic and were more likely to blow *themselves* up before an enemy.

He glanced at his old helmet, now residing on a small table near the closet. ANNIHILATOR was scrawled across the side in faded Sharpie. He'd stayed true to the moniker during his time in the desert, a one-man wrecking crew that'd eaten insurgents until Uncle Sam booted his ass. That was what the military had wanted, what they beat into him. Yet here he was, wasting his talents in a crumbling shit hole that hosted lame Valentine's Day parties overrun with politically correct artsy-types and dead-eyed "sober" geriatrics that looked down on him.

He sneered. He shouldn't be here; he should be out protecting the country.

A flash of light from the television scraped his corneas, momentarily blurring his vision. He blinked vigorously until his eyesight returned, but the headache swelled. He'd have to start banging on Jesus's door if the smell didn't dissipate soon. Or was Jesus at the stupid party trying to snag a piece of pussy pie for himself? Theo couldn't remember. Either way that little rat was getting a visit.

He focused on the show, remembering Afghanistan, remembering his first, and last, demerits. Theo had brought up his kill count when Commander Rose approached him, flanked by two MPs with their fingers casually on the triggers of their M4s. "Yes, and the United States appreciates your dedication to keeping it safe, however, it's not the deaths we're concerned with . . . It's the photos."

Theo was stunned. His weapons didn't discriminate. He set traps for kids weighed down by explosives, took out horses and dogs that were wandering where they shouldn't be, publicly executed an entire family that failed to stop walking toward his station. Book learning had never been a high priority for the Treadways, but even *he* knew his actions constituted war crimes. Yet Commander Rose was more worried about the fucking Polaroid collection?

Theo told him straight, "I like to remember as many of them as possible."

In retrospect, honesty had not been the best strategy. Commander Rose's upper lip lifted slightly, like a dog's does before turning you into a chew toy. For a few seconds there was only the sound of other infantrymen running around basecamp and the wind, but when the commander spoke again it was calm, measured.

"Get your shit. You're out of here tonight."

"And the pictures?"

"Always need good kindling."

A commercial to join the Marines ended, and with it his patience for anymore Weekend Warrior grab-ass. Annoyed, he rifled through the red gift bag, tossing decorative heart-print paper to the floor beside him. Tucked behind the chocolates and miniature bottle of cheap wine was an unmarked DVD in a white sleeve. It had one of those QR codes stamped to the front, probably for people who didn't have DVD players.

"The fuck?" he whispered. Given the theme of the night, he was hoping maybe Jesus had momentarily lapsed in being a useless slug and slipped the guests some adult entertainment. Probably not, but a man could dream.

He rubbed his vibrating temples, popped the disc into his old DVD player, and got comfortable.

For a few seconds there was only a black screen with some scattered snow. Slowly the camera faded into a posh den. Oak bookshelves lined the walls. Two leather chairs sat next to each other, separated by a small table with a highball glass and half-full tumbler of what Theo assumed was whiskey. The camera lifted, veered to the right just as a door opened. An older man in a gray cardigan entered the room, shut the door gently behind him. He resembled Mr. Rogers, but unlike the late, popular TV show host, no jaunty tune accompanied his steps.

The man took a seat in one of the chairs, adjusted the red knot of his tie before leaning forward with an elbow on his knee. He seemed like a father poised to deliver sage life advice. "Hi there. I'm Bob with the Department of Defense."

Theo raised the empty bottle in greeting. So much for potential scissoring.

"I'm glad you're here today, citizen. Our country needs you."

"Already been there, Bob. It didn't work out."

"Before you jump to conclusions, rest assured, I'm not asking you to take up arms. No, friend, we're utilizing a different approach, one that might seem odd at first, but exploring new horizons always comes with a dash of uncertainty."

Theo put the bottle to his forehead, hoping the coolness would ease the steady hammering inside his skull.

"We want you to *love the other*," Bob said, picking up the glass.

"How is this sexy?" he asked his empty living room.

"For over millennia, violence has been our core tactic when engaging with the enemy. Why wouldn't it be? Seems obvious, right? Fight fire *with* fire." Bob poured a finger of the whiskey into the glass, sipped, and savored the smoky burn. "Times are changing, though, friend. Our eyes are opening to revolutionary ways of engaging conflict without bloodshed. What we need to do is *love* our enemy. After all, they're our neighbors far and wide. They're *your* neighbors now."

Welp, it finally happened.

The woke patrol had stormed the collective brain of the American government, forced them to trade in the artillery for pacifiers and participation trophies. Love the enemy? What a load of fresh horse shit. If this was how they were recruiting now, then his fellow patriots might as well get on their knees and hope for quick deaths.

"Now, I'm sure you're thinking this goes against everything our nation stands behind. Might even seem like we're rolling over to expose our bellies, but trust in me, friend, this is the way. This is how humanity moves forward."

Bob polished off his drink. The corners of his mouth, pulled upward by invisible piano wire, unveiled a coyote-smile.

The room heaved, side to side, as if untethered from the building and dropped into a raging ocean. Theo's body temperature increased, coercing thick beads of sweat from every pore. He carelessly tried to wipe the dull sting of fresh tears out of his eyes, succeeded in making his vision worse. Vaguely, he felt as if there were thousands of eyes observing him, but that couldn't be right; it was just him in the room.

Clenching his jaw tight, Theo focused on the only anchor he could: Bob's voice.

"Everything's going to be okay, friend. Close your eyes. Breathe deep, in and out. Keep it steady. That's right. Just like that. It'll help ease that sledgehammer banging away in your head right now, the one sculpting a better you."

An orange arch bloomed behind Bob. The edges of the screen blurred and bubbled. His soft voice slowed to a molasses-drag.

"Relax your body. Soak in the essence of you and allow others to join. Achieve perfect harmony."

Rumbling filled Theo's ears. His muscles flexed rapidly. Warmth filled his groin, as the last of Bob's words looped in his head. Any anxiety he'd had was now being washed over with a sense of purpose, usefulness and need, like being scooped up and cradled in the loving arms of a cooing mother. The sound of IEDs and the cries of his friends as they crawled through the sand, shredded limbs trailing behind them, now nothing but echoes of someone else's nightmares.

He breathed deeply, sucking the air from the ducts into his body, and felt something new, something greater than the sum of his parts latching to the walls of his stomach, growing in his lungs. No, not growing, moving. Crawling. Tickles and stabs, like having your organs tattooed. It swam and skittered through his intestines, his bladder, absorbing stomach acid and ascending his esophagus only to rollercoaster back down into the cavern of his pelvis. A thick, euphoric honey spilled into Theo's bloodstream, but it wasn't alone. Millions of microscopic lifeforms began claiming his body.

Only for a second did Theo feel the distant tug of fear, his mind urging him to grab the nearest knife and dig the little bastards out, but the instinctual need for self-preservation was smothered by a tapestry of lustful, husky voices repeating a mantra more in line with Bob's speech:

loveconsumerecreateloveconsumerecreatel oveconsumerecreateloveconsumerecreatel oveconsumrecreate...

The insatiable need to become one with everything, to share this gift with the world that would lead them hand-in-hand to utopia, filled his chest. Theo let the feeling wash over him. Eyes glazed and tendons loosened, every nerve ending buzzing, Theo succumbed to the comfort of it all, sank into the static.

Oblivious to the world, he didn't hear the front door groan open, the heavy boots stepping across frayed carpet. Didn't realize three people had entered the room until they were right in front of him, obscuring Bob, who'd become warped scanlines. All wore gas masks. One held an AR-15 assault rifle.

Sunspots exploded in his vision, but Theo could tell that whoever they were, these couldn't be the neighbors Bob and the multitude of voices within wanted him to embrace. Who could love someone with a ribbed elongated hose protruding from between large beady eyes that took up most of the face they were set in? A test, maybe? To prove he could love even the ugliest of creatures.

Heart hammering, eager to overcome this challenge, Theo tried to sit up, felt himself pinned to the couch by cold steel. "Easy."

The third in the trio, holding a particle meter at his side, turned to the one in the middle furiously jotting notes onto a tablet with a stylus, asked in a garbled, insectoid voice, "I thought this was supposed to make them all namaste and shit? Ol' boy looks ready to eat us alive."

"He should be docile," Ron said without looking up from his scribbling. "Are you peaceable, Mr. Treadway? Do you hold love in your heart?"

loveconsumerecreateloveconsumerecreate loveconsumerecreate.

AR-15 increased the pressure. "What the fuck is wrong with his face?"

"Dude is all pupils." Meter Man reached for his own tablet hanging under his arm by a pleather strap. "There's no iris left. What's that mean, Ron?"

"Interesting," muttered Ron, writing faster.

"That's your theory? Interesting? This guy's eyes are about to pop and that's all you've got?"

When he finished, Ron slipped the stylus into his shirt pocket, crouched in front of Theo. "Would you prefer I panic?"

"I'd prefer a real answer."

"What you really want is an answer that makes you feel better." Ron held the tablet up, snapped a photo. "Mr. Treadway, I'd like to ask you again. Are you at peace?"

The bug man's words were faint, masked underneath the canopy of buzzing. Theo thought he'd heard his name, but could he even claim that moniker now? He was beyond trivial designations or false proclamations of family. For the first time in his life, Theo felt real brotherhood, and it was filling him by the second. He would love these creatures before him, usher them into their new forms, undo and remake them.

Ripples flowed across Theo's face, pushing the skin forward. His vision expanded. The room became a pixelated distortion. Heat flooded his veins. Everything felt wet and heavy, as if he were doused in a thick coat of slime. Sensing the warm bodies before him, the organisms within Theo made themselves known in a torrent of brown vomit that sent the bug man scurrying backward like a swatted roach. Speckles of bile spattered the gun still pressed into his chest.

AR-15 glanced over at Ron. "Interesting."

Meter Man gagged, pointed to a splatter of upchuck between Theo's legs. "You guys seeing this?"

A civilization swirled in Theo's lap. The once-microscopic organisms were now the size of pinheads. Tethered together by the faintest strings of vibrant red, Theo's new biological family coiled over themselves, desperate for affection from those before them. They lashed out across the crotch of his jeans, the tattered fabric of his couch cushion. Their love had been rejected, but Theo knew this trio of insects just needed coaxing. Once they'd felt the rush of bliss that came with sharing their bodies, they'd be unable to resist the passion.

Until then, Theo scooped his expelled family into his palm, welcomed the writhing beings back into his throat.

Meter Man unfastened the straps of his gas mask. "That's it. I'm done."

Ron grabbed his wrist. "Don't. If the vents are still active, you'll end up like . . . "

"Can't . . . can't breathe. Oh, Christ this mask smells like puke."

"Let's get back to the van. We weren't prepared for this situation."

"Yeah, no shit," AR-15 snapped, turning to address them.

It was all Theo needed.

He felt the weight lift from his chest for just a moment, grabbed the barrel of the gun, and jerked it to the side. Instinctively, the man's finger jerked the trigger, punched a hole into the couch above Theo's shoulder.

Before he could fire again, Theo rammed the stock of the rifle forward, smirked when he heard it smash pelvic bone. AR-15 crashed into the television, bounced his head off the back wall, and went limp.

The one with tablet ran for the door.

"Where the hell are you going?" Meter Man shouted, ducking under Theo's swinging arm, which now had dozens of thick, pulsating veins throbbing beneath transparent skin.

Bob's message had been to love the enemy, but deep inside Theo knew that wouldn't be enough. Not until their blood mingled could they really coexist.

Theo was never the most flexible. He was tall, thick, and wide in frame, the type of man you send in to knock down doors. This wily little creature that'd broken into his home, rejected the kindness of his family, might've been quicker, but Theo was patient.

He dodged another barrage of uncoordinated swings, the particle meter brushing his beard, then brought his fist down like a hammer onto the top of Meter Man's head, causing his knees to buckle and sending him face first into the carpet. Theo heard a loud crunch from inside the mask followed by a throaty grunt.

Theo crouched behind him, undid the already loosened straps of the gas mask, tossed it in the corner. Weak hands tried batting away the inevitable. Blood gushed from the man's shattered nose. The sound of weeping threw Theo off. Didn't he know this was the only way to achieve peace, to become one in the same thriving ecosystem of their new humanity?

He dug his knees into Meter Man's shoulder blades, pinning him to the damp carpet. With both hands clasped around the man's throat, choking off his blubbered pleas, Theo yanked backward, working the neck like an old, rusted lever. He relished the feel and satisfying bubble wrap pop of tendons and muscle as the flesh began stretching, tearing.

loveconsumerecreateloveconsumecreate loveconsumerecreate ♪ ♪ ♪

Had Theo's grip not been so tight, he mused, the screams Meter Man may have emitted would be a sound unlike anything to previously befall human ears. Dark blood steadily rained onto the carpet until, finally, with one hearty twist and pull, Theo wrenched the head away from the shoulders, spine trailing up through the back of the man's torso, its bottom half hidden in the chest cavity.

Theo dropped the head. He shoved his hands into the burbling neck stump, pulled open the gaping hole of meat, and expelled the new contents of his stomach—a viscous sallow secretion—into the still-kicking corpse. He wasn't sure how long it'd take, but Theo felt certain that soon enough a new life would spring forth, Meter Man resurrected as another body to bring them closer to heaven.

"You . . . Oh, shit," said a voice from behind him.

Theo turned, viscera slathered across his mouth.

Seated in the shattered husk of the television, AR15 sat up, tried to push himself out of the debris, slicing his hand on a stray shard of glass. "What . . . what the hell are you doing?"

"Becoming one," Theo said. He slammed his foot into the man's crotch with such force the man's pants ripped open and his dick tore off into the treads of Theo's boot.

Muffled screams fogged up the eyes of the gas mask.

Theo mashed the man's cock into cherry jam, then grabbed Lucinda, raised her above his head and sneered, drooling yellow goop onto the scratched and stained entertainment center. The beings roiling throughout his body thrummed with anticipation.

Ron screamed, dropping the tablet. He opened the door to the hallway and raced out.

"This is all for the greater good," Theo said, still fixated on AR15. "We're learning to love one another."

He buried the axe in the man's face.

2

The power went out with a thunderous pop, abruptly cutting off Moroder's theme for *Midnight Express*. Sighing, Ansel Friedl tossed the well-used issue of Cheri to the side, relinquished the stronghold he'd had on his dick, and tightened the loose drawstring of his sweatpants. Outages weren't anything new. Using the microwave and the dining room light at the same time goosed the wiring. Summers brought rolling blackouts. Too many appliances running at once tripped the breakers daily, which meant the V-Day shindig downstairs was probably sucking up enough juice to force their decaying diorama of a building to fold in on itself.

It was all part of being an unlucky tenant of Sunshine Spires. Eroding away on the outskirts of Mesa Tranquilo, CA, the three-story affordable housing project was nestled in between an empty factory that used to manufacture fiberglass insulation and an apocalyptic park full of playground equipment better suited for a mad architect's museum. Across the street a desolate strip mall barely clung to life with a few stores still open to the public. Behind the complex, like some forgotten Hollywood backdrop, were miles of wilderness. It beat sharing space under an overpass or stuffing oneself into a storefront alcove for a few hours, but not by much.

Unless this incident was isolated to his unit. The power snuffed for not paying the utility bill on time. Shit, was he late on another payment? He glanced over to the wire basket on the dining room table overflowing with coffee-stained envelopes and junk mail. Could one hold the answer to why he now had to enjoy the tastefully posed models of a long-forgotten smut mag in the dark? And if it did, did he even have enough in his account to get the lights back on?

Ansel yawned. Such mysteries were best solved another day.

His old roommate, Lenny, a hippy turned government security guru for better pay, would nag Ansel to sell off some of the rarer records in his collection when he was hurting for cash. Lenny also built tiny cities out of fast-food containers, moldy laundry, and crust-laden boxers for the horde of roaches that took shelter in his room, a testament that one could possess a brilliant mind and still be really fucking gross.

Besides, parting with his first pressing of The Residents' *The Commercial Album* would border on blasphemy. On a good month, Ansel would have enough from freelance gigs, but the work wasn't reliable. More and more he'd have to nag Lydia at the co-op to give him a few eight-hour shifts and pay off the lingering bills with the extra cash. A method Ansel had regularly employed until they removed him from the schedule completely last month, leaving him no other choice but to start eyeballing vinyl titles he might be willing to part with for the sake of housing.

Or you could work faster, old man. Put yourself out there more. Hustle.

His phone lit up with a text from Julianne, his only friend in the building, asking if he wanted to join the chorus of complaints to property management about constant power issues, the rhythmic thumping in the walls from the sound system that'd been set up for the evening's festivities, and the new smell making the rounds. She'd already wrangled a few others, but another body couldn't hurt.

There was nothing he'd love more than to watch Jesus cringe at the sight of a handful of angry tenants waiting outside his door, but if Ansel were honest with himself, confronting the building's slumlord frightened him. They'd already had one heated confrontation over Jesus's nephew continuing to park in Ansel's assigned space whenever he visited. Another might land him an eviction notice, which, given he'd torched every goodwill bridge left in his life, meant bus benches and piss-soaked alleys were the only lodging in sight. He supposed he could take refuge in one of the abandoned stores nearby, but the longevity there would be questionable. Not to mention someone might've already staked their claim. Ansel wasn't a fighter, wouldn't know the first thing about defending himself beyond flailing his limbs before running in the other direction. With his luck, he'd get hit by a car while fleeing the attack.

Staying true to himself, Ansel ignored the text. Besides, he didn't smell anything, and the storm of dated pop tunes would end eventually.

He thought about throwing his headphones on and hitting the sack to music on his phone, whisked away to slumber by Tangerine Dream. If inspiration wormed its way into his near-arthritic fingers before sleep overtook him, well the muse could wait till morning to dust off the old Moog synth. Wasn't his fault the place was stripped of electricity. Nothing he could do about that.

Sure, but you could've been finished already. Missing the deadline was your fault.

With a faint hum that made the building shiver, the power limped back to life. Light illuminated the tanned legs that formed the heavenly V Ansel had been admiring before being plunged into darkness. Moroder's track crept into its proper RPMs, filling the living room with an aural kaleidoscope of entrancing synthesizer and brass instrumentation.

"Well, shit," he whispered, feeling the guilt of laziness gnaw at his conscience.

Recently, he'd taken on a couple composer gigs, hoping he could sock away enough cash to keep snagging Record Store Day releases and still manage to afford this dump on his own. Short film gigs from a few of his old buddies that had made the turn from FX maestros of the late '80s and '90s to straight-to-streaming directors, and even a few up-and-coming young filmmakers. The latter always told him how much they enjoyed the scores Ansel churned out back in his prime. Most were lo-fi pieces with minimal composition. Meant to set the mood, but not distract. Still, they dug 'em and reached out with more enthusiasm than Ansel could remember encountering when the songs were fresh. Problem was, the work wasn't consistent, and lately he'd started getting worried that word-of-mouth would label him unreliable.

He'd noodled a bit throughout the last few weeks, hoping to send the tapes to said directors, but nothing stuck out as memorable, and if he wasn't excited about the work how could he expect them to be? Besides, he couldn't afford to transition from his beloved four-track recorder to a new, fancy computer program just for the sake of speed; didn't want to struggle with that learning curve.

Deep down he'd hoped this might signal the first step of a

comeback. Alcoholic composer finds sobriety and crafts award-winning emotional score was the back-in-the-saddle arc he fantasized about, an erasure of the last decade of failure.

He moved to the archive of music that'd grown to kaiju-like proportions over the years, looking for new tunes, something loud to get the blood going. Earlier in the day, he'd taped pieces of cardboard over the vents to create a bit of soundproofing. Bad enough the walls at Sunshine Spires were elder-skin thin; he didn't want to draw further attention by sending sounds rocketing through metal tunnels.

He threw on *Cosmic Thing* by the B-52's hoping the upbeat tempo would release some of the old musical mojo, but after a few moments, the coy smile of the bombshell on the cover of the magazine seemingly making eye contact with him, Ansel found himself yearning for a different kind of release. Surely, once he cleared his mind of distractions, he could finally settle into a rhythm and get to work.

Half an hour later, instead of composing, he was lightly napping, floating in the mild current of a lucid dream until the sound of trampling feet yanked him back to reality. He checked the time. Almost eleven. People were probably calling it a night, shuffling toward their popcorn ceiling and particle board cells, the prospect of romance dissipating faster than cheap cologne.

He pulled his hair-tie out, unleashed the greying locks that always made Ansel feel a bit wizardly, and yawned, eager to drift back to sleep. Everything would return to its moldy standard by sunrise, and then he'd finally knock out those tracks.

A flurry of fists pounded on the door.

"Son of a bitch," he groaned.

Ansel opened the flimsy door, let the lock chain catch, and peeked out through the crack.

Had it not been for the slime-green dye job, paint and clay-spattered red coveralls, Ansel would've slammed the door shut as the person with the half-face respirator tried shoving themselves through the gap. "Ansel! Open up!"

"Julieanne? What's going on? Why're you wearing that?"

"Please just let me in. Hurry!"

He stepped back, undid the chain. Julianne pushed past him.

"Close it," she demanded, handing him an identical painter's respirator. "Put this on."

Ignoring her, Ansel took one step out into the hallway, trying to figure out why she sounded frantic. The lights were flickering, which wasn't a surprise. To his left, he watched a couple of unfamiliar tenants carrying pink, heart-shaped chocolate boxes disappear into a unit farther down the hall, slamming the door behind them so hard plaster drifted from the ceiling. This was followed by screaming and what sounded like glass breaking. Bad couple's fight. Ansel hated when the neighbors fought; it was flat-out rude.

Looking to his right, he saw Mark, the bodybuilder who was always out front with his weights in the early morning, kick his way into the far stairwell, the blow from his sneakered foot nearly tearing the door down. Dude was ripped, but twitchy like he'd just snorted a rail of bath salts. Muscles Ansel didn't even realize existed in the human body pulsed beneath a thick, bronze spray tan. He screamed the lyrics to The Everly Brothers "Love Hurts" with a bizarre stutter as he made his way to another part of the building.

Out of nowhere a hand grabbed Ansel's shoulder, yanking him back inside the apartment. Julianne got in his face. "Shut it. C'mere."

He closed the door and relatched it. "You okay?"

"No. I dunno. Maybe. Will you put it on, please?"

Ansel glanced at the respirator in his hand. "First, what's happening?"

She scrunched her nose, eyeballed the apartment. He worried he'd left more than vinyl sleeves and dirty dishes scattered throughout. "It doesn't smell as bad in here."

"Thanks?"

"There's something going around the building. Intense and septic."

"Shit and chemicals are the standard scent here. The day it smells like roses is the day I know I'm having a stroke."

"This is different. It's caustic."

Ansel sniffed dramatically. "Smells normal to me."

Julianne studied him. Her eyes narrowed, thinking. "Yes, it *does* smell like the usual shit in here. Why?"

She tore her eyes away and inched through his tiny living space, sniffing with purpose. She stopped under the ceiling's heat vent and pointed. "What's that? Cardboard?"

"Impromptu soundproofing. Working on some stuff. Didn't want to bother Nico upstairs."

"Nico gets mad at birds. Soundproofing isn't going to appease him."

"Said he'd chop my head off with his katana if I kept him awake with my keyboard again."

"It's a miracle he hasn't cut *his own* head off."

"It's good. Has a Sisters of Mercy vibe. Wanna hear it?"

"Your decapitation?"

"The new song."

"No."

"You're starting to sound like my ex-wife."

"Shut up."

"Mrs. Friedl, is that you?"

"Ugh. Stop."

There was a loud boom out in the hallway. Ansel instinctively moved to the door to investigate. Julianne grabbed his wrist. "Wait."

"Just gonna check the peep hole." He peered through the fogged-up lens of the aperture. A rheumy eye stared back. A low, rumbling groan accompanied it.

"Help you?" he asked.

"I love you," said the man on the other side of the door. "You'll love me too. If you open yourself to us."

The doorknob creaked left then right.

Ansel turned to Julianne, mouthed *what the fuck* before turning back to the door. "You got the wrong place, buddy."

The eye retracted, revealing a gaunt, sweat-coated face. Smiling, the man on the other side opened his mouth wide, flexed his throat muscles, and unleashed a stream of brown liquid. Stomach sludge obscured the view.

Ansel's heart raced as he backpedaled into Julianne.

"Who was it?" she asked.

"Don't know. Guy's drunk as hell though. He just threw up on my door."

"Are you serious?"

"I would not lie about such a heinous atrocity perpetrated upon my domicile."

Julianne spun him around. "There's a rat's nest in my vent. I asked Jesus to clean the fucking thing out days ago. Surprise! He didn't. Tired of waiting for that lazy dick, I stuffed a metal lockbox up there to keep them from getting into my place. I never use the heat anyway. I use blankets. Blankets are greener."

"Greener than freezing to death at night?"

"Death is the greenest you can be."

"If you're dead you can be rat food, which . . . also green."

"I don't want to be rat food. With their little dagger teeth and gross tails. Disgusting. Anyway, yeah, I blocked it off with the shoebox. But that smell still kinda got through, you know? Started getting a little dizzy, so I threw this on"—she pointed at one of the mask's filters—"and went to Jimmy's to convince him to come with me to see Jesus. I was rallying the troops. Did you get my text?"

"No," he lied.

"Jimmy opened his door and holy shit did my eyes burn. Everything's starting to reek like embalming fluid."

"The rent's cheap for a reason. What happened to Jimmy?"

"He was off. Talking really slow and staring at me in a way I didn't like."

"He smokes a lot of weed, Julianne. No offense, but what're you getting at?"

"I don't know yet. When was the last time you talked to Lenny? Or Carol, for that matter? Where's she been?"

Ansel didn't want to talk about Carol. The complex busybody just lived to write up reports on noisy tenants. Her husband had died a few years ago. Heart attack while changing a lightbulb, she'd told Ansel one night after cornering him in the hallway, her desperation for small talk rolling off in waves. Now she dedicated herself to the role of hall monitor, writing up daily Neighborhood Watch reports for Jesus. Ansel took a wide berth whenever she approached to avoid getting a lecture about his music or having unsolicited gossip dumped on him. And Lenny left him with backpay on utilities he couldn't afford. He also left him with those weird roach hotels and Brylcreem stains on the bathroom rug. Guy was a capitalist knobslobber despite the hippy ideology he used to peddle, a stooge forever waiting for someone to tell him what to do. A solipsistic narcissist who most likely only tipped service-staff ten percent because he liked to pinch pennies the asshole way. The only good thing the guy ever did was never complain about Ansel writing music. *Probably made him feel cool.* That was the way of a vindictive non-creative—befriend others with talent to supplement the lack of your own imagination.

"Fuck Lenny."

"But didn't he have some type of relationship with the building owners? I remember seeing him here a few months ago with a couple of dudes who definitely weren't sleeping in this hovel. They looked official. Clean-cut. Checking windows and stuff, messing with doors. Maybe he can help or knows what's going on? Can we call him?"

"I don't even know how to reach him. He's somewhere making a steady paycheck."

"Then why was he here?"

"Booty call from Mrs. Grimes on three? He screwed her once. Cried afterward."

Julianne tapped her temple. "Is there a section of your brain that houses gross, irrelevant details no one asked for?"

Ansel shrugged.

"Okay, well, I'm off to kick in Jesus's door. This is more than dead animals in the walls. Something is fucked here, and I'm not trying to spend the night in my car. You coming?"

Ansel stared at the door, wondering if the man was still outside. He didn't see anyone. Guy must have decided to go bother someone else. He thought about encouraging her to stay with him, but he could see by the way she was staring at the door, squinting angrily, as if she could see right through the building's walls all the way to Jesus' office, that she wasn't about to spend any more time here than necessary.

"Maybe?"

3

Theo stormed down the hall with Lucinda in one hand and a severed head in the other, its mouth open in a grotesque yawn, lovebugs swarming the still-warm tongue. He cooed to it, promised things would be better. "We're going to love the world like we've never loved it before," he grumbled. To a casual listener, his words were mostly ululations and slick smacking noises. He knew this on some level—the level that told him his own tongue was three sizes too big and dangling below his chin—but he didn't care. He could feel his thoughts, all of them so beautiful they were nearly orgasmic, as if his brain were cumming inside his skull.

Voices rang out down the hallway. Was it the man who'd gotten away? The one who'd arrived with the tablet, the one who questioned Theo's feelings before scuttling off in fear? The one who'd come into his home as he inhaled utopia into his lungs? He hoped so. He needed to love that man. Needed his head and his heart and all his important parts to fill with more of their kind. Needed them like he needed more muscles on his feet. And with that thought, he stopped. The skin split open on his forearm, widening like a ruptured anal gland. The gristle snapped and the bones crackled. So many new organisms in there. Bubbling, roiling, squirming within their gossamer red threads, pushing out to freedom. Hungry for warm bodies.

Theo caught a glimpse of himself in the reflection of an emergency fire extinguisher case. He was ripped, rebuilt for the future civilization. His entire being hummed. Weeping holes scattered across his flesh pulsated. Theo strained, forcing all his muscles to press outward toward his skin. He felt those creatures inside helping him, forcing his guts around. Every vein on his body

21

bulged with the effort. Finally, with a thick splash, his intestines forced their way out his asshole and collected in a pile between his legs. He strained again, pushing other slick bits of insides through his anus. They exploded out to the floor, sliding around in blood and mucus. The collection of organs stank of bile and rotting meat, but he grinned at it all anyway. Organs were unnecessary now. His new family provided all the sustenance he needed.

loveconsumerecreateloveconsumecreate loveconsumerecreate

Voices drew his attention to the end of the hallway. Theo watched excitedly as a man in a white suit decorated with garish red hearts stumbled out of his apartment, gagging and batting away some invisible foe. The man was choking. Tears spilled down his cheeks. He stepped into Theo's path, coughed out, "Holy fuck! You look like a walking hemorrhoid, man! What's wrong with you? What's wrong with the air in here? I can't fucking brea—"

The man's head split down the middle as Lucinda descended with a rush of air. The two halves of his head slid off his shoulders and hit the floor just as his body crumpled into a pile of broken dreams.

Theo smiled through the blood-flecked teeth that hadn't fallen out. He yanked up the man's body, which weighed nothing thanks to his new sets of extra muscles, and puked all over it, depositing the organisms into the dead man's neck cavity. Some were bigger now. The size of quarters. Seeing them burrow into their new home filled him with pride. *This is true love, brother.* He dropped the man again.

New voices coming from the nearby stairwell. He lumbered toward the door, nearly tearing it off the hinges as he opened it. The potential converts were on the next level up. He ascended like an angel rising to meet God.

Heaven smelled so wonderful.

Ron heard the stairwell door fly open and wedged himself back under the stairs, the Beretta he'd brought—and failed to use—clutched tightly in his sweaty, quaking hands. It had to be Theo. No one he'd seen so far exhibited that amount of strength. Come to think of it, though, Ron hadn't really seen anyone else yet. Not since he'd given the order to release the gas and excused himself from Jesus's office to start testing. Maybe the big bastard was a one-off. A defect they could terminate without too much bureaucracy. *Should get the Wolves to deal with the issue.* No one would shed a tear if those nutjobs were gutted and left for dead; it'd be several less alt-right loudmouths to worry about down the road.

The behemoth stomped up the stairs. The door above opened and slammed closed, leaving Ron alone again in his hidey-hole. Downstairs the bass from the party plowed ahead at full speed, masking any other noise in the building.

He tried to steady his breathing—a lame and useless attempt to calm himself. All it did was fog up the gasmask, which was already chock full of spit and tears. The smell reminded him that maybe it was time to finally see a dentist; lately the bathroom sink looked like a crime scene after he brushed his teeth.

"What went wrong?" he muttered. "Too much adenine? Phosphates?"

Who the fuck knew? He was a puppeteer now. His science days were far behind him. He'd traded in his lab coat for a corporate corner office as soon as his superiors made the offer. That he *had* understood the chemistry behind much of the initiative was what had given him the edge to make the lateral jump, but that was a decade ago, and he was so bogged down with needless red tape of late the current science was passing him by.

These days his job was analyzing people and slotting them into spaces where they'd be the most useful for the program. Like Carol, and how he knew she'd be the perfect subject for their little limb regeneration study. He'd read her right, as he did with most people. It had nothing to do with understanding current genetic coding or untangling chemical chains. Because of that, he'd tried to explain what a misstep having him lead this new clinical trial would be, but C-suite handed the order down with less details than they dropped on the baristas who made their afternoon lattes.

That being said, he needed to contact HQ, fill them in on the current fiasco. By now the signal jammers were certainly on, ensuring no one could call in or out, but he'd dropped his tablet when he bolted from Theo's apartment, and a quick glance at his smartphone showed him the touch screen was smashed; both were loaded with frequency-hopping software needed to bypass the jammer. Without the tablet or his phone, he was screwed.

Now, back against the wall with piss-soaked tactical pants, his heart flirting with a coronary, Ron wished he'd gotten one anyway. He'd never been the type to push back against the rules. Stepping over the line when it came to work was too risky. Unemployment wasn't an option when a chunk of his check every two weeks went to help his sister Elaine live some quality of life within the walls of their parents' house back in Rhode Island.

He thought about the way she'd looked beyond him last time he visited, which wasn't often. How could he? He needed to work to keep up with her medical bills. She nodded along politely throughout their conversation, but her gaze was transfixed on the snow drifting lazily onto the front lawn. He wanted to ask what was so damn interesting about the snowfall. Didn't she realize what a pain in the ass it was to get anywhere in weather like that? Before he could ease back into the mode of older brother chiding younger sister, though, it hit him. Although the weather was a hindrance from his point of view, for Elaine it offered a new landscape, something beyond dim hallways and retrofitted ADA ramps.

She needed something to look forward to, a change in her life no matter how small to keep her going, which was why despite not feeling qualified for the job, Ron hadn't put up much of a fight when he became the lead on Project Honeypot. He knew it'd come with a fat end-of-year bonus. With that, he could fund sprucing up the house, maybe even take Elaine on a small vacation and still be able to keep the insurance leeches satiated.

However, Ron currently had a bigger problem to resolve. If this field experiment ended up an unsalvageable disaster, he could wish those dreams farewell. His only choice was to retrieve the tablet from the sticky carpet upon which it now lay, hope it wasn't damaged, and get what results he could. This wasn't a disaster, he told himself; it was merely an obstacle that required a little creativity to overcome.

The trick was not getting decapitated along the way.

Theo was upstairs spreading the word with his axe. A shred of luck Ron didn't want to take for granted. Hesitation meant worse than death. It meant being hijacked by a bacterium not even the eggheads at HQ truly understood. All he needed to do was flag this unexpected turn and ensure the building's lockdown procedures were a go. The Wolves would probably have to adjust their hard-ons the second the metal shutters came down.

He slipped out from his hiding spot. The possibility there could be more like Theo wasn't lost on him, but the only other option was waiting for someone offsite to notice they'd lost communication. That wouldn't do. That wouldn't get Ron his deeply desired bonus.

A moment later he was back at Theo's unit. It was a bloodbath. The two men who had accompanied him earlier, Chavez and Keany, had become mostly pink gruel swirled with dark red blood. A miraculously intact limb stuck out here and there. Chunks of meat bubbled and congealed. Somewhere in the crimson goo, Ron thought he saw a tiny conga line of puckered mouths open and close, like babies eager for a milk bottle. Did a tongue just lick the air? It was hard to tell through the crust inside the gas mask.

He found the tablet near a twitching combat-booted foot. The screen was shattered, but he thought maybe the damage was superficial—a hope that was quickly dashed as he watched the apps flicker across the screen, stuck in an endless loop of opening and closing.

Dropping to his knees, Ron waded into the paint-wheel of sludge that used to be Chavez. Or was it Keany? Didn't matter. He dug his hands into the still-steaming slop, felt bones slip through his fingers along with something else that tried to wrap around his gloved hands. He made a mental note. The specimens were no longer microscopic bacteria but growing into what they'd seen on the video Odyssey brought back.

Bulbous organs squished in his fingers like water balloons. "Where is it? Where is it? Aha!"

He withdrew the second tablet from the pile of human muck and felt his heart sink. It was also smashed. "Well, shit . . . "

He dropped it with a sigh and a plop, closed his eyes. *Breathe, Ronnie, and focus on a solution instead of fixating on the issue.* That's what Dr. Parker always told him during their weekly session. Maybe Theo, high off the spree of orgiastic violence, had left his phone behind. If it wasn't locked, Ron could use that. Swap the SD cards, try to install the frequency-hopping app somewhere else.

He scanned the destroyed living room. A sunburst of blood coated the ceiling. The TV was a shattered box of glass and plastic, wisps of smoke still trailing from the ragged slash in the screen. In between the overturned couch was a coffee table that'd been snapped in two. Old issues of firearm magazines and dirty plates were strewn around. A weathered, battered ballistic helmet sat upside down in the debris. If there was a phone hidden in this miniature blast zone, Ron wasn't going to find it without hours to spare and a few extra hands.

What he did find, though, was Chavez's AR-15.

Ron picked up the rifle, turned his attention back to the human stew, wondering if one of his former associates had brought a phone with them.

Ron leaned in for a closer look, grimaced at the polyps clustered around the stump of the arm. That's when the mouths appeared again. Tacky, swollen tongues licked the air. One of the arms swept back and forth along the carpet, flinging bits of meat and skin around the room.

Ron resisted the urge to blast a few rounds into the creatures. They'd known the gas would cause alterations in brain chemistry; that was kind of the point. The rats were promising, working together to build one massive living space in their glass home. But Theo . . . that was unexpected. The aggression, the augmentation of muscle mass. The fact the lovebugs were growing in the bio-soup. None of this had occurred in the early stages, which meant there was some kind of trigger within the building.

The best kind of sample would always come from a live specimen, but Ron wasn't keen on getting close enough to Theo to snag a chunk of warm tissue. That would be offering his head up for permanent removal. He eyeballed what had started to pool around his feet, pulled the tiny vacuum-sealed flask from his backpack. Carefully, Ron collected as much of the liquid as he could, avoiding the swirling daisy chain of pruned mouths seeking out his body heat. He wasn't sure how long they'd last without a live host, but he also wasn't eager to rent out his abdomen.

He tucked the sample collector into a pocket of his bag that had a small cold pouch. The shutters hadn't come down yet. Thinking he could still get to the Wolves before lockdown, Ron hustled out of Theo's and started toward the front door.

Deep grumblings shook everything around him. A painfully boring painting of a beach sunset fell from a nail, clattered to the floor. Something unseen slammed into the wall inside one of the other units. Deep, throaty moans filled the hallway.

So much for Theo being a one-off.

Remember, Ron. Think positive. Sure, you may be surrounded by two dozen or so maniacs, but such results could be a boon to the program. After all, the initiative was about human psychological modification. The aerosol with its mysterious alien components wasn't turning them into the loving flower children they'd hoped it would, but it *was* affecting them. It was still useful.

Adapt and overcome.

Another scream, lustful and high-pitched, rooted him to the dingy floor. Several of the doors flew open, tenants spilled out of their units, all racing for the building's north side lobby doors like teenagers in a mad dash to get to the front row of a concert, most of them nude or missing half their clothes. An older man in a shredded purple robe that shimmered under the hallway lights limped as fast he could, throwing terrified glances behind him. Ron watched impassively from just inside Theo's doorway as the Hefner lookalike was driven to the ground by a figure with enough coarse back hair to qualify as a shawl.

"True love is to be united," someone shouted in the fray.

They reached the door as one, slammed into the thin wood. Amidst the confused scrabbling, a thin, greasy teen wearing a fishnet top yanked the door open. Cool night air and bullets greeted them all. The kid's head snapped back, splashing blood and brains onto his neighbors before disappearing under tangled limbs. More bodies tried to shove through the gap. Gunfire trenched flesh, keeping the group from leaving. Most turned and ran, fleeing down the hallways back to their apartments. A few kept trying to get out the door, choking on the newly altered air in the building.

Ron continued to watch. A metallic click and whir rattled the ceiling. The steel security shutter dropped down like a modern guillotine, severing the foot from a woman lip-locked with another tenant, though only one of them seemed to be having a good time. She held the man to her, clutching tufts of chest hair, grinding her bare crotch against the thigh of his jeans like an overexcited dog. A couple that seemed to have fallen straight out of the pages of a vampire romance, all billowy shirts and tight leather pants, began dragging the dead kid toward their unit where a ghoul in a matte black suit waited, pale hands crossed in front of him. The one-legged woman slithered after them, begging them to suck on her tongue, leaving a trail of red slime in her wake.

The hallway became a stifling hotbox. Ron was grateful for the gas mask, but it didn't muffle the howls of lustful frenzy competing with screams of pain, nor did it hide the wet splatter of vomit and rhythmic squelching that arose from the spontaneous orgy making its way into the rooms around him.

Within the mass of gyrating bodies, a pair of eyes found Ron idling in the doorway, then another, and another, until several heads had spotted him.

"Ah, fuck," Ron muttered.

4

Vern Kloppenborg picked up the still-gushing leg, underhanded it at the three pack members standing at the bottom of Sunshine Spires' porch steps. "Turn this into your next fleshlight, Jimmy!"

McKay and DeFanti sidestepped the airborne limb, laughing as they watched Jimmy Simpson bat it away. It landed with a wet thud, bounced a few feet across the asphalt where its getaway was finally stopped short by the tire of an old Astro van.

Now that they'd stopped blasting the freaks inside, Vern could get back to enjoying the red-blooded American rock 'n roll blaring from his truck, which they'd backed up as close as they could to the entrance. Easier to grab weapons that way. They'd brought out everything they had. A few .22s, standard shotgun, Glocks, milk crate full of homemade pipe bombs in case things turned silly, and of course everyone had their own AR-15. Nothing fancy like those spooks Vern had seen enter the building. Just good, practical firepower.

Vern knew the Wolves of the 2nd Amendment were on as many government watchlists as there were letters in alphabet soup. He was proud of that. It meant the Wolves were becoming a name. Unlike so many other groups cropping up across the U.S. that hid behind message boards, divulging dreams of their utopia in secret meetups and yelling on social media over petty grievances like mask-wearing—supporters who were only down for the cause as long as it didn't mean leaving the safety of their gaming chairs or couches and generally being blinded to the bigger picture.

The Wolves were about action. Boots on the ground. Boots on the necks of anyone who opposed their right to live freely, but this hands-on approach wasn't cheap. They needed funding to forge ahead, so when the man in the sweater showed up on Vern's doorstep one crisp Saturday afternoon with a job offer and checkbook, Vern holstered the .357 he'd been holding out of sight and asked where and when.

The sight beyond the doorway reminded him of roman paintings where dozens of bodies writhed in front of a backdrop of flames, fused together in a parade of penetration. He wasn't sure what these people had been hit with, but it couldn't hurt to dangle a little blackmail in front of Uncle Sam's stooges in return for some insight into their research for future endeavors.

Vern patted the body cam clipped to his flak jacket. "Everyone fully charged?"

His pack responded in the affirmative.

One step closer to keeping the country and their families safe, he thought.

5

Theo smelled sex in the air. He smiled, a maniacal rictus of shredded lips and missing teeth. It signaled that his—no, *their*—acolytes were finding each other throughout this decrepit rat maze, creating life as he stalked the halls, helping the lost ascend on the spot. But where were these loud lovers of the new paradise? Surely, Theo could assist them in their transition to Valhalla.

The door to his right seemed to pulse like a pregnant belly. In and out. In and out. Dripping with condensation. Was he imagining this? No, he could smell the rutting, could taste it. Urgent, animalistic, and musky, enough to exhaust veteran sex workers. Yes, this was the love nest. He wanted to celebrate with his new family, open them up to their true potential.

loveçonsumereçreateloveçonsumeçreate
loveçonsumereçreate ، ، ، love

"We're bringing the love tonight," Theo spit, swinging Lucinda into the lock. The door exploded open. He careened inside with purpose, kicking over chairs, tossing aside tables, his cock aching as if on the precipice of a massive orgasm. A cat darted across his path. Theo brought the axe down, but the orange tabby vanished before the blade even hit the floor.

The bedroom door beckoned him. Moans of pleasure sent a tingle through his pelvis. Lucinda made fast work of the barrier. Inside the room were two masses of fat and skin undulating like albino worms on the bed. They rolled over each other, bloated maggots crying in ecstasy. Teeth and assholes, all swirling in a miasma of people-pudding, like dessert toppings on frozen yogurt. Former humans, now something else. *Something perfect, something necessary.* "I love you," he said, towering over them.

31

"Help us," one of the forms pleaded in a garbled, panicked voice. "What the hell is happening!"

Theo took in the room, with its eggshell paint job and thrift store ocean art. A sallow mist fell from the overhead heating vent. Its smell would suffocate most people, send them running, but not Theo. He inhaled deeply, inviting more to settle in his veins. The euphoria was addicting. Life changing. Ripples swam up and down his neck, like thick grubs wriggling under his skin. He arched his back and roared as his shoulder muscles were devoured, replaced with more of the powerful organic storm within him, growing so that he could shepherd their flock.

The coital mass on the bed reached out. Its hand split in half, now resembling a macabre V. "Help us," pleaded a voice.

"Don't worry, baby," Theo said. "Of course we're going to help you."

Lucinda chopped the mound of flesh into a hundred globs of slick meat. Blood arced like strong ejaculations in an underground home video. Theo swung and swung until the bodies were mere oatmeal on a cheap duvet. The marble-sized creatures that hadn't been turned to pulp began to consume their brethren.

He turned to leave but stopped when he heard the sucking, wet sounds of something moving before him. The sludge that was once two dead people folded into each other and rose to the ceiling in a pillar of ichor threaded with pink striations that lit the beast up like a monstrous circulatory system.

"Do you know your job?" Theo slobbered.

The beast dipped its upper parts, like a worm nodding yes, and crashed off the bed.

Theo patted its anterior bulges. "Go! You have work to do. We both do. We're going to love everyone so fucking much."

Theo smiled like a proud parent as the beast slithered off into the hallway and went to spread its affection, leaving a path of bloody slime in its wake. Maybe their paths would cross again. Maybe not. For now, he had his own crusade to worry about.

6

Two floors below, Ansel fidgeted with the respirator, trying not to let Julianne catch on that he was feigning incompetence in an effort to avoid going out into the hall and showing his face to Jesus. "Sorry. My fingers aren't what they used to be. Are you sure this is going to fit?"

"The straps are adjustable, dude," Julianne snapped, grabbing the mask. She pulled the plastic clips back as far as they'd go, put the mask onto the lower half of Ansel's face, and tightened it. "There. Now don't start telling me you need help with the rest."

Ansel slid the scuffed plastic eyewear on. "Fine, fine. Wouldn't it be easier to just use socks or an old shirt?"

"No offense, but how often do you actually do your laundry?"

Ansel looked away, embarrassed. "I do my—"

A massive quake shook the building. Knocks and bangs ran throughout the vents overhead before ending in a metallic shudder like an old furnace coughing out its last breath. Ansel and Julianne stared at each other for a minute before she walked over and tore one of the cardboard "soundproofing" flaps off the vent in his kitchen.

Slowly, she waved her hand back and forth. "I think whatever they've been pumping in just gave up the ghost."

"Great!" Ansel began trying to undo the mask. "Maybe they fixed it."

"Jesus doesn't fix shit. He applies Band-Aids, if that. Let's go."

Julianne opened the door, and Ansel followed her out into the hallway once again. The faint trace of chemical fog still lingered, and begrudgingly he was grateful for the face protection. He'd gotten strep once as a kid, and although he wasn't the cleanest by any stretch, the sack of needles that had sat in his throat for weeks was enough for Ansel to give any potentially serious interactions with bacteria a wide berth.

Aside from the dull background thump of the Valentine's Day party music below, it was eerily quiet on their floor, as if all the commotion had abruptly come to a halt. The usual annoyances of couples fighting, units packed with more bodies than they could reasonably accommodate, and 5.1 surround sound systems blasting video game machine guns were all gone. It was the quietest Ansel had ever heard it.

"Wow, almost peaceful for once," he said.

He followed Julianne down the hall to the elevator. She tapped her foot furiously, waiting for the doors to open.

"Stairs," he offered.

"Fuck that. This is the one amenity offered by this shithole, and I'm gonna make use of it."

As they waited for the elevator, Ansel took his cellphone out of his pocket. "Gonna call the office just to let Jesus know we're coming."

He dialed, noticing he had no signal. Not exactly a surprise for Sunshine Spires but still annoying.

"Stop. Don't. That'll give him a chance to prepare. I wanna clip this lazy sack of shit off at the knees."

Ansel shrugged, tucked the phone away, and attempted to do the same with the growing fear that he might lose his home. "Don't have any service anyway."

Julianne aggressively thumbed the elevator's call button. "Christ, this thing is slow."

As they stood waiting, new sounds seemed to emerge all around them, something close to mewling. Beyond the mewling there was moaning. It sounded baritone and sad.

"You hear that, right?"

"I wish I couldn't. Sounds like the most depressing sex I've ever heard."

The doors to the elevator opened. Both he and Julianne went rigid. The interior was wet and smelled of copper.

"Is that blood?" he asked, pointing to the smear on the floor.

"This place was already hell, and now it's sunk deeper."

She stepped inside, keeping clear of the red splatter carpeting the floor. On the wall, a flyer for the night's Valentine's Day soiree had been slashed into ribbons, the winking anthropomorphic heart sliced in half.

Ansel followed her in, cringing as his New Balances absorbed some of the chunky gruel. Before the doors could close, he saw someone coming down the hallway toward them. He stuck his hand out, forcing the doors back open. "It's Bruce. Hey, Bruce! We'll hold it for you!"

Bruce bellowed back with the fury of a man who'd just lost his pension on the poker slots. As Bruce drew closer, Ansel could see the old car salesman wasn't exactly himself. For one, he had bulked up significantly. His shirt and pants were ripped like an old Hulk comic. Additionally, his hands were completely missing, and in their place, wedged into bloody stumps with a pink, taffy-like substance wound around the handles, were a meat cleaver and pizza cutter.

"Okay, something's wrong with Bruce," Ansel whispered.

Julianne peeked over his shoulder. "The fuck did he do?"

"Don't know. Don't care. Just . . . you know . . . close the door."

"Yeah. Good idea."

Julianne began her rapid-fire assault on the CLOSE DOOR button.

"Now would be preferable."

"I'm trying."

"Try faster. Please."

"Oh, now it's urgent!"

Julianne fingered the button like she was fifteen again burning through incel mouth-breathers on *GTA* online. "Fucking close, you broken cock-sucking piece of shit!" she screamed.

Bruce's mouth opened and unleashed a fountain of puke. The cutlery he'd wedged into his stumps slithered out, directed by vicious serpentine pastel cords.

Ansel jumped back as the blade of the pizza cutter sparked off the closing metal door, and then they were descending.

7

The doors opened on the first floor. Ansel and Julianne were still plastered against the back wall, expecting something hideous to leap inside like a rabid coyote in a chicken coop, which would be preferable to the cartoon monster they'd just encountered. It took until the doors started to close for Ansel to stop them. Together, they emerged into the hallway.

"The fuck was that?" Julianne asked.

"Bruce is not all right."

"You think? Let's get to Jesus's. There's no way he can weasel out of this."

The air was hazy on the first floor. Even through the respirator, Ansel could smell a trace of something foul. Maybe this floor always smelled bad, and he just never gave it a second thought.

"Is it darker down here?" he asked.

Julianne scanned the overhead fluorescent bulbs. Half of them were out. The other half were flickering. "Power issues. I don't know why I expect anything less here."

They found the property manager's office at the end of the hall. The name JESUS GONZALES was stenciled across the mesh-wire glass. A piece of steno pad was taped to the wall beside it with office hours scrawled in sloppy gel pen.

Ansel knocked. No answer.

Julianne said, "Screw niceties," and opened the door.

Inside, the room was sparse. A metal desk. Ancient desktop PC. The office blinds were drawn, engulfing the space in shadow. Were it not for the glow of the computer screen, it would have been hard to see anything at all. A calendar featuring some women in bikinis hung on the wall. The date squares were blank. Jesus clearly wasn't using it to keep schedules; he just liked the photos.

"Well, he ain't here," Ansel said. "Maybe we could call corporate or something."

"Fuck all good that'll do. You ever call it? They just have a machine to gather up grievances. Ten bucks says they never even listen to it."

"There's gotta be a clause in the lease about fixing shit that's broken. Whatever's going on isn't just a legal issue. From what I've seen, there might be an emergency."

Julianne moved to the desk, started rifling through papers. "Maybe there's a direct line we can call, jump that stupid voicemail box no one ever checks."

As she searched, Ansel moved toward the window, spun the tilt wand that opened the blinds. His tongue clicked involuntarily. "Huh . . . Hey, Julianne, what's this?"

Still rifling, she said, "What's what?"

"Why is it blacked out?"

She dropped a collection of papers she'd been holding, stared at the glass. "I dunno. Wait, it's not blacked out. It's some kind of metal shutter. What the fuck?"

"Gonna get a look from the outside," Ansel responded. He left Jesus's office and made his way down the drab and stinking hallway toward the lobby doors. When he got there, he noticed they were also now covered on the outside with corrugated shutters, and much like the elevator, he found himself standing in a pool of what was definitely blood. "Okay, weird." When he put his ear to the ribbed metal, he could hear voices outside. Electronic voices, like those on walkie talkies.

He made his way back through the massive blood puddle until he was back at Jesus's office. "You're not gonna believe what's out there," he said to Julianne.

She was trying in vain to get into the computer but finally gave up, waved a piece of paper in his direction. "Look at this."

"What about it?"

"It's today's date. With a shit ton of exclamation marks next to it. Nothing else. Like an urgent note-to-self."

"Yeah, I'm getting the sense something is off. The front doors are blocked. There's blood—"

"Blocked? How?"

"Steel shutter."

"Are we completely locked in?" she asked, her eyes widening with concern.

"I have no idea. There are fire exits, right?"

"This fucker set a trap. We're trapped!"

"I'm sure there's an explanation. Look . . . maybe this just opens." He reached for the window lock and spun it. But when he pushed on the glass, it wouldn't budge. He pushed harder, shoving with all his might, but the window wouldn't open.

Obstinately, he picked up Jesus's office chair and hurled it at the window. It bounced back into the room without harming the windowpane.

Julianne pressed on the glass. "This isn't even normal glass. It's thick. Real thick. Like, bulletproof thick."

"I don't get it. Why would they lock us in?"

"You tell me."

"You can open the window in your place, right?"

"Sure, but I live on the fifth floor. Almost the same as being locked in."

"Try the phone."

Julianne picked up the office phone receiver and held the earpiece to Ansel's head. There was no dial tone. In disbelief, he tried his cell again but still couldn't get service. "Fuck. Okay, look, there's a fire exit in the stairwell on this floor. Let's give it a try."

"I'm losing my patience with this place. Should've never moved here."

"Why *did* you move in?" he asked.

"My parents are nice, but their love language is suffocation and lecturing. College, college, college. They never shut up about it. I barely limped out of high school. Spending another four years in a classroom when I'd rather be building a blood cannon or set for my shorts sounded like a nightmare. Besides, living with them until my thirties? No, thanks. This was the cheapest place I could find. Why did *you* move in?"

"The cheap part, mostly. But it always seemed—"

"Almost too good to be true?"

"I dunno, below market value, I guess. That type of luck still exists, you know."

"Sure it does." She exited the office and turned right toward the far stairwell.

Ansel noticed now just how dark the whole building seemed. It was always dim, sure, but this was different. It looked like someone had removed most of the lighting fixtures.

When they reached the stairwell, Julianne stopped abruptly on the second stair.

Ansel came up close behind, nearly shoved her forward. "What's the—Holy Fuck!"

Splashes of champagne and shattered pink glass glittered on the stairs leading up to the next floor. Half an upended sheet cake slid slowly toward them. Sitting at the top of the stairs, one hand stuffing her face with gobs of frosting while the other caressed the head of the man feverishly lapping at her clit, was an elderly woman Ansel vaguely recognized. Blood pooled underneath where she sat, mixing with all the smashed chocolates around her.

Julianne's mouth opened, but words failed her.

It wasn't just the two of them. Another man, knees pressed into the concrete steps, thrust into the one going down on the cake lady. The lion tattooed on his back, ostensibly poised for attack, now just looked like it was trying to get the hell out of there.

"Someone must've spiked the food table at the V-Day party," Ansel whispered. "A few drops of high-grade LSD or whatever synthetic shit they lace weed with now, maybe."

Julianne pointed at the sex show. "It doesn't explain the bizarre anal beads creeping from that man's asshole, tickling his hips and the backs of his knees."

A sudden *clomp clomp* resounded from the landing directly above them. Heavy footfalls descended toward where they stood. It was accompanied by a low growl followed by something wet and pink splatting on the ground next to them. It was a human chest, flayed off its body. Two pierced nipples bookending a gully of wiry black pubic hair. Winding their way throughout the meat were orbs about as big as human eyeballs, except instead of pupils, these had vertical slits full of jagged teeth.

Lion Tat glanced over his shoulder, finally noticing them. "More the merrier." He pulled out of the man who was determined to make cunnilingus an Olympic sport. His hefty, vein-ridden cock bobbed against his thigh, leaking strands of viscous precum.

This time Ansel pulled Julianne by the shoulder. "Come on."

They rushed to the fire door, found it locked. "Fuck!" Ansel yelled.

The footsteps rounded the landing, coming down toward them. *Clomp, clomp, clomp!*

Ansel spun around, panicked, looking for a weapon. There was nothing useful. But there was another door. A beacon of hope in their current situation. "Basement. This way!"

The gargantuan noggin burst like a soggy pinata.

"Escapee down." Vern turned the volume up on the truck's speakers. "Stranglehold" filled the night air. The fleeing, now headless, former resident of Sunshine Spires fell to the cement with a *thunk* and *splat*.

DeFanti threw a fist up. "Hot damn! You see that dome explode, Vern?"

Vern liked Morgan DeFanti. She was smart, agile, and unassuming, with a lanky frame most men took for granted right up until she slid a switchblade into their throat or the barrel of a gun underneath their chin, fishing their wallet out and disappearing into the night. McKay and Simpson were good guys, but Vern always got the impression they leaned hard on the libertarian side, wanted to be part of the cause because it allowed them to move freely throughout the world with minimal consequences. To Vern, that just boiled down to them wanting to be pricks without any blowback.

Morgan was a true believer.

And damn good with the guns.

He popped open the cooler they'd set next to their artillery, grabbed a Lone Star, and let the cold beer glide down his throat as the rest of his pack blasted holes into the building. He still wasn't sure what the government creep's goal was here, but he was sure of one thing:

No one was getting out alive who wasn't supposed to.

8

To live and die in a sex swing, Ron mused.

He'd put some distance between himself and the ravenous horndogs before ducking into an open apartment. Being fucked to death and reborn as a horny alien ghoul was not an appealing end. It wasn't lost on him that this could've still happened the moment he locked the door, but hesitating was a sure death, and this was merely a possible one.

The man before him flailed around, wrists and ankles cuffed to the support chains of the toppled pleasure device.

Damn shame they won't be able to cart all these specimens back to the lab.

An even bigger shame that he was the only one seeing this. Next go-round he'd remember to budget for body cams. Eliminate the reliance on the tablets, which had almost gotten him killed twice already.

Still, at least they were learning something along the way. Ron just had to make sure the research data made it back to the lab. He pulled a fresh sample kit from his messenger bag.

"You're going to change the world."

The man lifted his head from the carpet, leaving an ear behind. A pained moan slithered through split lips. Thick strands of liquefied face dangled like shredded paper. Ron took note that not all the test subjects reacted with accelerated muscle growth or intense arousal mixed with bloodlust.

All that came with the sample kit was a syringe, biopsy punch, and a dozen containers. It'd allow for micro-data collection, but Ron wasn't the bare-minimum type; he especially couldn't be one now. He wasn't an in-and-out clock-watcher collecting a paycheck. He was an integral part of revolutionary science. You wouldn't know that by reading the reports. Samson, the project's brain, referred to most of the team in reductive titles like "lead" or "coordinator." Dull vagaries that most of the directors would gloss over when going over the documents during their morning shit. The lack of recognition aggravated Ron daily, but now, they couldn't relegate him to another faceless cell in a spreadsheet.

Ron rummaged through the kitchen, hoping to find a suitable knife. The more time went by, the more he felt his confidence grow. He could do this. This was his chance to stand out, not be seen as a seat-warmer, and with that would come the bonus he needed to get Elaine out of the dark cove of their family home and onto a beach with some goddamn sunshine, seawater, and a drink that had a stupid umbrella in it.

Ron started to itch with irritation. He'd found nothing but random junk, a bag of sporks, and empty Tupperware containers crusted with old food. "What the fuck do you eat with?" Ron shouted into the living room, yanking out more drawers and dropping them to the floor. "Never mind, I know the answer."

He was about to start in on the closet, convinced there had to be something useful within, when he noticed the duffel bag. MAINTENANCE was stenciled across the olive canvas in black marker. He pulled out a variety of tools, feeling more and more like a back-alley surgeon by the minute. Buried underneath the wrenches and assorted screwdrivers, he finally found what he needed.

The teeth of the hacksaw were rusted and chipped, but when your only other option was a fork-spoon hybrid, you were thankful. In his pre-med classes, he'd watched videos of human dissection where the doctor explained it was important to cut into a body with finesse, respect. Your fellow human deserved kindness even posthumously. Despite the path he found himself on, Ron agreed, but time wasn't exactly plentiful given the apocalyptic orgy occurring in the building.

Back in the bedroom, the sex swing's occupant had managed to free one of his arms. The metal handcuff thumped against the carpet as he slowly pulled himself toward the entryway, leaving a trail of fingernails stuck in the carpet. Lovebugs began pushing their way through tiny slits in the nailbeds.

Ron stepped wide to avoid the man's grasping hand and the mouths at his fingertips.

Before getting to work, he grabbed the leather gimp mask from the foot of the bed. Dead or not, he didn't think he could handle looking into another man's face while sawing through his neck. He may have been riding the high of determination, but Ron took no pleasure in dismembering a body.

He planted a knee in between the man's shoulder blades to steady himself. Leaning back every so often to dodge the arm flailing about like a striking cobra, Ron pulled the mask down over his specimen's head. The thick leather sloughed off gobs of buttery flesh as it concealed the man's face.

Knuckles grazed his temple. "I'm going to have to do something about that arm."

When it jerked in his direction again, Ron snagged the wrist, quickly cuffed it to the other set of handcuffs still secured to one of the posts. The lovebugs wrapped around the metal rod, seeking warmth.

He took in a deep breath, grabbed the man by the hair, and slid the hacksaw underneath the pulsing throat of Sunshine Spires's longtime maintenance man. "Okay, here we go . . . "

9

"**D**id you know this place had a basement?" Julianne asked.

Ansel fumbled around trying to find the light switch, annoyed at the sluggishness of his fingers. When had that started? Was that why his compositions weren't as fluid? Why the music itself sounded so unsure these days? "I didn't, but I'm not surprised," he responded. "My guess is this is where the electrical room is."

"No, that's on the eighth floor. I know because it hums all night long."

"Okay, well, the fact remains we found a basement and neither of us know what's down here, but this is the only part of the building that doesn't sound like the porn parody of a massacre, so does it really matter?"

"Jesus, dude, calm down. I just thought you might know since you've been here longer than me."

Ansel shrugged, reiterating that he had no idea what was at the bottom of the concrete stairwell.

He wouldn't admit it, but even he'd been caught off guard by his outburst, a childish response to a logical question. Insecurity had been bubbling in the back of his mind for the last few months. Ansel knew the longer he took to produce a slice of music for someone's independent project was another day toward losing the gig. The nostalgia young and seasoned creators had for his work on titles like *Eat of Her Flesh* and *Sundown Showdown* would only grant him so much time to dick around before they got frustrated enough and dropped him from the project. The marionette-creep of his fingers was a reminder not only of his age, but proof he was no longer in his prime, and maybe no longer capable of producing anything worthwhile.

And Julianne was young. She was hungry. There was a whole life of experiences and creative opportunities ahead of her. Deep down in his sensitive-to-anything-but-white-bread guts, Ansel felt jealous.

Halfway down the stairs, Julianne grabbed his shoulder. "What the hell is that noise?"

"Maybe Bruce is finally using that pizza cutter?"

"No, asshole." She pointed toward the black rectangle of a doorway at the bottom. "Listen."

A wet, thick wheezing drifted up from below, like an elderly cat preparing to spit up a ball of fur.

They reached the bottom of the stairs, cautiously stepped through the door. A hallway hooked to the right, opening into a massive concrete space littered with fast food boxes, shower curtain rods streaked with gummy fluids, and candy wrappers. All of it circled a lone hospital bed. A sallow bulb hummed overhead. The floor was stained with splotches of acrid yellow that Ansel could smell was piss.

Sitting in the bed was a massive heap of flesh.

"Is that . . . " Julianne cocked her head to the side. "Is that fucking Carol?"

The last time Ansel had seen the complex's self-appointed Neighborhood Watch, she'd been several hundred pounds lighter and wasn't missing her left leg and right arm. Soiled wax paper covered the still-weeping stumps. Her one intact leg scratched a hypnotic rhythm against the sodden fabric of the mattress.

"I take it back," Ansel said. "I'm suddenly very grateful for the mask."

"Fuckin' *told* you."

"I guess now we know where she's been."

Extroversion wasn't Ansel's strong suit. He couldn't name most folks who lived in the building. The freaks they'd run into having a messy threesome on the landing were grotesque versions of people he'd ascribed titles to. Captain Beefheart Wannabee, Asshole Construction Worker, and Library Lady, shorthand monikers for strangers that required little brain power on his part. He'd only started talking to Julianne because he'd noticed her *Fire and Ice* T-shirt and they got to bonding about rotoscoping. Turned out she was an animator, and her love didn't stop at cartoon animation. She'd been working hard at sculpting, tinkering with animatronics, and trying to get her own FX business off the ground. All of which were expensive undertakings, hence her current residence.

She'd been a big influence on his decision to put himself back out there as a composer. Especially after he'd seen the reception to her five-minute short film, *A Rest in the Void,* about a young woman's escape pod getting lost in space. Despite the bleak premise, the banter between the main character and the unit's AI as they propelled farther into the darkness of space really kept the piece from dovetailing into complete despair. There'd been talk about turning it into a feature, which she was firmly against; it wouldn't work as a longer piece.

"I thought she'd moved out," Julianne said.

A rusty bucket balanced on Carol's globular belly. She withdrew a spoonful of slop that resembled moldy spaghetti and crammed it into her mouth, chewed with an immense smack that reminded Ansel of the feral raccoons that ate from the dumpster out back.

They both jumped when Carol's head snapped to the side, regarded them with beady eyes reduced to black pinpricks that were buried under puffy, sweat-damp eyelids. "They ain't grown back yet, but that don't mean they won't," she gargled, fighting for breath. "Y'all took too much last time! Get some more chow in me, though, and I'll be as right as the good book. God rewards those who work hard without complaint. Work, work, work. Gotta earn your keep and if you do right it's off to the heavens. Where there's probably good eating. Now get me my food! I'm starving!"

Carol's swollen belly spilled over the sides of the bed, folds of flesh that nearly touched the ground. Like giant wings of corpulence, swaying ever so gently. Her neck folds hid chunks of food that had turned gray. The bed dipped downward from the stress of the weight. An inhuman bulk that had not graced her body before. This was all new somehow. An experiment in glandular swelling. Ansel thought of inappropriate jokes about whales he'd heard as a child, and a sadness welled inside him. Overweight was one thing, but this wasn't normal. Someone or something had ballooned her nearly to death and then taken her limbs for God knew what reason. This had been done on purpose.

It was then he noticed the tubes going into the back of her leg. They connected to some motorized contraption on the floor next to her. It hummed like a pump. A tiny green light winked on and off, indicating power. Beyond that he couldn't tell anything about it.

Julianne took a few steps forward. "Carol, are you okay?"

"Hell are you?" she wheezed.

"Julianne, from the eighth floor. Remember, you told me I was a busybody last month."

"Right. You're all busybodies. Wait . . . " Their former neighbor stared, as if she'd finally realized they weren't whoever was keeping her down here. "You're not with the company?"

"No. What company? I'm here with Ansel from 3-B. There's something going on in the building. People are changing."

Carol started thumbing the button of a small remote that Ansel hadn't realized she'd been holding the entire time they'd been standing there. "Dying? We're all dying, sweetie. I'm gonna go sooner than later if these bastards don't hurry on up with the rest of my dinner."

Ansel couldn't stop staring at the bucket rising and falling with every strained breath she took. Marinara sauce streaked its sides like crusty rivers of dried blood. Rogue noodles pasted to the rim dangled wildly.

He really didn't want to be around for the next course.

"Not sure when they plan on coming back," Carol said. "Don't have a clock in here."

Ansel stepped back from the bed. "It's close to midnight."

Carol grunt-belched her disapproval at the news. "Damn, that is unfortunate. Do me a favor, would ya? The TV stopped working a few hours ago. Mind giving it a good smack, see if it comes back on?"

Ansel went over to a massive Zenith television that'd been set up on a small dresser. A single cable snaked out the back to an extension cord. Damn thing probably stroked out when the power went out. He messed around with the buttons, while Julianne pushed for more information.

"Carol, who did this to you?" She gave the slightest tug to one of the tubes in Carol's leg, and Carol howled.

"Leave it!"

"Okay, okay. But tell me who did this?"

"I did."

Julianne narrowed her eyes. "I don't understand."

"Well," Carol said, attempting to readjust herself, "when Hollis died, most of our money was coming in from his cable company pension, and a lot of it went to funding my stepdaughter's rehab stays." She tapped the side of her nose to illustrate the point. "Hollis had heart, but he was too soft on her. I cut her off. It was only right, but what was left of the nest egg barely covered me for six months."

"I swear I used to know how to work one of these," Ansel muttered, still fiddling.

"After that, I was going to have to find a real job. Quilting isn't a very lucrative business, especially when I'm not on social media. Besides, I can't compete with a lot of the younger folks. Talented and attractive. A privilege I've never had."

Ansel unplugged the TV, re-plugged it in, and banged the sides of the massive box.

"I tried talking to Jesus, but I'm sure you know what trying to get through to him is like. He just gawked at me from across that desk of his like I'd gone in and shown him my backside for a laugh, said there was nothing he could do. Company rules are company rules."

"C'mon, you old bitch," Ansel said, putting a little more force into swatting the TV, thinking back to all the times his old man would do the same, getting angrier and angrier that he was missing whatever western flick was airing that night.

"Then a few days later, this older gentleman shows up at the door. A little plain, but cute in that 1950s sort of way. He said management informed him of what he called 'my unfortunate situation,' and he came all the way down to personally make me an offer. The company that owns this building also works with the government, leasing a lot of their properties for projects. Did you know that? I didn't. He didn't go into much detail. Quite honestly, I'm glad he didn't. I don't need to know. What I wanted to hear about was how this would help me keep a roof over my head. Darlin', would you mind helping me here? This damn thing broke not too long ago."

Ansel continued to fiddle with the TV but wasn't getting anywhere. "Nothing in this stupid building ever works," he mumbled.

"Sweetie . . . " Carol continued.

"Oh, uh, yeah of course," Julianne said. "What do I need to do?"

"Just take a hold here." Carol held up the arm with the wax paper. Up close she could see it was being held in place with a zip-tie. "Just don't grab the end of where my arm used to be. Only got so much mobility till it grows back."

"I'm sorry? Grows back?"

"You heard right, love." Carol chuckled. "That was the trade-off. My body for shelter and a chance to contribute to my country."

"I know I heard that wrong," Ansel said, peering up from the television.

Carol nodded to a darkened corner of the room where a plastic tub sat, an orange biohazard sticker slapped across the front. "You got your masks on. Go take a look."

Julianne met Ansel's gaze. Her eyes went wide, and her head tilted and her lips went tight as if she were trying to summon up a latent superpower. But he got the gist of her expression. There was no way Carol was telling the truth.

Based on the entire set-up around them, he bought into the experiment bit. Limb regeneration was another thing. A breakthrough like that would've made the news and a shitload of company men quietly rich. And it sure as shit wouldn't be taking place in a dark basement littered with dirty dishes and diarrhea stains.

"I'll take your word for it," Julianne said.

"Your choice, sweetie. Hey, you are quite pretty, you know that?"

"Thank you," she said.

Ansel could see something was wrong with Julianne but couldn't quite put a finger on it. The way she smiled with pathos felt real, but he could see her hands trembling in fear. She was struggling with what she was seeing.

Julianne touched the old woman by the shoulder, searching for sympathy within herself, trying not to visibly cringe at the wet fabric or the stale body odor drifting up from Carol's unwashed girth. The revulsion was a bit of a surprise. Julianne struggled with her own body image, championed body positivity whenever she could, but in the moment, there was nothing but a growing instinct to recoil.

She wondered if it had less to do with the woman's physical state, more about how the closer Julianne got, the harder Carol bit into her bottom lip. She expected to see a line of blood start running down her chin, congealing with the crusty tomato paste any second.

"Talented and beautiful," Carol said. "You're a lucky one."

"Uh, yeah, thanks," Julianne said, tugging a bit harder, fighting off the mental image of becoming Carol's lunch. "Can you sit up a bit more?"

"You're doing great. Downright delicious."

"How the hell did people operate these back in the day?" Ansel brought his fist down on top of the TV.

Carol's half-arm came up and around, gripped the back of Julianne's neck, and pulled her forward with enough force to make her cry out as her face collided with the woman's cheek.

"There was an old myth about cannibalism, that if you ate someone, you took their power. Maybe the same can be said for beauty."

At the same time, a dull green glow illuminated the room.

"Hey!" Ansel shouted. "I got it to work—Oh shit! Let her go!"

Carol's tongue performed a manic dance, leaving snail trails of spit across the bridge of the respirator's bulky nose.

"So hungry. I've always wanted to try something delicate. So painfully hungry."

The woman wept as she repeated herself again, spiraling into a desperate mantra. Fighting off a wave of nausea and the bizarre strength behind her old neighbor's amputated arm, Julianne brought her fist into the woman's monolithic bulk half a dozen times.

It was about as effective as punching a vat of marshmallow fluff.

Slowly, Julianne felt a subtle tug on her scalp followed by frenzied slurping and succinct pain. Heat flushed her face as she realized Carol was gobbling her hair up like egg noodles. She tried to steady herself, slipped forward into the flesh-rutted valley between Carol's distended breasts.

Through a mouthful of her hair, Julianne heard Carol elicit a muffled moan.

Something grabbed Carol by the sides of her skull and pulled. Julianne prayed it was Ansel coming to save her. The moaning grew into horrid sounds made of primal climax and rage, nearly drowning out all the screaming.

Clusters of agony erupted across Julianne's head. Wet tearing filled her ears.

"Whatever you're doing," she screamed, "fucking stop, man! Try something else! Hurry!"

* * *

Ansel let go of the human vacuum that'd become Carol's cranium. Fire flared in his arthritic hands. *You useless old bastard*, he thought as his only friend in the building was slowly being eaten alive hair-first. He scanned the room for anything he could use as a weapon.

Then, as absurd as it was, it occurred to him. The biohazard box.

Quickly, he popped the lid off. Mask or not, the smell of rancid meat engulfed him. She hadn't been lying. Arms and legs in various states of decomposition filled it to the brim. Sitting atop the pile, though, was an arm with most of the muscle dissolved, radius and ulna both broken and jagged at their ends.

Screams and squelches continued behind him.

He'd written the music for countless films where the human body was destroyed in thousands of ways, some gruesome and others downright silly. Mouthfuls of popcorn devoured while passively watching simulated deaths—sometimes on a loop to match the right sounds to the visuals—and laughing most of the time. He was always amused by those scenes.

He grabbed the meaty arm with the exposed bones and attacked. All he felt now when the tapered ends of bones punched through Carol's temple was just how damn difficult it was to stab someone in the head.

The old woman's appendages, both stumps and full-length, went wild. Ansel pressed down, driving the arm bones so deep in her head that brains began oozing out around the puncture site. When he finally let go, all that remained was a flaccid hand hanging askew from Carol's gore-drenched dome. Her body bucked a few more times, a final jig of death that made the hand look like it was waving.

Carol's mouth relaxed, allowing Julianne to escape. She sat on the floor, hair dripping with stomach bile.

"Here, let me help you up," Ansel said.

"Just . . . give me a fucking minute."

10

"**N**ot all heroes wear capes or uniforms. The government thanks you for your service, citizen."

Ron saluted the freshly decapitated head in his hand, warm blood still dripping onto the carpet. He briefly wondered if he should remove the gimp mask before packing it up but decided it really didn't matter when he could hear Theo getting closer. Besides, he quickly pulled the mouth zipper shut as a few familiar tendrils started unfurling from behind the man's pale lips.

The screams were now few and far between, which meant most of the tenants were likely dead and now shambling, horny corpses, piloted by an alien force.

A shame.

They all held unique information within themselves. How they interacted with the lovebugs was all promising data—even the one in the basement. Many nights had been spent on that one. He'd asked if they could get her out ahead of time, but Samson had forbidden it. For the sake of national security, they wanted zero surviving tenants.

He'd studied the layout of the building every night leading up to the project launch. Entries and exits were minimal, which at the time was fine. There hadn't been a plan B or exit strategy because everyone was supposed to turn docile, experience a newfound desire for peace and love, man. Ron made a mental note to not be so lazy next time. It'd nearly cost him his life this go 'round.

It wasn't all doom and gloom, though. He'd finally found a smartphone in working shape. He grabbed a thin nail from the toolbox and popped the SD card out of his own phone and placed it in the new one. It powered up, and all it took to unlock it was to place it in front of a picture of the unmasked gimp-masked man that hung on the wall.

It took a couple of minutes of digging around the memory files, but he finally got the frequency-hopping app up and running. "Please, please, please," he whispered as he keyed in the emergency HQ phone number, followed by the requisite security codes. After several seconds of soul-crushing silence, the sound of a dial-up internet connection tickled his ear on the other end before ringing.

"I'm not sure if any of you know this, but things have gone south in here. Over."

There was a crackle and hiss before a voice cut through the static. "Perimeter is secure. And you don't need to say 'over,' fuckstick. This isn't Fallujah."

"Well, I'm glad that pack of yokels can manage to follow basic directions, but in here things are very *unsecure*. I need an evac."

"No one leaves. That's the order."

"That applies to the tenants, not me."

"Applies to everyone until we hear otherwise."

"So you're aware of what I'm dealing with here?"

"Of course, dipshit, there are more hidden cameras in there than a Chinese brothel. Doesn't change a thing. No one comes out. Nice head, by the way. You trying to smuggle out a new sex toy?"

Someone chuckled in the background.

"I have to bring the samples back! You want this project to work, we need to figure out what went wrong."

"No can do. Sorry, man."

"What am I supposed to do then?"

"Pray?"

Laughter erupted in his ear.

"Whose orders?"

"Classified."

"Bullshit. Samson?"

"Classified."

"We can't figure out why the project failed without the samples. You and the donkey braying next to you might be assholes, but you're not stupid."

"Just put them down somewhere. We'll find them."

"Fuck off. I'm bringing these in and dropping them on Samson's desk."

"Evac is off the table. Now if you'll excuse us, there's a trio of wannabee vampires sucking more than each other's necks on camera seventy-seven. Have a good day."

Fucking surveillance-jockeys were getting off on the little bit of power they had. *Wouldn't be as smug with that mutated giant smashing through their little panel van out on the street, popping their heads off.*

"I'm cleared for any and all information regarding this mission," Ron said. "Just tell me if these are Samson's orders."

"For the lead guy on this, you really don't know shit, do you?"

"Listen, bring the ground shutters up for a second and let me out of here. Have the control team stand down. The samples I've got in here are valuable."

"Hey," said a voice in the background, "tell him to try the roof, see if he can fly off into the night."

"You hear that, little birdy?"

Ron ended the call, clipped the phone to his belt. Hacksaw in hand, he made his way out of the apartment and down the dark hallway. He'd find his own way out of the building. That wasn't the hard part. Not getting ripped in half in the process was what worried him.

11

Theo could sense them everywhere, the ones who still needed to be loved. All around him, ensconced behind paper-thin walls. Their bodies ready to receive the seeds of his people like fresh soil. He just needed to smash his way into their lives, bringing the pleasure and pain that came with rebirth.

He knew there were others like him in the building. Envoys chosen to guide the course of their species' kidnapping into an opportunity to spread. Given the rampant cries of change he heard as he stalked the halls, Theo had no doubt the rest were delivering on their promise to hijack these fumbling meat sacks, and in time, the landscape of this world would be theirs like so many before it.

He kicked open the nearest door and let himself into the musty apartment. An old man sat before him in a wicker chair. He was nude, his legs spread. Gray pubes dangled down to his knees. His chest cavity had been torn open, and gray intestines dropped to the floor like dead snakes. Yellow mucus dripped from his mouth, the telltale sign of someone who'd breathed deep of the gas. Someone now controlled by the sentient microorganisms invading his brain. "You here to suck me?" he breathed, tapping the head of his dick. "You can have this body. I don't need it anymore. Yours looks better anyway. Stronger. Why don't we trade, huh?"

Theo wanted nothing to do with him. He raised his axe to hasten the geriatric's progress but stopped when the man thrust his hand into the gaping wound on his torso. This one was chatty, controlled by thousands of his kind who found joy in communicating.

"Body is full of mud," the man said. He pulled out a handful of black goo and threw it on the ground. The smell of diarrhea was a cheap shot to Theo's heightened senses. He opened his mouth but inhaled through his nose anyway.

"Do you want to literally fuck my shit up?" The man laughed. "These things have such a narrow understanding of everything around them, don't they?" He reached inside his split belly again and hoisted up a handful of liquid feces, threw it on the floor. "Nothing but waste."

"Have you seen a man who looks like a bug?"

"Everything I've ever seen is inside me. Come and take a peek, brother." The old man yanked another handful of shit out, threw it at Theo. It hit him in the face. "Have we begun to amass yet? Where will our center grow? Take us there."

Theo took the man's head off. He could find his own way down to the party.

"I don't think you're ready yet."

Theo exited the apartment, spitting hot fecal smears off his lips. Even with the stench of excrement stinging his nostrils, he could still smell Ron in the air. He took off down the hall with only one mission in mind.

12

Julianne leaned against the concrete wall, felt wetness slide down her belly under her shirt. Liquidized fat from Carol's exposed insides had made its way down into the coveralls. Warm and thick and heading toward her waistline. Julianne pulled the zipper down, tore off her shirt, and scrubbed the goop away from her navel.

Ansel's gaze zoned in on the generic black sports bra. When was the last time he'd seen a woman like this who wasn't photographed and showcased in pages printed in the '80s?

She turned away from him. "Ugh, Jesus, dude . . ."

"Sorry." He put his nose to the wall, feeling ashamed. "I wasn't—"

"Yes, you were. You think I made it this far in life without clocking that shit? A few seconds of glancing feels like an hour, but half the time I don't bother saying anything because if I do, I end up in a shallow grave somewhere."

"I said I was sorry."

A circular orange stain adorned the front now, like someone tried to draw a pumpkin using actual pumpkin pulp. She tossed it to the floor, zipped back up. "What was all that about limb regeneration and the government?"

Ansel faced the room again, stared over the preternaturally massive corpse on the table. "Yeah, I heard all that, too. And she thought we were in on it. What's going on?"

"What's going on is this apartment was cheap for a reason. I'm beginning to suspect they needed free guinea pigs. Thing is, those people on the stairwell, that torso, it didn't look like anyone had new limbs. It looked like they were melting, splitting open."

"I thought I saw a jellyfish crawling out of that guy's asshole."

Ansel ran his hands over his body, feeling for abnormalities, any suspicious lumps or cuts. "I think I'm okay. I don't feel different. And no one offered me any deals moving in here. Not for money or food or anything else."

Julianne was already heading for the door that led back to the stairwell. "We need to get out of the building. Any way possible. There should be a fire escape door at the end of one of the hallways."

"Honestly . . . " Ansel gestured at the room. "Starting to think this is the safest place to be. Those things didn't follow us in here, and all we've come across is Carol. Besides, the lobby was locked up. Same with the office. My hopes aren't high for the emergency exits."

"What're you suggesting?"

"We wait."

"You're kidding."

"This is the only time we've had to take a breath and think about the situation. We're safe in here. The door is solid. It should hold. I say we wait until the authorities arrive. If there's one thing I know about Jesus, it's his safety comes first."

"You're forgetting that ominous date I found. There's no way he wasn't involved. And this door was unlocked. Do you see a way to lock it from our side?"

"So we block it."

"With what? The box of body parts? The TV that's practically the size of a boulder?"

Ansel glanced over at Carol's body. "Not exactly."

Laughter broke Julianne's face into a dozen angles. "Ansel, I'm not going near her again. No. God. Damn. Way."

His embarrassment deepened. He was just doing what he thought was logical based on the information they had. She didn't need to make him feel stupid. "I'm not going back out there."

Her demeanor softened. "I understand you're scared. In here we can control the situation, but—"

"Yes!"

"It's a coffin in the long run. Do you remember when Pretorius Valentine emailed you?"

"I still think that name is fake," he said.

"Unless his parents are mad scientists, yes, but you were nervous. Your inbox had been empty for a while and here was this underground director getting good buzz reaching out to *you*. What happened?"

"I was going to delete it. I thought it might be a joke or a scam."

"And then?"

"You told me to respond. That if I got back a reply asking for money or that my niece's great-uncle's nephew's aunt had been abducted and the only one who could help me was a Nigerian prince, then it's a scam."

"Was it?"

"It was not."

"Exactly. Then that led to getting another gig and another."

"I already said thank you."

"I'm not finished. I'm trying to put it into context for you. When you're too scared to keep moving forward, that's when you need to, and right now we need to keep going or we'll die in this concrete box."

"What're you suggesting?"

"If the doors are all locked, we break through the walls, even those things out there. Whatever keeps us from the outside, we tear right through it. Don't you want answers?"

Ansel nodded.

"Me too. Let's fucking go."

DeFanti put her rifle scope to her eye and aimed at the third floor. An enormous body moved in front of the windows. "Either they got some thick ol' tenants in that building or something else is going on. You seeing that . . . thing . . . up there?"

Vern stared through his scope and followed DeFanti's trajectory. Something was definitely moving around the building, but it was hard to tell just what it was. He lowered his rifle and shrugged. "Looks big."

"Big enough I might need a whole magazine to take it down. What do you think it is? A sasquatch? That what we're dealing with here?"

McKay pointed at the severed leg still cozied up to the van's tire. "That ain't hairy enough to be a 'squatch. And lookie at the tattoo of a fish with legs. That there is something much worse than a 'squatch. That's a libtard."

DeFanti pretended to puke before chuckling. She finally put her rifle back against her flak vest, where a patch depicted Jesus Christ firing off crucifix-shaped bullets from atop a red, white, and blue Appaloosa. "Big fucker, whatever it is. What you think, Vern? Maybe we could mount its head in the rec room back at the clubhouse."

"Don't know. Don't care. All I know is if it comes out here, we shoot it."

"Amen to that," she replied. Then, "Hey, what if someone tries to go in?"

"What do you mean?"

"Like, what if somebody's mom comes to visit? What do we do?"

"Real simple, sweetheart. If it's near this building, we kill it. Going in or coming out. That's the job."

"Amen," she said again.

"God bless America," McKay added.

The Wolves of the 2nd Amendment howled to a moon obscured by clouds, fired a few rounds in the air, and went back to watching the shit show.

13

Ansel tried the fire door again for good measure. Still locked. At a loss for what to do next, he followed Julianne back into the first-floor hallway, content to let her lead the way. The doors to the rec room were closed, but the sound system raged on. The amps they'd set up along one wall rattled a few of Ansel's decaying teeth. He'd be shocked if anyone were still in there dancing. In all the chaos, someone must've forgotten to pull the plug.

Ansel pointed down the hall. "We could try . . . "

"No way. You hear that?"

"Modern pop isn't really my thing."

"Listen a little harder."

Ansel took a few hesitant steps down the hall. Underneath the indecipherable vocals and galloping bass were throaty yips and growls like coyotes in a canyon.

Julianne clapped Ansel on the shoulder. "You want to check it out, you go first."

Ansel peered around where they stood. Monstrosities weren't waiting to turn them into dinner, but they'd left behind plenty of evidence that they'd been there. The scuffed hardwood floor was smeared with blood. Vibrant, candy-speckled vomit was splashed across the walls. Where someone had gotten a machine gun, Ansel didn't know, but there were more bullet holes than a militia firing range.

"Maybe we try going up a few flights, see if we can get onto a balcony and flag someone down."

"He's thinking!" Julianne proclaimed, throwing her arms wide like they were on a high school theater stage.

Before Ansel could respond with a quip, Julianne was already back in the elevator, waving him to follow.

61

They picked the fifth floor at random. The ride up was an exercise in mounting tension. Ansel expected the car to stop at any second, doors wrenched open like the lid of a tin can for a hungry pack of deviants, but instead of the metal doors sliding open into a maelstrom of gnashing teeth and spurting sex organs, their destination was a lonely corridor.

Julianne moved to the closest unit. "I don't know who lives here, but I also don't care." She pounded on the door. The booming of her fist resounded down the hallway. "Open up!"

"Avon calling!" Ansel shouted.

Julianne stared at him. "What?"

"Nothing. Something my dad used to joke about when I was little. It was a makeup—"

"I know what it was. I've seen movies." She banged again and added a kick with her foot for good measure. "If you're not some kind of psycho monster, open up!"

"Maybe sounding like a SWAT team isn't helping," Ansel said.

They waited for an answer and when nothing happened moved on to the next unit. This door was different. There was noise behind this one. A wet slapping sound that could have been two people fucking or another Carol smacking their food like a giant baby.

"Sounds like someone playing with Jell-O," Ansel said. "I vote we find another door."

The slick Jell-O noises grew louder. The door opened, and a long, pustuled arm shot out. Firm, spindly fingers gripped Ansel by the bicep and yanked him inside. He was gone before Julianne could even scream.

But scream she did. "Ansel! Open up! Open the door, you fuckers!"

14

F uck Samson, Ron thought. Fuck him so hard. He may have been CFO on the project, but Ron had put years of blood, sweat, and tears into this company. He put this team together, not that creatine-obsessed mouthpiece. The wall-eyed ex-Navy officer played on his phone through most of their interviews outside of Luau Burger, leaving Ron to carry the entire conversation on his back. Made up of people who were the best in their fields, and unconcerned with attaining any kind of celebrity status, they worked around the clock to make breakthroughs in national defense measures. Everything from augmenting the human physique, regenerative tissue, accelerated mitosis, attuned sensory receptors, building humans into weapons.

And then, the discovery of extraterrestrial biologics. The key to unlocking it all.

It was his ticket to the executive floor. If he was going to switch from the lab to the corner offices, he was going to make damn sure he got all the incentives that came with it, as well as a paycheck for Elaine's medical bills. They were so close he could taste it. So close to perfecting the toxin. Either the aerosol cocktail had been miscalculated or something in the building, some foreign agent, had fucked up the expected results, but it could still be saved in the long run. It could be amended. It could be useful. He'd seen what these dregs had become. These scrawny, substance-abusing, basement-dwelling, wishy-washy losers of humanity who actually believed they could get a two-bedroom in this town for under $1,000. He could still save the research and data from this test run, use it to make sure the next one was perfect.

He thought of what the voice had said on the phone. Go to the roof. See if he could fly. What fucking pricks those guys were. But they weren't wrong; the roof was not locked down. No one expected the tenants to go there but rather congregate on the lower floors. So yeah, the roof would be his salvation. How he'd get down, he didn't know, but he'd cross that bridge when he got there.

He exited the unit. Shut the door behind him. In the hallway were two bloated former humans licking each other. He couldn't tell if they noticed him, but he kept quiet as he eyed the elevator behind them. Could he get into it before they focused their attention on him?

"Easy, Ron, easy," he whispered to himself. He placed his back against the hallway wall and inched toward them, doing his best to hold his breath, wondering if the smell of the blood-covered severed head he carried would attract them.

The two people were naked, grasping at each other, frantically kneading one another's skin. They were covered in thick charcoal veins that raised up off their backs and shoulders. The veins pulsed with their heartbeats. Their musculature was swollen, their legs bowed to the point of breaking. They licked and licked and licked, fat green tongues swirling over graying flesh and rippling muscles. Were they roommates, lovers, two randos who just happened to meet in the hallway and felt the need to devour each other? Ron didn't care; he just wanted to get by them.

He took another step as one of them reached out and grabbed him.

"Join our communion," the putrid anomaly wheezed.

Ron raised the hacksaw and swung to free himself, but his movement was blocked. Another arm had him, and he was being pulled closer.

"Join us," the mutant said through gobs of phlegm.

Together they started hiccupping, conjuring up whatever foul soup remained in their guts. He pivoted to avoid the massive arm coming toward him like a crane of heavy flab. The meat paw smashed into the drywall, dug a foot of it out before swinging around to club Ron in the back of the head.

A millisecond of blackness. Pain spread throughout his skull. He stumbled sideways. Another heavy hand forced Ron to his knees, eye level with the beasts' crotches. The male was engorged, his dick gnarled like the branch of a tree dying from blight. Before he could scream, something ripped his mask off, and Ron's head was turned toward a gray-and-white vaginal chasm that had ballooned to the size of a soccer ball.

"Feel the love," the mutated experiment cooed.

Ron screamed as his head was forced into the vagina. He wished he was still wearing the gas mask, realizing just how exposed he was to this biological nightmare. The top of his head entered the slick hole, then his forehead.

The sight of the hallway gave over to blackness as he passed completely into the vaginal cavity. He held his breath, feeling the slick insides of this squishy prison pass down over his nose, then his lips, until his head was fully inside, and he could not see nor hear. The top of his head hit bone, keeping him from going farther. He grabbed both of the mutant woman's legs and tried to pull himself out, but he was being held in by a force he couldn't overwhelm.

He felt organisms tickling his skin. The lovebugs looking for a way in. But his orifices were pressed tight against flesh. Still, they multiplied, swarming his head like roaches outside a dumpster, searching for a way in. Hungry for Ron to join their tribe.

He whimpered, trying to conserve his air, when he felt the swollen, bent dick of the mutated man hit him in the chin. The penis worked its way up into the vagina, over his mouth and to his nose, and then began slamming into his nostrils. Again and again. Harder and faster. When that didn't work, the monster cock began trying to probe his eyes, demanding entry into his head any way it could. Long and aggressive strokes. The fist-sized mushroom head moved down, dug into his throat, causing Ron to choke and cough.

This is how I die. He panicked as his head wedged farther inside a woman than he'd ever been. But then he remembered the hacksaw. Except he wasn't holding it. Where was it?

The monster cock was hitting him underneath the chin now, slamming his head up into the mutated woman's uterus. Everything was tightening on him. The monster cock was shoving him upward, pushing his shoulders into the vulva, the balls bludgeoning his Adam's apple.

He clawed the floor under him, fingernails tearing at cheap blue carpet, hoping for salvation. He found it. The hacksaw.

He swiped up at the woman's body, level with his face, and sliced into her. The dick continued to beat his face inside the vagina, but he sawed at the flesh before him. Zipping the teeth of the saw over her abdomen. Back and forth, as fast as he could, his lungs aching for air, about to burst. He felt skin tearing, peeling apart. He felt muscle separate and cleave. He felt the zig-zag cock hitting his chin.

With his other hand he grabbed the mutant's balls, squeezed. The fucking stopped for a brief second, and he used it to his advantage, slicing the creature's testicles off. Even through the walls of his biological cage, he could hear screaming.

He went back to work, knowing he was down to the last few seconds of air in his lungs. He sawed up and down on the woman's abdomen, slicing and cutting and knifing until the saw teeth nicked his nose. With all his might he pushed his face forward, slipping through severed flesh, thrusting through slickness and blood and dangling intestines, ultimately freeing himself like a man emerging from behind a waterfall.

He saw his mask against the wall and slammed it back over his face just as his lungs gave out and forced him to suck in the building's contaminated air. Another breath and the spots in his vision stopped zooming around. Another breath and his heart rate slowed, his testicles loosened, all involuntary shaking subsided.

The two mutants clutched at their privates, rolling on the ground, covered in blood. Lovebugs erupted from their new orifices like uncovered vipers' nests. They weren't even making noises anymore, just experiencing their pain the way insects would.

"Thanks for the party," he muttered and made his way to the elevator.

Once inside, he pressed the button for the top floor and wiped a thick wad of gray jizz away from the eyes of the gas mask, whipped it to the floor. Inside the dark translucent ejaculate were smaller lovebugs, swirling around, hoping to find a fertile home.

Ron brought his boot down.

15

Julianne's knuckles were starting to crack and bleed from pounding on the door. She tried to scream Ansel's name, but her throat was still sandpapered from the fight with Carol. Every effort came out scratchy and muffled, like the final whispers of a terminal lung-cancer patient. Without warning, music blared from within the apartment, Sinatra's "That's Life" quieting the sounds of Ansel's struggles inside.

For such a shithole complex, Julianne was surprised the door didn't collapse the first few times she threw her shoulder into it. Kicking the door handle didn't help much either. The brass knob maintained its position, mocking her.

She had to find a way in.

The unit to the right was locked, but the door beyond that sat slightly ajar. Hazy light spilled out into the hallway. If she could get out onto the balcony and hop back to fourteen, she might have a chance of saving Ansel's ass.

Julianne knocked as she pushed the door in and crossed the threshold, not bothering to wait for the a-okay to trespass. She heard a TV nearby:

"Unlike our species, these creatures appear to have mastered the art of synchronicity, of unity . . . "

Calling out was off the table. She wasn't eager to have a repeat of Carol. The living room was dark ahead of her except for the pale blue glow of the television set. It was enough to illuminate the shapes tangled on the floor. The carpet squelched underneath her shoes as she inched into the room.

" . . . no violence. No bitterness among them. These species live together in harmony."

Three people sat on their knees, backs to her, watching the

scene unfold on the television. A gift bag from the Valentine's Day party was tipped over on the floor, revealing an open DVD case. The man on the TV had a soothing voice. It flashed to what looked like mites on flesh. Then flashed to B-roll of people laughing and kissing. This must've been what had been playing when Ansel had managed to get Carol's television running. She felt like she'd walked into the middle of an art film with zero context.

The scene on the TV changed again. Purple liquid cascaded down a rocky cliffside into a massive pool where thick tufts of electrified strands folded and unfolded into one another like lightning filtered through cotton candy. Within the swirls of pink, thin translucent mouths grazed each other, transferring a honey-colored substance between them.

The camera zoomed in.

"Lovebugs, as we've been calling them, are able to achieve this kind of fully immersed community through whatever this golden discharge is, a biological mucus that contains similar proteins to dopamine, as well as numerous elements and chemicals we've yet to decipher. This syrup allows the lovebugs to connect themselves, even connecting from a distance through crimson strands similar to human synapses, to become a bigger part of a singular network, a hive mind, allowing the species to achieve their goal."

The trio on the floor hadn't noticed her enter. They sat mesmerized by the TV, their arms and hands rubbing each other like lovers initiating a threesome.

Julianne tip-toed behind them, behind the couch, as she made her way to the sliding glass door on the other side of the room.

"Surprisingly, the creatures weren't fearful of the rover as it approached," the show's narrator continued. "They were curious in the same way we were. We've yet to fully understand how they've achieved such complex movement and understanding without displaying any kind of central brain."

"Motherfuckers," Julianne breathed, "they infected us. They're using us as hosts."

It was just like people in power to decide how the less fortunates' lives should be used. They told you you had freedom, but did you really? The men with the money would always fuck you in the end. Your body meant nothing to them, your art meant nothing, your dreams meant nothing. All they wanted was your contribution, be it your money or your life.

Julianne unlocked the balcony door with her thumb as quietly as possible, pushed forward gently.

Not that she expected anything different to happen, but her heart still dropped into her gut when the rusted metal of the track rubbed against the torn rubber at the bottom of the door, emitting a raspy groan.

The closest person turned their head toward her. Julianne didn't recognize the woman's face, but it was hard to ID most people when their eyes had been replaced with pulsating wads of neon pink. The woman's mouth puckered and chewed, like she was on MDMA. Yellow goo drooled down her chin, which seemed to move ever so slightly on its own. Her hands were two sizes too large, rippled with tendons and muscles.

"Four is always better than three," she said, unfurling a tongue pocked with tiny extra mouths. "Join us?"

The man in the middle rose to his feet, cracking and unfolding like a beaten accordion. Julianne knew him. Gorman. In fact, she realized, looking around the room at all the weird memorabilia he collected for "historical" purposes, she was in his place. He was a real dick she avoided at all costs.

When he'd found out she worked in film, he'd harassed her with film 101 questions. Who directed *The Shining*? Had she ever seen *Dark Star*? Questions meant to test her knowledge because surely someone without a turgid worm sprouting between their legs couldn't possibly know about cool shit.

"Kubrick's movies are beautifully shot, but ultimately cold, and no, I haven't seen the other one," she'd said.

Unfazed, Gorman had switched gears, launching into a long adoration of the 1930s propaganda film *Triumph of the Will*. The way he'd talked about it, like he was reciting a love letter, set her teeth on edge. *Tell me you're a bootlicking Nazi without telling me*, she'd thought. When he'd finished gushing about it, Julianne had thrown a "Cool, bud," his way and gotten out of the laundry room so fast she'd almost left a cartoon dust cloud.

She could see from the framed flag on the wall behind him now that her assertion had been correct.

Gorman took a step forward. Julianne noted the way he seemed unsure on his feet, as if he'd suddenly forgotten how to walk. It was when he came even closer that she noticed the crusted blood encircling the top of his head.

The other two stood behind him. Both wore tattered fleeces with an emblem she didn't recognize. When they spoke, it was through the fat polyps decorating their faces like someone had gotten blitzed in the morgue and turned the cadavers into a craft project.

"Only the start of our little nest."

"A loving triad."

"Infinitely together. Forever in love."

Julianne slid the balcony door open the rest of the way. Only a slight reprieve from the crushing humidity within the building. She made for the edge of the railing, muttered, "Fuck," at the massive sheet of bamboo walling off the other side.

The threesome emerged from the dank pit of Gorman's apartment, shedding their clothes. Oozing holes peppered their body, reminding her of the thumb-sized craters in her grandmother's back when she'd caught shingles in a care facility. Only there hadn't been sentient red strings unspooling from inside the pockets of infected flesh, searching for another body to cling to.

Like now.

She yanked on the makeshift privacy screen. No luck. She peered over the railing, tried to see if she could reach around and swing over to the other unit, but it was out of reach. The other balcony was separated by a roughly foot wide gap.

Screeching tires and blaring dad rock caught her attention.

Below, off to the right, a pickup that was more rust than blue careened around the corner, headlights cutting an odd angle across the side road. She couldn't see who was driving, but based on the abrupt wail of the brakes as the truck came to a halt, they weren't here to save the day. The words *Judge Jury Executioner* were stenciled in red, white, and blue on the side of the vehicle.

Someone in full black Kevlar and what appeared to be a Halloween wolf mask rose from the bed of the vehicle, an ugly black firearm aimed directly at herself and Gorman's conclave.

Julianne wanted to shout for them to wait, that she wasn't infected, but she'd seen enough of these cosplaying work-for-hire militia morons to know shooting first was their signature move.

She dropped, covered her ears, prayed to the stars and the moon and the old ones and anyone who would listen.

Bullets ground up meat and obliterated glass. The force blasted one of the pink-eyed goons back into the apartment, took the sliding door's frame with him.

Gorman's waist hit the railing, pitching him forward. Julianne finally realized why his head looked so odd. The cap of his skull slid off. His brain winning the race to the bottom as the hunk of soft tissue splattered onto the asphalt. The things inside it wrapped around the gray matter like razor wire.

The remaining person—the woman—was more fortunate.

Her right arm had been blown off along with an ear, but the pulpy wounds only revealed more suckling mouths and malicious fibers. She pulled herself toward Julianne with her working limb.

"Love can survive anything," she said. "Even in death, true love lives on."

She rolled onto her back. Then, hand trembling in eager anticipation, she gripped the flesh under her belly button, tugged downward.

"Let us taste you. Assimilate and know pleasure you couldn't even conceive of. Together we can create eons of life."

Unlike what they'd seen so far, this lady was cute even with an ear dangling from a strand of meat. Had an alien life form not hijacked her body and used it as a tool for full-on assault, she might've considered asking her over for a B-movie marathon, but as it stood, getting violated on a balcony in the middle of the night wasn't terribly romantic.

More wisps of thin tissue unspooled from her nasal cavity, the corners of her eyes, and the fresh wounds. Still getting used to the missing arm and damaged muscle, the thing driving the body now righted itself, staggered forth clumsily, like a marionette with most of its strings cut.

Julianne didn't want to touch it, didn't want to risk getting infected, but remaining slumped in the corner guaranteed she'd be this things "lover" in just seconds, and she was certain whatever this was, she couldn't get a prescription for it at urgent care.

When she was close enough, Julianne grabbed the bony wrist and forced herself up, hoping the nuts in costume were still down there. She threw her shoulder into the woman's chest, knocking it to the balcony's edge.

Automatic gunfire rang out, turning the woman's head into a crimson cloud.

Taking her chance, Julianne ducked back into the apartment, nearly tripping over the man inside.

One of the bullets must've clipped his spine. He lay prone on his back, grasping at the air in a spreading pool of blood. "Come to me, darling." His flesh rippled, as if bugs were crawling under his skin. Which was probably true, she realized, even though she hadn't understood the program they'd been watching on TV in its entirety.

Julianne searched the room. There was no way she'd make it to the next-door balcony with those gun nuts patrolling the base of the building. She'd have to find another way to get to Ansel.

Then she saw it, smirked.

If there was one thing Julianne knew for certain, after years of encountering oddball men, it was at least one in every ten had a weapons collection. And Gorman appeared to be that one. Resting underneath the flag thumbtacked to the wall like a forgotten umbrella was a sizable sword. Engraved on the hilt was a tiger roaring triumphantly.

"Oh, that? That's just my sword," she could hear him saying with smugness. "No big. Anyway, my favorite movie is *American History X* ... No, I'm not racist. Geez!"

Julianne grabbed the heavy steel, unsheathed it.

The man on the floor gazed up at her, his eyes rimmed by pulsing sphincters. "Bake in the furnace of our desire, my dear. I want to fu—"

The blade cleaved his face into two steaming halves.

✳ ✳ ✳

The brain hit the ground first, splattering bits of tissue across the asphalt. Then came the body, which crumpled like a sack of wet takeout upon impact, forcing all but Vern to take a few steps back.

No way anyone could've survived such a swan dive into the ground, but assuming the brain spackling their combat boots belonged to the body before them, it wasn't too big of a surprise that the pile of limbs was still moving around, eagerly. The head itself had been shoved into the chest, its mouth opening and closing, trying to emit words, and failing spectacularly.

DeFanti pulled the snarling wolf mask up to get a better look. "Damn, this joker is still kicking. What's going on in there?"

They all looked to Vern for an answer—they always did.

"Not sure. If I had to guess, judging from all the shit we've seen so far, an in-house bioweapon." Vern pushed the broken arm away from the face. It flopped backward. "Probably testing it out on these poor bastards."

"Should we be wearing the other masks?" DeFanti asked.

"We're okay out here, I think," Vern said, "but grab the 95s from the truck. Maybe we should document what's happening, see if someone inside can give us a bit more information."

"The fuck for?" Simpson asked. "Did you see what's in there? What's right in front of us?"

"Leverage," Vern said. "We could make a fortune dangling this in front of those government cucks."

Simpson held his hands up. "Vern, I respect you, but we're not equipped to fight monsters, brother. You said the job was just to shoot anyone leaving. I assumed you'd meant people. And shit, we've already gone through half our ammo."

"Scared, huh?"

"I'm trying to be practical."

Vern looked at McKay and DeFanti. "Well?"

"I'll get the 95s," McKay said, heading for the truck.

DeFanti nodded.

When they were ready, McKay and DeFanti headed toward the fire escape.

Vern stopped next to Simpson. "I get it. Not everyone is built for this. You and your limp dick can stay and watch the truck."

Then he pulled the wolf's head down over the medical-grade mask and followed his two best soldiers into the monster party.

16

They'd hoped by cutting the proteins with low-levels of serotonin and adding the video message meant to lull them into a languid stupor, the process would dampen the overzealous lust that overcame the creatures they'd brought back to use in Project Honeypot.

He peered up and down the destroyed hallway, wishing he'd had some VapoRub to salve the lingering odor of the woman's vaginal juices. Limbs were scattered about like forgotten doll parts. In the middle of the vomit- and blood-streaked floor was a torso, its abdominal cavity mostly blown out, but as Ron got closer, he noticed wisps of pink threading itself through the nest of mauled meat.

Crouching, Ron retrieved a Tech-Ease 20X illuminating flip-out magnifying glass from his messenger bag. Closer inspection revealed the tiny mouths he'd grown so accustomed to stuck to the searching pink strings like microscopic Christmas lights. As long as there were a few left, they could sustain themselves for a time, but without anything grander to latch onto would likely result in them cannibalizing one another. The substrate of the planet Gemein, where they'd discovered the lovebugs, was a biomass fusion of proteins and nucleotides. A living surface, in a sort of fashion. But here on Earth, soil killed them; these things needed flesh to propagate. *Funny how something so advanced on a functional level isn't able to realize it could cause its own demise.*

Then again, humans were pretty fucking clueless, too.

Ron admired their determination for survival for a few minutes before continuing toward the stairwell, wishing he'd had something more than a rusty hacksaw. As soon as he hit the first step, he heard the rushing sound of boots.

"Hey!"

Ron turned to see three of the rent-a-militia goons they'd hired to guard the exterior lots now standing at the end of the hallway. They looked ridiculous in their wolf masks, like a political cartoonist's rendition of a right-winger. He figured the one in the middle, cradling a rifle like a newborn, had been the big dick behind the shout.

"What are you doing in here? Your job is to be outside."

"We're getting the truth." Big Dick aimed the large ArmaLite rifle in his direction. "Something crawled off the balcony, and it don't look like anything I've ever seen before."

Son of a bitch.

They'd been so focused on securing obvious exits that no one had given half a thought to unconventional escapes. Granted, no one thought to forecast gorilla-levels of strength or that anyone would literally try to smash through a wall to get out.

Containment was going to be a nightmare. In movies they always bombed the infected town to quarantine, but nukes weren't a line item on their approved proposal. This wasn't the '60s or the '70s. They couldn't just pin the devastation on some bumbling contractor and hire a director to falsely claim the thing lurking in the woods was some method actor in a rubber suit, prepping for his latest flick. He had to get someone on it now or they'd be paddling up shit creek with their hands.

"How long ago?"

"Maybe an hour. Don't change the subject!"

"You want to be useful? Go after the thing you saw. Empty those guns into it, bag it, and bring the leftovers to me."

Big Dick took a few steps forward. "Ain't going nowhere, Hoss. Already did that and the Wolves of the Second are making a citizen's arrest. Starting with *you*. Now set your purse down and walk toward me. Slow. Got some questions for you."

Ron burst into laughter. "You work for me, you podunk shitheel!"

"Not anymore. Now move."

Ron did as the redneck instructed. Part of him would love nothing more than to draw the rusty hacksaw across his leathery throat, but it wasn't worth the risk of getting shot to pieces. If nothing else, he wanted to survive long enough to drop the head onto Samson's desk. The ultimate eat-my-ass. Here's a lifetime's worth of research.

Ron smirked to himself. None of these guys knew what to look for. All they had to go on were a few monsters they'd gunned into oblivion. Kind of shocking, honestly, that this trio of good ol' boys storming the rundown castle with their modern-day pitchforks, hard at the thought of burning the monster at the stake and being the heroes of their sad little stories, hadn't run into more of a resistance.

Ron stepped toward a ragged stump of neck. Coagulating blood squelching underneath the rubber soles of his boots. He could see the tiny pink strings prodding the air, searching for a new home. He feigned accidentally toeing the neck toward Big Dick. "You're absolutely right. I'll tell you everything."

They didn't see the thin pink lines excitedly unfurling from the depths of the corpse on the ground, worming their way up his pant leg, probing for the warmth of their bodies.

For the first time since everything had gone to shit, Ron smiled.

Then the screaming started anew.

17

Nothing left to kill.
Nothing left to love.

But the chorus could not be satisfied. It rolled on like an endless spool of tickertape.

Loveconsumerecreateloveconsumerecreate
loveconsumerecreateloveconsume
recreate . . .

Theo smashed through every door that was still closed. A few times he'd managed to find someone who was in throes of permanent ecstasy, but as the night went on, it was more and more darkened abattoirs or rooms where his kind had figured out how to manipulate the bodies, become what they needed to play their part in the great coupling. Serpentine creatures, bulbous monstrosities, ambulating mounds of flesh, and so much more.

All those mouths. Hundreds of eager lips pulsating, calling to him. Tongues beckoning him to complete his transformation. The ones that were already in him yearned to connect with others, but the mission wasn't over yet. He needed to continue spreading their word, herding everyone to ascension.

Then came the sound of gunfire, glass shattering. The soul-tickling sound of screams.

He was only a few feet below it.

Theo continued toward the promised land.

18

Ansel felt wet, rubbery skin tightening around his neck. His mask broke off and he smelled unfiltered rotten food and heard goopy, smacking noises all around him. He fought for air, thrashing at the sinewy arm around his neck, tearing at loose flesh with his fingernails. His foot kicked out and a drinking glass teetered off the coffee table before him and shattered. With his last moment of air, he grabbed a shard and sank it into the appendage holding him down. There was a hollow wail and the arm retreated, slithering across the living room floor, and disappearing into a nearby bedroom. The door slammed shut, shaking the walls so hard family pictures fell from the walls.

He stood, massaging his neck, feeling the chaffed skin near his chin. "Fuck was that?"

Ansel felt like he'd just been assaulted by Plastic Man, but that couldn't have been real, had to have been a misfire in his brain from the trauma of the attack. Trailing behind the elbow looked to be a cluster of red wires.

He was starting to lose it, to get angry, to cry. His mind reeled and his knees buckled. It was all too much. He'd just wanted to listen to some music, go to bed, and wake up refreshed enough to write his own in the morning. Now, he was stuck in this mess with nowhere to go and on top of that feeling useless. Every choice he'd made so far was wrong. Nothing he'd done had helped get them closer to escaping the building.

This was the life of Ansel Friedl. Enough of a space cadet to bumble into situations, but never more than an innocent bystander to whatever happened next. The stress and fear that came with grabbing the wheel and righting his own path was crushing. Easier to let life happen and let people know at least it wasn't your fault, which, as he was beginning to realize, was making the mistake yourself anyway.

Through the walls, he heard Julianne's barely audible voice. She must have gone into an adjacent apartment. Had she been captured too? He needed to get to her, needed to figure out how they were going to get out of this charnel house. He glanced at the bedroom door, wondering if the long-armed beast would return, wondering how he'd fight it off again. From behind the door came the low mewl of an animal in pain.

"Good. Fuck you," he muttered.

He made for the picture window and stopped when his foot kicked something soft. The bloated remains of a child. Its gender was unrecognizable, owing to its head being completely missing from its body. Its arms and legs curled up like that of a dead spider's. Someone had broken every bone in its body. Something big. Something that had enough time and limbs to crush all at once.

Ansel held back tears as his stomach dropped. Understanding that at any moment now this could be his future.

Without even realizing he was doing it, he grabbed a throw blanket from a recliner and covered the dead body. "Sorry, kid."

A television was playing on the wall, spouting off about a NASA rover having discovered some kind of alien bugs on a hidden planet or whatever. Seemed like the start to some old 1950s sci-fi movie. "These lovebugs work in unison as a sort of microbial farm team, growing food for their young and ensuring every egg is tended to. They never stop procreating, and are always stimulating one another . . . "

The image flickered like a filmstrip, the sound cutting in and out. Scanlines disrupted the screen, reminding him of the old days of VHS. If he didn't know any better, he'd say someone or something was hijacking the cable feed.

None of that mattered right now. He had to get back to Julianne. Had to make sure this time he would be in control of his own fate.

The picture window looked out onto a fire escape. A second column of windows to his right provided access. Just as he unlatched it, there was gunfire from the parking lot below.

"Jesus!" He flung himself to the ground as glass rained down on him.

From outside, he heard Julianne's voice clearer now. She was so close.

"You can do this, you can do this." His pep talk did little to encourage him, but he leaped up anyway and yanked the window open. A voice from below yelled up at him, but he did his best to ignore it. For a brief second, he saw Julianne two fire escapes away, behind a now-shredded bamboo screen. Bullets were pinging off the railing in front of her like cheap fireworks.

"Julianne!" he screamed, but the gunfire drowned out his voice.

Risking a look below, he saw a man in cheap MARPAT pants and shirts with dime store jingoistic slogans on them. Not actual military, more like back-alley mercenaries. Thank God this idiot couldn't shoot straight with that ridiculous Wolfman mask on.

Julianne was in trouble, and if he didn't do something fast, she'd be .223-caliber Swiss cheese.

He fell back into the room, stepped over the dead kid, and reached for the door to the hallway. That's when the bedroom door flew open and that gray, fetid arm shot out and barred the exit.

"Oh, c'mon!"

He raced back to the fire escape and ducked outside, just in time to see Julianne retreat into whoever's apartment she was in.

The arm whipped across the room, shot out the window, and speared him in the balls. Exquisite pain raced up his stomach, making him gag. Falling to his knees, he called out to his friend, hoping she'd hear him, even though he knew he could do nothing to help her.

The arm expanded, wrapped around his ankle, and hoisted him into the air, dangling him a dozen stories above the parking lot below.

The gunfire stopped, and Ansel heard an amused voice below say, "Sweet baby Jesus!"

All Ansel could yell back was, "Don't shoot! I don't wanna fall!"

The man in military cosplay lit a cigarette, leaned onto the tailgate, ready to enjoy the show.

19

The split halves of the dead man's cranium rocked back and forth between Julianne's feet. His body continued to move, arms and legs flinging wildly like one of those blow-up tube men outside of car dealerships. The other occupant crawled one-armed as her insides spilled out of her shredded belly; intestines snaked under her knees, catching on her high heels, which yanked them out with a squelch.

That wasn't the worst part.

Fist-sized polyps rolled around in much of the woman's digestive tract. Connected by fibrous red strands, the creatures began reinserting themselves into the vacated abdomen. Her left eye slid from its socket, replaced by another sentient tumor.

Julianne started to shake. She'd never been shot at before, had never seen this much blood and gore before. There were actual fucking brains on her pants! She felt warm viscera in her hair, and now this woman's body had been taken over by what? A new kind of cancer? One that could pilot a dead body?

The death grip she had on the sword could have crushed stone. She didn't dare drop it.

Was Ansel still alive? Was she on her own? Had whatever pulled him into the room already turned him into one of these monstrosities?

She needed to find safety and she needed it fast. All she had to do was finish off the woman crawling around with her guts out, lock the door, call for help—somehow—and wait to be rescued. This was America, after all. The police would come get her. They were here to help.

Right?

Who was she kidding? She was on her own. If officers showed

up anyway, they'd probably ask her what she did to provoke the attack.

With a wheeze that sounded like an octogenarian's fart, Intestinal Girl's face fell into the floor with a crunch. Whatever these things were had terrible motor skills. Good news for Julianne. She launched herself over the wriggling body, chain locked the door, and returned to dismantle this poor thing that had once been a person.

When she'd finished, the entire carpet was a reddish-brown lake. She hadn't killed the thing, wasn't sure if it could die really, but at least in pieces it struggled to push itself off the floor.

Julianne kicked the head out onto the balcony.

Next, she pulled out her cellphone. Still no service. Of course. She remembered that Ansel had already tried. Maybe Gorman had a landline? Guy like him probably didn't trust technology. Unless he was the new kind of neo-Nazi, using social media to foment the Fourth Reich. Either way, she raced around the room searching for a phone, ultimately coming up empty.

That's when she heard the voice. Ansel's voice? Could it be?

It was coming from outside, out where that lunatic was using them as target practice.

Sliding up against the wall, she eased herself nearer to the open rectangle that had once been the picture window. Warm dusk air wafted into the room, what was left of the curtains blowing gently in the breeze. She peeked out, saw the gunman far below staring up at an area of the building not far away from her. She poked her head out, felt her face start to sweat.

It was Ansel.

He was screaming, held aloft by a snake. No, not a snake, an arm? An arm with dozens of those fleshy strings using it like a demented hand puppet.

"Can't be real. This shit isn't real," she muttered.

The arm toyed with Ansel, dipping him up and down like a teabag in some Earl Grey. Only there was no tea, just air and purple striated skies in the distance. From below, the gunman whistled the way lonely, sad men whistle at pretty girls on the street. The kind of whistle that exemplified how big the hole was between their ears.

Without any thought, Julianne stepped through the shattered window and locked eyes with Ansel. `"What are you doing?"

He yelled back: "I heard your voice. I was saving you."

"I was saving *you!*"

"I don't need saving."

"You fucking sure about that?"

From down below, the whistler added: "This is better than that stupid fiancée show my wife watches."

"You need to get down!" Julianne yelled.

The arm let go of Ansel for the briefest second, then snatched him up again. He screamed in horror. "I can't! I don't know what to do."

Her heart sank as he started to cry. She'd seen men cry before but not like this. They cried because she wasn't interested, or because their dog died. She'd learned long ago that, deep down, men had the emotional fortitude of a house of cards. It looked good all set up but crumbled in a cheap wind.

This was worse, though. This was a man facing death. Not a man like Gorman, who thought he was invulnerable, but someone who despite being a bit of a doofus was a good dude. He knew no meant no and didn't continue to harass or attempt to convince afterward.

His eyes pleaded with her, but there was nothing she could do or say to save him, and he knew it. He chewed his lip, thinking, hoping, probably praying even if he wasn't religious.

"What do I do?" She felt nauseous as she spoke.

"Help me?" he pleaded. "Please."

"How?"

"I don't know."

The arm lifted him to the floor above her. "I don't know what to do!" she screamed.

"I don't want to die! I don't want to fucking die!"

She was crying now, clutching her stomach, afraid to turn away as if she owed him that much. They weren't lifelong friends, but Ansel was the only one she didn't despise in this dump—someone she could share ideas with and who despite his shortcomings bestowed a little industry wisdom onto her every now and then. She'd hoped at the very least he'd get his little cult revival, see how appreciated his work had been beyond Reddit posts and the occasional Letterboxd review.

"Make it stop!" was all she could get out. "Whoever's doing this, make it stop!"

"Why is this happening?" Ansel cried.

"The lovebugs!" she yelled. "It's on the TVs. The bastards are rationalizing our deaths. But I don't know how to stop it!"

From below: "This is definitely better than that stupid fiancée show!"

Julianne couldn't help herself as she leaned over the balcony and screamed, "Fuck you, loser!" at the man below. Then, connecting with Ansel again: "Wait! I've got a sword. I can cut it off you. I'll be right ther—"

And that's when the rest of the creature pushed its bulk through, shattering what remained of the glass door. Its head had grown twice over. The left side already a burst watermelon, spurting yellowish and red fluids, the right a pulsating mass of fat veins threatening to free themselves at any moment. Bouncing off its chest of mangled muscle and hair was the thing's jaw. No tongue. No teeth. Just a deep tunnel of ribbed, slimy tissue.

Ansel's shrieks were like nails on a chalkboard as it brought him closer to its mouth. Julianne went mute. Stunned and unable to turn away from the gory circus act about to take place, she felt her nausea grow as it ejected a torrent of brown fluid into Ansel's wailing mouth.

The arm flung him closer to Julianne. She reached out, climbing halfway onto the rickety railing of the balcony, stretching for all her worth, noting in her periphery that something else was approaching from behind Ansel. The other arm, its growth made possible by all the creatures wielding it like a horrid extension. Should she tell him? No, absolutely not. She just needed to grab him, swing him in toward her, into Gorman's apartment where they'd both be safe. They could try to clean him up in a shower.

"Almost . . . reach . . . you . . . " Ansel said, his fingers splayed out, eager for hers.

"Stretch!" she yelled.

The second hand cuffed Ansel's other ankle. His eyes fell, sad, resigned. "No," he whispered.

"Ansel, grab my hand."

The creature yanked Ansel away from her, just far enough out of reach, toying with them both.

Tears streaked down Ansel's cheeks. He was hyperventilating, coughing up bile. The arms spread his legs painfully wide. "Oh God no," he pleaded.

And then he screamed as his legs were pulled apart, ripping the stitching in the crotch of his pants.

"No!" Julianne wailed.

Ansel's shrieks were like sirens on the wind. The arms opened his legs more, slowly, centimeter by centimeter, enjoying the torture. Blood arced out of his rectum, rained down on the man below, who clapped in enjoyment. Then another centimeter, tearing open a gash in his perineum. The next centimeter, breaking the subpubic bones—the sit bones. Another centimeter, tearing into the scrotum, splitting the testicles, causing them to spill out and dangle lifelessly. Then another centimeter, ripping a tear up the middle of Ansel's abdomen, letting loose all the intestinal stuffing inside.

Ansel screamed so hard his voice reached registers only dogs might hear.

Yet another centimeter and the tear in his abdomen stitched over his belly, ripping open his core. Gray and pink guts fell to the ground below, erupting like water balloons.

A foot more and the tentacles exposed his rib cage.

They tore the body apart one last time, skin tearing toward his head like someone ripping off a hangnail. Ultimately his head remained on the right side of his body, all of which was nowhere near the left side.

The arm lifted Ansel's remains high in the air and finally let one half go. It hit the ground with a sickening, soupy crack, exploding a miasma of pink and purple goo all over the concrete.

Julianne fell, crying, back into Gorman's apartment. Far below, a lone hired gun was trying to send a video of the action to everyone he knew.

20

L ike the wired bolt of a Taser, the pink threads hit Vern square in the crotch, dug through his pants. He screamed, yanking at the fibers now connecting him to the dead body parts on the floor. "Get it off!"

Ron seized the opportunity to leap forward. With one hand, he knocked the wolf mask askew, while the other yanked the gun away. McKay and DeFanti were stunned, marveling at their leader, now falling to the floor, blood hosing out his lower back.

"Fucking shoot it," Vern wailed.

His most loyal followers finally raised their guns and aimed, waiting, making sure to avoid hitting the wrong target. It was enough hesitation for two more ropes of gelatinous proteins to fire out of the mutilated corpse parts and catch them each in the face, snaking down their throats. Bullets sprayed the ceiling as they each fell to the floor.

McKay, eyes bulging and pink, managed to get her gun up to her temple. "I'm not joining you fucks." Her brains coated the hallway's cheap wallpaper.

The other two fought to pull the pink cords from their throats to no avail. Then, in some unspoken move, they each grabbed the other's thread and pulled. Each string finally came out, attached to some large chunk of organ. Both men died, their eyes rolling back in their heads. The pink ropes snaked their ways back into the bodies again and wiggled as they rooted around inside the corpses, eager to jumpstart their new vessels.

Ron moved to the wall and stayed silent, watching the dead men flutter about.

He picked up the first merc's gun, remembering how the man had said things had been coming out of the upper floor windows and walls. Not only had he been left for dead, but the exits were compromised, and the exterior lot was possibly crawling with lovebugs.

His only means of egress was the roof. If he could get there, he might be able to phone a friend, as they say. He'd deal with corporate hanging him out to dry later, after he survived.

21

Back in the hallway, Julianne held the sword close to her chest, listening to the walls creak. It was hard to tell what was the building settling and a freak trying to convert her to its parasitic commune.

Maybe they were one in the same.

She shook her head for the hundredth time, trying to erase the vision of Ansel's death, but it was like an image drawn in permanent marker on a white wall. No matter how hard she tried to scrub it out, some semblance of it remained.

Now, she moved toward the room where her friend's killer resided. She wasn't really sure why she was going there. Driven by anger and a bit of madness maybe. Whatever was in there had killed an innocent man, and she hated it for existing. She wanted revenge, and she wanted to take it out of this world.

She'd gutted fish with a knife before; she could cut this beast with a sword.

The doorknob was slick with a gooey, off-white sludge that dripped to the rug of the hallway. At this point, Julianne couldn't be bothered to care anymore. She grabbed the handle, pushed the door open. Rotten air rushed out at her, hot and coppery. From inside came the sound of labored breathing, immense wheezing like the lungs of an asthmatic filtered through a massive amplifier. Something large and deadly was inside, sucking in air and breathing out death.

She held the sword in front of her and entered.

"You're mine, fucker."

The entryway was covered in shattered glass from picture frames that had been knocked off the wall. Her Skechers crunched them underneath as she moved past the tiny kitchen, spying the open picture window across the unit from her. More of the ochre ooze dripped off the kitchen counters, collecting on the floor in pools. The stench reminded her of the guys in her senior class that didn't bother to shower after the gym. The kind of odor that clung to clothes like mold on forgotten food. This was that smell, perhaps combined with a hint of vomit and trashcan ketchup.

She passed the kitchen and followed the trail of goo to the unit's bedroom door. She knew this layout because it was exactly like hers. The bedroom connected to a small ensuite bathroom, then a closet with barely enough room to keep a week's worth of clothes in. The outside balcony stretched to the bedroom window, but if she took it, she'd be seen before she could get inside. The bedroom door was her best option. Fling it open and attack.

She held her breath and thought of her mother. Then her father. They both still sucked, so she switched her thoughts to her childhood dog. That was better. Wimbly had been a sweet mutt, and she still missed him. Then her thoughts went to Ansel, and she kicked the door open, charged inside.

"Fuck you!"

She was instantly flung back against the wall as the arm shot out at her like a wild firehose with a morning star affixed to the end. She hit the floor, the wind knocked out of her, the sword cartwheeling away through the air. Her chest heaved as she struggled to breathe, her mind trying desperately to decipher the scene before her.

It was Ansel. Or at least half of Ansel. The half that had been pulled back into the room. Half of his face was melded with that of another man she didn't recognize—no doubt the owner of the apartment, a now-demented Stretch Armstrong.

Viscous goo covered the taffy-like body. The stench of aggressive body odor was everywhere.

Another arm reached out and grabbed her, wrapped around her arms, and pinned her to the wall.

"Alsh lvd u," Half-Ansel-o-pus gargled. "Ths we be togshr fevr."

The beast shifted toward the foot of the bed, and in doing so, exploded bloody fecal waste at her. It slopped across her face, and she wretched, struggling not to vomit. She didn't dare lose control and give this thing an edge.

The arms tightened, threatening to rip hers off.

She whipped her head about, finally found her breath again,

and managed to choke out a string of nonsensical noises that were half pleas and half bespoke slurs for sideshow freaks. The monster before her couldn't care less about any of it. Instead, it unfurled a thick, bulbous intestine from underneath its belly. It undulated toward her, and she saw an opening at the end, like a small mouth.

"Oh no, no, no," she cried, realizing it wasn't a mouth at the end, but a urethra. "Don't you fucking touch me," she spat.

"It's all about the union," the beast said. "We will make a world of trust and unity and unbridled procreation. The proliferation of a species that protects one another, guides one another, becomes one another. Our kind does not stop. We only grow."

Half-Ansel-o-pus lifted his tentacle dick and flicked it at her, launching gobs of yellow spunk at her already shit-covered face, coating her hair and ears. The hot stink was too much to bear. She flung her head down and threw up in the respirator with such force her stomach contents had no choice but to spray from one side of the mask.

The tentacle dick seemed to take on a life of its own, slithering down and rolling in the vomit that had managed to escape its plastic containment like someone twisting a limp French fry in mustard. Now coated in Julianne's half-digested lunch, the dick raised and rolled back toward its owner, probing gently into Half-Ansel-o-pus's own mouth.

"Dlllsssshhh," he said. Then, moaning, he began to suck his own tentacle dick, all the while staring at her with eyes half dropping out of his head. The other half of the beast, the man who owned the apartment, used his one bloody eye to look her up and down, lingering on her chest.

Julianne struggled against her binds but couldn't free herself. Her thoughts reverted back to Wimbly, hoping if there was an afterlife (which she never believed) that at least she'd get to pet him again.

Half-Ansel-o-pus fucked his own mouth with delight, gobs of dick residue dripping down his chin.

Knowing scumbag men like she did, Julianne figured she had one option that might work.

"Cum for me," she whispered.

Half-Ansel-o-pus leered at her, the corners of his eyes rising in a smile.

"Yeah, that's it, you cum for me. You cum so hard for me."

The creature fucked its own mouth faster, its head bulging like a balloon inflating, its moans jumping up an octave.

"Cum so fucking hard for me, you slut." She shuddered with each word, wanting to die inside, but hoping this strategy would work.

The dick went faster, harder, faster, harder until the beast wailed in delight.

"Cum for me!"

And then it did, and black and red sludge shot out of the monster's mouth, erupting up to the ceiling.

Both tentacles holding Julianne fell away, and she was free. She bent and found the sword, watching as the unknown half of the monster rolled his droopy eye back in his head, basking in the most fucked-up orgasm she'd ever witnessed.

She swung the sword and chopped the dick off at the base.

Half-Ansel-o-pus screamed and punched her with all its legs, sending her through the cheap drywall of the bedroom and into the living room. Every bone in her body felt like it was broken, and it was only the panic of being eaten alive, or fucked to death, that forced her to roll over and try to stand. All bones seemed to be working, but a section of the ceiling came down on her back and pinned her to the crunchy floor.

Through the dust of falling drywall and not-up-to-code popcorn ceiling asbestos, she saw the massive thing that was once Ansel (and once some other guy) scuttle out into the apartment's hallway and disappear.

She thought of Wimbly again and laughed hysterically. What else was there to do?

22

The elevator doors opened, and Ron stepped back, gun raised, waiting for something horrible to jump out. The elevator's lights were snuffed. Anything could be in those shadows. "I've been killing all night," he warned the darkness. "Give me an excuse to keep doing it."

He gave it another two seconds and decided it was empty. He stepped inside, hit the close button. Noise exploded above like a sudden stampede just as the door dinged shut. He thrust his gun out to stop the doors from closing, redirecting his gaze to the elevator's ceiling. The broken light had been smashed and the access panel next to it was torn open. Through the hole, he saw the blackness of the elevator shaft above him. Sounds drifted down that made him nervous. Things were moving about up there, banging on the walls, rippling the elevator cable. Wet, violent gagging echoed down followed by the unmistakable burble of someone upchucking.

He couldn't see it, but the smell hit Ron with gusto.

"To hell with this."

He left the confines of the elevator and speed-walked to the far stairwell. Climbing five flights of stairs was not something he was excited about, but then he was also not excited about death, so beggars couldn't be choosers.

The interior of the stairwell was just as dark; the emergency lighting had kicked on, but the bulbs were smashed out. Something had been here already. He waited, tilting his head upward to catch remote sounds. There was nothing suspicious, at least for now.

He took the stairs slowly, gun raised, finger on the trigger. He'd never had any formal firearms training in his life and hoped the action movies he'd watched in college were based in some semblance of reality. Point, shoot, and run. John Woo had better know what he was talking about.

He'd had friends from high school go the military route, do tours in Iraq, but he'd never seen the sense in taking down pawns on a game board when the real target was always the brain moving them. And brains were easily taken out with the push of a button these days. He had no interest in soldiering, but he did have an interest in those brains, those power players controlling the world.

Neurology offered more for his appetite. That and astrophysics. Two endeavors that had given him a leg up when it came to finding work. Looking to the stars for new life, new brains, new futures. Samson had snatched him up straight after graduate school.

It had been worth the insane amount of course work and thesis papers.

There'd also been Mila Tottono. That was her name. The girl he'd chased into the major. Met her during a tour of the college, asked her what she was interested in career-wise. They'd gone on a few dates. They banged after the third one. The sex was great. He was in love. But there was no fourth date, and she stopped taking his calls. Man, how he wanted her, and later hated her. What had been so wrong with him? He was a nice guy, right? He'd taken his hands off her head when she'd told him to stop shoving her chin into his balls.

Sophomore year she'd been in one of his classes and actually came up to him. "How have you been?"

"Mila? Great! Didn't know you were taking this, too."

"It's a requirement for the major."

"Of course, of course. Hey, would you want to grab a coffee and go over notes sometime?"

She actually said yes that she'd like that, but the following week she was hanging on the arm of some other guy in the class, and they never shared a coffee.

Nights in the dorm were spent lonely and angry. But he studied and he dreamed. Get the money, get the girl, save the world. The single man's narrowly focused mantra.

He realized he was on the fourth floor, his legs burning. He kept going, hearing his mother's voice in his head. "You said you'd come visit for Christmas, but you didn't. Why do you lie to your mother?"

"I said I'd come if I could make it, Mom. I couldn't make it."

"Work is more important than your mom? Your sister? You know she looks forward to these visits."

"No, Mom, it's just that I'm in charge of some high-profile stuff here. I can't just up and leave. People are depending on me. Besides, you all benefit from it."

"You hate us. We're an embarrassment to you. Two old people and a disabled girl. Nothing we offer can make you more successful."

Ron bit down on his tongue. It'd be easy to start screaming, but this wasn't something he needed nagging him throughout the project. "I'll be there as soon as I can. You know this. We have the same conversation every year, and I usually show up."

"Always at the last minute. Us left wondering if you'll show. And then as soon as the sun comes up the next day, you're gone."

The phone creaked he was squeezing it so tight. They were the ones who forced him into a lifetime of straight As, embarrassing him for the C he'd gotten in Phys Ed. Because his body should be as sharp as his mind if he was going to make it in the world, and that meant never taking time off or accepting silver medals.

Now they wanted him to drop everything in the prime of his career 'cause it worked for them. The friends they'd paraded him in front of as a kid had all moved away or died. No one left to be in awe of their biological show-pony, so of course he had to change course to accommodate them. They'd given up on Elaine, which pissed him off even more. She was disabled, not suffering brain damage. There was plenty they could do for her, but instead they treated her like some overgrown child, refusing to let her even try to help herself. Ron knew how demeaning it could be. He needed to get her out of there and on the beach already.

Seaside sunsets and margaritas in the future, sis.

"I need to go."

"You're gonna let us die alone and unloved and for what, some work? Not even a girl. A girl I could understand. You like that girl from school. Mila. You talked about her for years. You still talk about her."

"Mom, that was a couple dates in college."

"You obsess."

"I don't obsess."

"Then call her."

"I can't fucking call her! She wanted nothing to do with me, and it was ten years ago!"

"Well, don't worry about her. She's probably miserable."

He couldn't handle it. He punched the wall and gripped the phone hard enough to crack it. "Who cares how she is? She's not with me, so who fucking cares?!"

"Your language, Ron. Such anger."

He took a deep breath, let it out. "I'm not angry, Mom. In fact, I'm working on a project right now to eliminate anger, eliminate jealousy, and make it so everyone gets along. We found something out there, Mom, and I can't tell you what it is yet, but it's going to change the world. It's delicate and unknown and needs lots of research, and that's why I can't commit to coming home yet."

"You certainly sound angry to me. I don't think you got over that girl. But she was just a girl. There are others."

"There are no others, Mom! She was the one, but she fucked me over! But maybe the lovebugs can bring her back to me."

"What bugs?"

"Nothing. I'm gonna get fired if I say more. Look, trust me, Mom, my work is important. I'll visit you soon."

"Do you still love me?"

"Oh, fer fuck's sake."

"Do you?"

"Yes, Mom. I love you."

"Yet you do it from far away. That's gratitude."

"I gotta go, Mom."

"Make me a promise, Ron?"

"What?"

"Find love someday, my baby boy. Find real love. You need it in your life. You more than anyone. You can't just rely on our love to get you through this. You need more."

"You have no idea, Mom. Bye."

His legs were burning when he reached the roof access door. Sweat dripped down his back; his ankles were swollen. He shook his head, clearing away the intrusive fantasy of Mila naked in bed with him.

He spoke with exhaustion, near delirium from the trek up the stairs. "She'll love me again. They all will."

He pushed open the door, stepped out into the cold night. Steam roiled out of a nearby exhaust vent. Two helicopters circled the property at a distance, like vultures waiting for a wounded animal to die. Lights from below spilled upward to the purple clouds above.

He took out the stolen cell, and his face exploded with pain.

His body slammed to the rooftop, a tooth tearing out of his gums and bouncing across his chest. A massive shadow stepped into view, a human with a fist still balled up and ready to strike again, the other hand dragging a blood-covered axe.

Theo.

"Little bug! I'm glad we found each other."

23

When the stench of burst bowels and rancid fuck-juice finally became too much, Julianne got to her feet, using the sword like an old man's flamboyant cane. She prodded the rope of flesh left behind by Half-Ansel-o-Pus with the tip of the blade. Up close, she realized it wasn't really an arm anymore. More like multiple umbilical cords twined together with rudimentary mouths crafted by a blind child turning its nightmares into art. A tiny pink tongue probed the air, nibbled the tapered steel.

She wanted to tell what was left of her friend—if this even was his limb—that she was sorry. She'd really tried to get here in time, but this was one of those moments in life where doing your best was great and all, but it meant nothing. It bummed her out that she'd never hear the score he'd been working on for *Funeral Shroud*, never get to see him resuscitate his career.

Absentmindedly, she sliced a quarter of the fleshy purple hose away as it had found her shoe more enticing than the sword.

Her ears hummed and rang, reminding her of the time she'd forgotten earplugs for a Plutonium Christ sewer show. Feedback from the guitar had ricocheted off the concrete walls, slammed her eardrums. After that, she made a note to always keep a pair in her bag should she ever find herself at an unconventional venue, a production that happened to have a lot of gunplay, or fighting monsters determined to invade every hole in her body and leave her impregnated with their spawn.

Despite the ongoing drone in her head, Julianne could still hear the chaos swarming around her. Every floor sounded like a mosh pit at a swinger party. Getting out was going to be an obstacle course designed by Ed Gein and H.H. Holmes.

She'd seen that rat-faced slumlord, Jesus, at the V-Day party, and thought he'd been sweating from the lack of AC and all the bodies swaying to music, but only now did it finally click. He knew what was happening. And since things had gone down so fast, he no doubt had an escape plan in mind. Unless his boss was more than happy to watch their underling trampled under the thrusting bodies of dozens of horny maniacs, which Julianne could totally get behind given his attitude.

His office had been devoid of personal belongings when she and Ansel searched it. No coats, no Thermos, no phone charger, nothing that would say he was still at work. He'd definitely packed up in anticipation of something. But other than lack of belongings, nothing else had stood out. No faux bookcases or trapdoors leading to a secret escape tunnel. She thought briefly about trying the windows in his office again, but even if she did miraculously open them, the armed bozos outside were probably still jerking each other off to pictures of Chuck Norris and she wasn't eager to get blasted into oblivion the moment she emerged.

That left the rec room.

Most of the tenants had been packed in there when the change occurred. The ones who hadn't wandered back to their rooms with the hope of getting laid were likely partying in a different way now. She held the bloody sword up. Chunks of flesh and body hair clung to the blade. It was good in close quarters, but what Julianne needed was something powerful.

"I'm, uh, not super great at goodbyes, dude," she said, staring down at what was, hopefully, left of Ansel, "but for what it's worth, I really did like your music."

She wiped a few tears away, headed down the hall to grab her latest creation before going back downstairs. She'd been working on it for a new short film.

A DIY flamethrower.

24

Theo smashed his fist into Ron's face for a third time.

"Loosen that kisser up for me, honey bun."

Defiantly, Ron spat a gummy wad of blood and teeth into the monster's face. Theo picked a few incisors from the curls of his massive beard, popped them into his mouth like mints. "Ah, fuck it. You'll have enough holes for the whole family once we're finished here and I take you back downstairs. Besides, there's more to love when you're in pieces."

The sight of the man ass-scooting away from him, blood staining the front of his shirt, made Theo's groin ache. Eager lovebugs wormed their way up and down his urethra, sending jolts throughout his hardened member. The ones winding around his brain whispered ballads of harmony and pleasure, nibbled at his mind to keep bringing everyone together in one place for an outstanding Grand Guignol sex party.

Overhead the dull clap of a helicopter drew closer. A blue-white beam of light hit the roof.

Theo was so focused on the sheer wave of pleasure from dominating a weaker being that he didn't notice Ron's hacksaw until its teeth raked across his shin. He wobbled, swung the axe in an upward arc, gutting nothing but air in a massive *whoosh*.

He stomped toward Ron, swinging the huge axe back and forth like a drunk with a flyswatter.

There wasn't a muscle in Ron's body that wasn't burning. He ached in places he didn't know were possible. Worst of all, he could feel himself slowing. Whether he wanted to admit it or not, the human body had limitations. Molasses invaded his reflexes. Eventually, he'd have to choose between getting chopped into an amputated sex doll or a disgraceful dive down eight stories.

Theo brought the axe down between Ron's legs. Tar and gravel chips sprayed. With a frustrated grunt, the rampaging behemoth struggled to pull the blade from where it'd embedded itself into the BUR membrane roofing.

Ron seized the opportunity. He swiped at Theo's bulging wrists, feeling elated when the teeth nicked one of the pulsating veins. Theo roared and gripped the wound.

Ron grabbed the phone and yelled into it: "You still out there, asshole?"

"Oh, we wouldn't miss this," said the teasing voice. "My biggest regret is you won't get to see how entertaining you look running around rooftops like a trapped animal."

"I've got a head in my bag."

"We've got lots of heads back at the lab."

"It's infected with lovebugs."

"We'll recover a corpse later and do the same thing."

"You're really looking forward to digging through all that rubble?"

"Demo is scheduled for after."

"My ass. You want the head or not?"

A pause. Then, "Okay, okay. The specimens haven't died in it yet?"

"No, been keeping 'em warm and nice and fed on this little adventure, but we need to get this to the lab soon before it chews its way out and up my asshole."

"I'd like to see that."

"Get me out of here!"

"Chill, old man. We're talking to the pilots now."

25

Dorian McNamara was an emerging auteur in the underground horror scene. *Tiffany's Rage*, an unsubtle examination of a young attractive woman's mounting psychosis brought on by familial trauma, made even the most jaded film critics take notice. But his talents didn't end there. McNamara also fronted the avantgarde death rock band Silhouettes at Dusk, known for blurring the lines between fake fighting and borderline sex acts on stage.

He also happened to be batshit crazy.

He'd contacted Julianne after seeing her short, impressed that she'd managed to portray the ominous encroaching light from another dimension as it split a black void with nothing more than painted boards and colored gels. He said she deserved an award, said he wanted someone like that on his team for his next project, *Demons of the Desert*, a film that dared to criticize American soldiers fighting the war on terror.

"I'm not a military expert," she'd said over video chat, "but did they even use flamethrowers during the Iraq war?"

Dorian waved the statement away. "They did. They used them to burn brush and trees and anywhere they thought an IED could be hidden. They set a lot of nature on fire. Can you make me a cost-effective working flamethrower?"

"Can't you just buy one?"

"There's too many legal hurdles and permits. And I wouldn't want to support those people anyway. This is guerilla filmmaking. We do it all ourselves, and I need you. So . . . can you?"

Julianne smirked. People were always asking her silly questions with very obvious answers.

"Of course I can."

Impossible and No weren't words that existed in Julianne's vocabulary when it came to creating what she needed. Disparate parts or trashed electronics were just puzzle pieces that hadn't found their companions yet. It had taken her a week to collect everything she'd needed. The trickiest part had been finding a reliable recipe for napalm that would make a truly hellish pop on camera.

She hefted the full pack onto her back, double-checked the metal ring she'd screwed onto the tip of the kid's firefighter super soaker to keep it from melting, and clicked the grill lighter affixed to the bottom on. The napalm mix would skim the top of the flame and light up anything within six feet. It wouldn't be on par with a dragon's belch the way a lot of high-end flamethrowers were, but she needed it to be functional for the sake of getting out of the building.

She stuffed a few bottles of lighter fluid into her crossbody bag and a half-full bottle of New Amsterdam and some rags for when the tank ran dry. The sword slid in between her belt and jeans.

Part of her wanted to grab her laptop and a few other keepsakes, but time was winding down faster than a lit wick of dynamite. She'd spent a few good years at Sunshine Spires. It was objectively a shithole, and she fought with management on a regular basis, but she couldn't deny the bizarre cast of characters inhabiting every unit had been amusing. She'd done some of her best work in this cramped little hotbox with missing patches of carpet, unpredictable outages, and constantly failing amenities.

The kitchen wall exploded. Plaster sprayed outward. Dozens of arms pocked with tiny hungry mouths searched for the warm body on the other side. Rhythmic banging vibrated the studs and plaster as the eager mutants slammed their genitals into what was left of the wall.

Run now, romanticize later.

Before her mind had the chance to picture a drawn-out, grueling fate, Julianne hustled out of the room and down the hallway, hopping over nude corpses.

A door to her right blew outward, sent her stumbling into the adjacent wall now spattered in spunk and gore. Hot, rank air wafted over her, followed by an oceanic moan. She kept going. Told herself there was no fucking way she'd seen a dripping wet tongue filling the doorway.

The stairwell was relatively clear save for the two mutants fucking on the concrete landing. The man's eyes dangled at the end of the optic nerves, bounced off his cheek in rhythm with the relentless grinding of his hips. His partner was supine, fingers packed deep into her spread asshole. Julianne couldn't tell what was worse, the fact the woman's torn rectum was stuffed with teeth or that the man was playing hide the salami with the newly formed mouth in between her breasts.

Conscious of her limited fuel supply, she stopped and swung the sword with more muscle than she knew she was capable of. The man's head fell to the floor as his body slumped sideways, spraying yellow ejaculate at her feet. The woman with the toothy asshole tried to rise, but Julianne slammed the sword into her neck and quickly sawed sideways. Blood spouted up, coating Julianne's face. The woman tried to roll her ass toward Julianne in one last desperate attempt to eat her. Julianne swung the sword again and cut the remaining ligaments holding the head on the body. The two bodies lay still except for the asshole mouth, which still smacked and bit at the air.

Julianne stepped back and admired her work. It may not stop them, but it sure felt nice.

She continued down the stairs.

Doors began slamming open on every floor. Slimy, hurried slithering created a cacophony of alien gibberish as the lovebugs tried to use the vocal cords of the tenants they'd devoured, reminding her of that nu metal singer in the Adidas tracksuit who used to scat over down-tuned guitars.

If upstairs had been hell, this was Satan's septic tank.

The first floor greeted her with viscous, ankle-deep sludge. She peered up to see a ragged hole in the ceiling. Pipes were twisted and snapped in half, spilling a waterfall of waste down onto the first floor. Splash Mountain if it were made of raw sewage. Fingers and other discarded limbs lazily drifted by accompanied by half-eaten heart-shaped cupcakes, bottles of cheap champagne, condoms, novelty sex games, and a penis pinata with a hole punched into it. Colorful fluids swirled throughout the trash like paint strokes.

To her surprise, the double doors at the front were wide open. A metal barrier beyond it had been shoved aside. She stomped through the muck, kicking aside severed dicks and a ridiculous set of fake tits.

Who'd been in charge of this Valentine's Day party, anyway?

Hope flickered in her chest as she got closer to the door. She may not have been able to save Ansel, but saving her own ass was just fine for the time being. Survivors' guilt could wait until sunrise.

Pain exploded in her side. Almost instantly, she felt herself levitate and then smash into the running river of organic refuse. Sour liquid rushed down her throat, cajoling a fresh gout of vomit from her already frayed esophagus. She blinked brown water from her eyes in time to see the mutant who had hit her lift her from the floor and slam her into the wall.

Reflexively, she brought the super-soaker up to turn this ugly bastard into a smore. He grabbed her wrist, twisted. Sparks of pain shot up her forearm, forced her to drop the flamethrower.

"You're so pretty," Jesus said.

Julianne couldn't help it. His face, once the narrow shape of a rat's, now resembled a prolapsed anus. She laughed at the sight of his tongue flipping around like a trapped slug. "And you somehow got uglier."

He reached up inside her respirator and pinched her septum ring between his thumb and forefinger.

She stopped laughing as the slightest tug sent a jolt of pain up into her skull.

"You would be a lot prettier without all this shit in your face."

The ring made a disgusting pop as it was wrenched through her columella. Julianne screamed louder than John Wetton belted the chorus to "Heat of the Moment," which was pumping from the sound system just beyond the doors. The respirator fell back in place as her right arm shot out, eager to plunge the sword into his throat, only to find it was no longer in her hand. Her closed fist hit him in the side of the throat, but Jesus didn't seem to notice.

"I've watched you since the day you moved in here. Never once have I seen you with a boyfriend . . . or girlfriend. You need a man in your life. Someone who can take care of you. Not pal around with that scrawny, washed-up musician. A *real* man."

A real man. The words rolled around in Julianne's head. She'd heard it so many times in her life that she wondered if it even had any meaning. What made a man real? Chopping trees down before speeding off in a lifted truck, road soda firmly tucked between his legs, annoyed that he had to go home and smash the same old pussy he'd been putting it to forever? Having a stance on "traditional" gender roles so rigid that any deviation would be met with childish insecure verbal and physical abuse, a constant cycle of tears, bruises, and unwavering resentment? She'd lived that already, and she knew those guys weren't real men; they were the products of fearmongering.

Her parents had lived out the nuclear family fantasy until she'd left for college and, much like Oppenheimer's invention, had erupted in a hailstorm of drama resulting in marital scorched earth. It was then that Julianne realized she'd been the plug for the tension in their relationship. They'd kept it together just long enough to see her head out on her own. "Mom and I . . . " Her dad massaged his scalp, staring off camera on the video call as if searching for a cue card. " . . . we haven't enjoyed each other's company for a long time. In all honesty, I think I was holding her back all these years."

Dad wanted the family rooted in his hometown of Ramona, CA. Wanted Julianne to know the history of where she'd come from. When she was little, he'd tell her stories about a colorful town brimming with characters, from an old WW2 vet that'd converted the front of his home into a neon sign graveyard to a couple of fellas who used to ride around on horseback looking to lasso anyone breaking the law.

It'd been fun when she was ten, but the older Julianne got, the more it seemed like those people were just into hoarding and good ol' fashioned vigilantism—she never bothered asking what color most of the "law breakers" were, didn't need to.

She knew her dad's real reason, though, and it had nothing to do with enriching the life of his daughter. Rather it had everything to do with the fact that country musician Big Craig Wade had grown tired of driving around the country in a converted van, playing to scattered audiences in remote bars. He didn't have that problem back home. Every other Friday night he'd fill up the Ramona Mainstage to a crowd of folks he knew by name. Christ, they even had a billboard up with his face on it, heavy black Stetson sitting high on the top of his head. "Ramona's finest country singer" was stenciled on the side.

Mom wasn't built for small town life. She'd commuted down the mountain to Poway every morning to her gig at Juice Electric, drafting and designing jobs to maintain fire safety throughout the utility's territory. Mom was a wizard in AutoCAD, and in addition to being talented in visual design work, she understood how everything worked from capacitors to fuse cutouts. Sometimes she'd sleep at the office, saying they were under pressure to get jobs out, and just bill whatever takeout they ordered to her card. Julianne often wondered if maybe she'd just needed a break from her father's constant desire to be the center of attention.

When they'd split, it had been more of a relief than a surprise. She'd given them her blessing, which they weirdly needed, and hoped they'd found their happiness. Mom took an early retirement, got a bunch of tattoos, and was now living the bohemian life in an old tour rig, while Dad moved Lucy, the bartender from Hot Shots Bar & Grill, into the house where she could dote on him and provide the praise his parents never gave him.

If she'd learned anything from all that, it was that people should just admit when things weren't working out instead of dragging each other down.

Fuck norms.

Jesus leaned his head back. The thin webbing of skin at the corners of his mouth split. Ochre fluid dripped down his chin as his jaw began to unhinge. His tongue was now dotted with crooked, horny mouths eager to find purchase on her body. Unceremoniously, his eyes popped out from their sockets to make way for more mouths.

"We don't need to see you to enjoy the fruit of your body, beautiful. Come join the family."

Jesus wrestled the fuel pack off her. It dropped into the river of shit with a splash. With his hand tight on her throat, he tossed her through the rec room doorway. Pain spiked her lower back. Her body tumbled over itself and stopped with a loud crack as the back of her head hit the sticky, fluid-smeared floor. Thick gusts of fetid heat blew over her body.

Shockingly, no one had destroyed the sound system. The song changed to Ginuwine's "Pony." Ripped red-and-white streamers of daisy-chained hearts dangled from the ceiling. Overturned tables and chairs became instruments of anal impalement. Julianne would've felt bad if those with the steel legs firmly wedged in their rectums didn't seem to be reaching some sort of cataclysmic climax from it. Their hips shuddered and rolled, arms working overtime if a hole wasn't available to catch the steady streams of baby batter leaping from their laps.

It was disgusting, but Julianne had seen enough creeps banging their boring members into another dimension to zone out. Nothing new to see here, folks. Just another dolt with impulse control problems.

Jesus stood over her, smiled when he noticed her watching the frenzied masturbators. "Everyone's having a good time. You will, too."

He pulled Julianne to her feet by her belt, so she could finally see where the thick canopy of humid rot was coming from.

Sometimes knowing was worse than ignorance.

She'd seen the creatures get as big as her fist, but the thing mouthing the air like an infant eager for a tit was twice the size of her Volvo. Its thick beige tongue made from melted human muscle glided over gray, grooved lips that had their own smaller mouths. The sight was so excessively absurd, her mind kept wanting to make jokes. Behold! The world's first kaiju sex toy!

Strands of pulsing membranes sprouted from it, disappearing into holes in the ceiling, the walls, the floor. A living spider web that absorbed everything it came in contact with and worse, if you could even believe that this could get any worse, were the bodies strung throughout like insects caught in a web. The fleshy strands of meat that connected the lovebugs sprouted from all the orifices they could, keeping each other together, growing hungrier by the second.

"I wanted this to be special," Jesus said, dragging his tongue up the back of her earlobe. "We're going to do this together."

* * *

Jimmy threw the sweat-soaked wolf mask onto the passenger seat of Vern's truck, searched the visor for the keys. He could deal with knocking other human beings around. Especially the ones who actively wanted guys like him dead. He'd seen it on all the social media sites and message boards. Encouragements of suicide or insinuations about the relationships he'd had with his sister. They came out in packs of condescending college kids to scream and spit in his face because what? He believed in keeping his people safe, and he knew there was an evil spreading throughout his country like cancer in the form of things like indoctrinating their kids into believing they should feel bad for being white or God forbid straight. Not that he'd really seen any of that in action. Only heard it from friends and other anonymous posters, but still, they wouldn't be talking about it if it weren't true, right?

He tore the glovebox apart. Some rabbit's feet charms and a few extra boxes of bullets, but no keys. Vern must've taken them with him. They'd been in there for hours, and given the sounds coming from inside, Jimmy Simpson figured the rest of his pack wouldn't be coming back out.

Stupid.

Going in there like that. They had families to think about. Catching a bullet was one thing. Whatever this experiment was, and like with most things he heartily believed in despite concrete evidence, the risk of bringing the disease back to their families wasn't worth the financial gain Vern hoped to achieve.

He continued tearing the truck apart searching for a way out. So singularly focused he didn't hear the heavy roar of the helicopters above.

26

The helicopter hovered a few feet from the edge of the building.

Two mercs in full special ops gear with night-vision goggles strapped to their faces sat in the open cabin of the Sikorsky, training their MK-17s at the roof. For a moment, Ron thought they were going to blast him *and* the axe-wielding brute, but when the bullets started eating up the roof behind him, Ron figured this was the best they could offer for cover fire.

He ran for the ledge and jumped.

When he felt his shoulder hit the cool metal of the cabin floor, Ron barely registered the pain. He was free. He could breathe again. The *whump* from the rotor blades eased the tension out of his muscles as he fantasized about the look on everyone's faces when he walked back into the lab, head secured in the bag for further testing. The champagne they'd pour for him already tasted sweet and acidic.

"Fuck yeah," Ron muttered, thinking maybe he'd nap all the way back. "I did it."

The helicopter pitched to its side. Gunfire filled the cabin.

Terror and rage swirling in his chest, Ron watched Theo pull himself inside. One of the operatives slumped against the far wall. The blade of the axe had split the man's head down the middle and was now wedged firmly in the stump of the neck. Blood belched from the deep gash.

"What the fuck is going on back there?" the pilot screamed.

"Get us out of here," Ron shouted back.

The other operative slammed another clip into his assault rifle, brought it up to blast Theo in the face, but the rampaging lunatic knocked the weapon out of his hands the way a disgruntled adult would a child with a squirt gun. Theo grabbed the straps of the man's flak jacket and slammed him ass-first onto the side of the axe blade that wasn't nestled in his co-worker's throat. The gunman's weight shoved the axe farther into the other man, flopping the two halves of his head onto his shoulders.

The merc's scream made Ron's asshole try to retract, but the part of him that loved research watched Theo drop to his knees. The impaled operative wailed as the delicate pouch of his testicles split under the pressure of Theo pushing down on his shoulders. Theo yanked the goggles off the man's face, tossed them aside.

"It's always better when you can see the eyes."

The bulging masses that had once been under Theo's skin burst forth, revealing mouths. Dozens of lashing tongues unfurled, lapped at their newfound freedom. He wondered if Theo was now more lovebug than human, an ambulatory vessel collecting new bodies for the cause.

Theo pried the man's mouth open, vomited thick strands of sallow, juvenile lovebugs into his throat. The man shook his head to get the vomit off, but Theo kept on spewing.

Which reminded him, he needed to get this head on ice asap.

"Are you going to get us out of here or keep flying in a fucking circle?" Ron snapped at the pilot.

The screams slowly became moans as the deposited lovebugs began mating in their new home.

The pilot eased the cyclic stick to the left. "We can't leave the area until that thing is contained or dead or . . . we run out of fuel."

Theo yanked the axe out of the merc's mangled crotch with a wet crunch, headed for the cockpit. Half a dick slid down the curved blade, made a *plop* sound as it fell into the growing pool of blood on the floor. More love bugs sprouted from his arms, wrapped around the gore-slicked handle.

"Give me your side arm?" Ron yelled.

"Ain't got one, chief."

Ron wasn't built for this type of confrontation. Beyond medical training, his real strength was his ability to take in information, strategize, and then send in more capable psychopaths to bring his plans to life. He'd relied on those talents for so long because for the most part, he'd never needed to do anything else. Now he found himself wishing he'd taken a self-defense course at the very least, or maybe hit the gym a few times a week.

The copter banked, made a sharp turn. Theo slid to the side but braced himself with the axe to keep from falling out of the open cabin.

An idea wormed its way into Ron's head. Hope filled his chest. You really did just have to stop and take a minute to think through the situation, assess your options. All the overbearing tough guy shit could only take you so far. But merging the two would always yield successful results.

Theo was so close to the door. He just needed a little nudge.

"When you take this next turn, lean into it, hard, and then right it as quick as you can," he said to the pilot.

He did.

A little too much.

As soon as Ron felt the helicopter shift, he shut his eyes and launched himself at Theo, shoulder first in his best impression of a defensive lineman. It happened so fast he barely registered making contact. He heard an *oomph* and then summer wind washed over him like a warm blanket. Weightless, how people feel when they achieve a victory against all odds. He turned to flash the pilot a thumbs-up and . . .

Wait . . .

He wasn't supposed to be outside the copter.

Shit.

The cab of the truck erupted in a geyser of glass. His spine collided with the top of the windshield frame, snapped like a whip being pulled taught. His right leg folded underneath him. Unbelievable pain overwhelmed him.

Seconds before he blacked out, Ron saw the helicopter pirouette in the air before crashing into the side of the building.

27

J ulianne's parents had always wondered where she fell on the spectrum of sexuality. "We don't care," her mom used to say. "We just want to see you happy." She believed them, and she was grateful—especially considering her dad's hometown. A lot of her non-cishet friends didn't have a support system. What irked her, though, was their insistence that true happiness only came from being romantically entwined with someone, that she'd be incomplete without a partner.

That was bullshit. She was just happy doing her own thing, spending time with her friends. When it came to sex, Julianne was more than capable of taking care of her own needs. The world she lived in came with an endless supply of toys and tutorials. Besides, once the post-nut clarity cleared the fog of horniness, she was able to go back to taking care of things that mattered, like creating art and memories with those closest to her.

Still, she hadn't emerged from her parents' soap-boxing unscathed. There was a period in her early twenties where she'd experimented with people across the gender spectrum, thinking maybe the next one would help her find this supposed need to attach herself to another person. Nothing ever lasted long, and in all honesty the sex, whether foreplay or more, was always a frustrating event of unsure hands poking and prodding uncomfortable areas of her body, going too fast or too slow, or simply not knowing what to do altogether. Plus, the emotional damage control that came with telling someone it was okay they didn't get her to achieve orgasm got old real fast.

She could make herself happy.

She could make herself cum.

Which was why being sandwiched between a massive pulsating

tongue monster and her rotting scumbag property manager felt like hell. She was running out of options, seconds away from biting into Jesus' face and risking one of those weird rectal creatures mating with her eye socket, when the helicopter came screaming through the ceiling.

Her world went nine different ways of upside down.

The sound of the thunderous impact nearly burst her eardrums, causing a blaring klaxon in her head. Chunks of support beams and popcorn ceiling exploded. The kitschy disco ball erupted into thousands of microscopic jagged mirrored glass shards firing into the floor. She was hurled into the air, flipping like a ragdoll, her legs and arms threatening to tear off her body. Pain swallowed her chest as she fought to breathe. A tsunami of fiery, rushing air pinned her to a surface she could not discern. Was she on the ceiling or the wall or the floor?

The wail of the helicopter's rotors made her entire body vibrate. Windows were blown out, doors were decimated, walls crumbled.

Her whole world was a warzone of concrete, steel, and splintered furniture.

She waited for blackness to engulf her, for her consciousness to wink out of existence, but all she knew for certain was that Jesus was now on top of her. A thick cloud of black smoke fell over them, enough to choke the average person, but her respirator managed to filter enough to keep her from passing out.

Somehow, she was still alive. But for how long? Was there a fireball explosion coming? Would the whirring rotors cut her in half?

Knowing she wouldn't get another chance, Julianne brought her knee up into Jesus's groin. The grin that spread across his face wasn't exactly the result she'd hoped for, but no man could withstand a nut-shot without acknowledging a bit of the pain that came with it. She used that momentary shock to shove him off her.

The gargantuan tongue was there, too, licking her back.

"Give me a fucking break!" she screamed, army crawling under a ceiling of drifting blackness.

Jesus squirmed toward her, getting closer. She grabbed him by the collar of his greasy, fluid-stained shirt, shoved him toward the eager, open mouth of the tongue mutant. One thing she could count on was these things didn't discriminate. A warm hole was a warm hole. Blind, confused, and operating on pure sexual need, Jesus rolled into the sticky, waiting tongue.

The tongue wedged into him, spreading his asshole to impossible lengths, as it lifted the useless bastard into its maw.

Thankfully, her flamethrower still sat in the flowing muck in the hallway. Before anything else could surprise her, she slid the straps over her shoulders and went back in.

Jesus had mostly disappeared into the mouth. Its massive, slug-like appendage continued to force itself up through his body. Intestines pushed their way out of his mouth like sliced meat through a grinder. His tiny cock bobbed sadly in a thicket of unmaintained pubic hair.

He was still grinning.

Julianne pulled the trigger. Orange flame spewed, coated the mother lovebug. Fist-sized blisters formed and burst on its lips. Jesus's body crinkled and blackened. Fat melted to the floor. The entire space around her erupted in shrieks as the creatures ignited.

Doing her best to conserve her fuel, Julianne torched sections of the wall and ceiling she knew would spread the fire faster, pumped another gout of flame into the bubbling mouth, and then hurried over to the crashed helicopter that was hemorrhaging the last of its gasoline.

The rotors were slowing. What was left of them, anyway. The blades had broken off on impact and left nothing but nubs.

She could see remnants of the crew inside. Meat and bone splattered throughout the cabin. The only distinguishing clues that these had been people were the glimpses of torn fabric and aviation headsets embedded in their faces.

Sparks burst from the instruments inside. Metal clanged off metal somewhere in the engine.

Julianne took a few steps back as pieces of ceiling fell around her. She fought the urge to hold the trigger down, wanting to make sure she wasn't about to barbecue someone who might need help.

"Love is the foundation of all species," growled a voice in the wreckage. "Unity makes us strong. Together we're everything."

She knew who it was before she took a few steps closer, before the bushy beard came into view. Theo's prized axe had lodged itself into his own pelvis. Close up, she could see his blackened husk crawling with frantic lovebugs searching for a new place to hide.

He'd scared her the moment they passed one another in the

hallway. She knew he thought she'd narced on him about his lumberjack trips into the surrounding forest even though it'd been none other than that old twat Carol. Julianne figured it was easier to let the unhinged ex-marine go about thinking it was her. She could defend herself if she needed to. Carol wasn't prepared to endure the wrath of a man with nowhere to vent his frustrations.

"Please," he said, "let us come to you. Let us—"

She turned the spreading gasoline into a lake of fire, then ran.

28

J ulianne stepped through the shattered front door and over the twisted metal barricade lying on its side. She staggered down the front steps of Sunshine Spires as fast as she could without tripping. It'd be pretty embarrassing to come this far only to get taken out by a twisted ankle. Screams spilled from inside the building. Whether from the fire or achieving transcendental ecstasy, she couldn't be sure, and she didn't give a shit. The important part was she'd made it outside.

Thick black smoke blocked most of the rising sun. The pyre at her back cast a deep orange haze that covered the parking lot and went as far as the decaying strip mall across the street. The mostly abandoned storefronts seemed unaffected by the all-out battleground that'd popped up overnight. Even the sign for Pho Me Up, the only place Julianne had ever seen open, continued blinking on and off. Its white-and-green neon glow contrasting with the inferno painting she'd emerged from.

A moan caught her attention.

Instinctively, her finger curled around the flamethrower's trigger. Every thought screamed at her to head straight to her car and get down the mountain. She wasn't obligated to play exterminator. That was the job of several entities that seemed to be non-existent at the moment.

It may have been a small town, but Julianne expected that someone would've called emergency services when everything went down, but the only sounds she heard were the crumbling building, the fading screams of the lovebugs being cooked alive, somebody moaning, and the steady *thwip* of the wind. No firetrucks or cop cars screeched into the lot. Not even a single ambulance. Parked on the corner was a black panel van with tinted windows and egregious antennae, but even that seemed empty.

This is what the end of the world feels like.

It's heat, and destruction, and a vast emptiness signaling anyone left was on their own.

Around the corner she found the source of the moaning.

She could tell that the truck belonged to the gun-humpers who'd tried to kill her on the balcony from the stickers plastered across the paint-chipped tailgate. FREEDOM ISN'T FREE! JOHN 3:16. AN ARMED SOCIETY IS A POLITE SOCIETY! FUCK YOUR STICK FIGURE FAMILY! The last one came with a grinning caricature shooting a man and woman in the head. And finally, one strange take on the Who Saved Who? pet sticker that featured a hefty .357 magnum instead of a cat or dog paw.

These dipshits always missed the point.

Julianne brought her attention to the crumpled body lying in a nest of shattered glass and crumpled metal. Inside the vehicle was an arm splayed across the dashboard, an American flag with writing within the bars tattooed down the forearm.

He didn't even seem to notice she was there at first. His hands worried the strap of his frayed messenger bag, like the movement of his fingers was the only thing keeping him alive. One leg had been snapped askew at the ankle, while the other was hidden beneath him. Blood trickled down the front of his mouth.

"Huh . . . huhlp," he said, glancing over to where she stood. "I need to get this to Samson."

He tried to sit up so he could get the messenger bag from around his chest. Glass crinkled underneath, forcing him back down with a screech.

"What is it?"

"A chance at peace."

Julianne took off her respirator, breathing in outdoor air for the first time in what felt like forever. She looped it around her wrist, took a step closer to the man, looked him over. His outfit was odd. He wore bloodied slacks with combat boots, flak jacket hiding most of the dull flannel tablecloth pattern of his dress shirt. There was no way this guy had been a tenant, which meant he was on the side of whoever did this to them.

"Please help," he said again.

"Why should I?"

"There's so much we can learn from this. We can finally reach perfect harmony."

She knocked his trembling hands away from the bag's zipper, opened it up.

Even with all the smoke, she could smell the rot slithering from the bag like some kind of ghostly vagabond. Using the barrel of the flamethrower, she opened the bag further. Resting inside was a severed head encased in a bondage mask. For a moment, Julianne wondered what poor bastard had suffered like this, become this man's prized token of research.

Then, slowly, three tiny love bugs emerged from the face. Two slid out of empty eye sockets. The third unfurled from the host's mouth. Their pruned rictuses seemed smaller. Cracks in their lips wept of yellowish fluid. The webbed membranes they used to move around were dried out and flaking.

Julianne didn't need a degree in anything to know they were dying. They'd used up whatever life this head once had. The head's blood was clotted, the flesh dry. It was no longer sustaining them. These things that had previously decimated an entire building now moved in aching jerks.

"There's a black van out there. Some of my colleagues should still be in it. They work for Samson. Take it to them. They'll know what to do. They'll make sure the program is a success."

"You killed all of them. Everyone inside."

"Their lives were meaningless before I came along," he said, coughing blood into his hand. "Better to die for something than rot away achieving nothing."

"What *something*?"

"Love. We did this for love. For the species to get along."

"You infected people with something against their will."

"We had to. You wouldn't have done it yourself. You'd never have gotten along otherwise, and the world would just keep fighting and fighting. What other choice did we have? Don't you agree the world will be better once everyone gets along?"

"It doesn't give you the right to use us without consent."

"Would you have volunteered? 'Hey, we found this alien bug that somehow makes living things come together.' Yeah, right."

"Even if your intentions are good, it still doesn't excuse it. You can't just take control of someone's body. It's not yours to control! It's my body! Not yours!"

"So then what, the human race just keeps warring till it destroys itself?"

"Maybe! Who cares! You don't get to decide for me! For us! And you know what? Yeah, maybe I would have volunteered. It's not like you asked. Lots of people want a pleasant society, but it's gotta work itself out on its own. If you force it, it'll just fall back into shit again when the drugs wear off or the . . . bugs . . . die. All you did was kill the people you wanted to save. All you did was force control of a situation that has no clear answer. You're the problem with humans, not the people who just wanted to go to a Valentine's Day party! I mean, fuck, why this place? Why these people?"

The man's eyes narrowed, tone going cold. "You're all bottom feeders. You're haters and elitists and busybodies and keyboard warriors. Addicts and psychopaths. You may say hi in the hallways, but you secretly hate each other. We chose you for that. You think you just lucked out on cheap rent and no credit checks? Julianne, you were perfect to move in. You live to fight."

"With Nazis, yes! With people minding their own business, no!"

"Your films are just fights, girl. Angry protests on the screen."

"You know nothing about me."

"I know you are a fighter, and that's why you're here. But I can save you. I can save you all. Just get this head back—"

"No!"

She wanted to scream at him some more, explain how wrong he was. That a lot of the people who died were some of the most vibrant and creative folks she'd met. Sure, others were downright assholes and creeps, but those types of people were inescapable. You couldn't control them or their desire to be total dicks. But you cultivated community where you could and brought the hammer down on the folks who were a real danger, like the nuts they'd hired to patrol the perimeter—idiots who resorted to violence because non-traditional approaches to resolution made them piss their pants.

You just had to do your best where you could.

And you certainly didn't need to murder a whole bunch of people to test your mad scientist hypothesis.

Julianne upended the bag. The head landed on the man's chest with a thud. Sensing warmth, the lovebugs started probing him for entry. It was enough for her to solve the final mystery. Why every mutant wanted to fuck so bad and puke on each other. The lovebugs could use a body for a bit, but eventually they needed untainted blood. The sex-crazed activities and vomit spraying they induced had nothing to do with love or communion or sick kinks; they just wanted a new body to feed on.

"No, no, no," the man said. "Not like this."

One of the lovebugs found a torn nipple, burrowed its way into the open flesh pocket. The other two went in opposite directions, penetrating the soft knot of his belly button with a pop, while the other gnawed at the gash in his temple, pushing the skin up and disappearing under a waterfall of blood.

He screamed, but seconds later his eyes glazed. His shattered pelvis tried to thrust outward only managed a stunted jerk to the left. He elicited a shrill whine, then his teeth clamped down hard onto his tongue in an attempt to hang onto his last shred of humanity. Then the tongue in Ron's mouth split in half and stuck to his chin.

The lovebugs had firmly rooted themselves into another doomed vessel. The man's legs were shattered, his spine snapped in half, his arms useless. His body would stay here and decay, and the lovebugs would die. Or would they find their way to another vessel? Maybe the poor bastard sitting in the driver's seat of the truck, his upper body crushed by Ron's fall.

"Fuck it," she said and pulled the trigger on the flamethrower. The man's body caught flame and started to sizzle and pop. He didn't scream or make any movements. He was dead when the first flames lit up his hair. She waited to make sure the lovebugs didn't escape.

They didn't.

Julianne checked the tank on her flamethrower. Limping, cut, bruised, covered in blood and black soot, she started heading toward the road.

The remaining bit of fuel was enough for a meet-and-greet with those fuckers in the van.

The Secret Eater

CODY GOODFELLOW

We buried Dad in the back field of the Hulder family farm on the Fourth of July. It was perfectly legal, but naturally, there were rumors in town that we murdered him. The suspicion became certainty when half the town showed up for the memorial service. That's what the trashy books and podcasts will say, if and when such things are written. We respected Dad's wishes as a lapsed Catholic by forbidding an autopsy; but by interring their mortal remains on the farm, we were keeping a promise he made to the land.

Terry Hulder passed the way he always said he wanted to go: astride his big red tractor. He died fighting a losing battle, though. Only a little more than half the acreage yielded marketable hay. A week before harvest, the fields were rife with invasive weeds. At seventy-two, he was on medication for hypertension and chronic pain, so he might have died of cardiac arrest in the freakish summer heat even had he not been overwhelmed by an allergic reaction and ingested a lethal dose of herbicide while spraying the fields. Mom called Mary because she was the oldest. Mary raced over, then tracked us all down and ordered us to gather at the farm, before she called 911.

I had already closed the bookshop and was drinking alone at home, watching TV, and knitting a hat for someone else's kid, so I got there first. Eric arrived last and wouldn't have come at all, but Mary told him to forget about the restraining order. She'd left a message with Liz in Toronto, who was busy coaching a hockey clinic.

The pale sun still shone into our valley at 10 PM, gushing rosy light off the face of Pioneer Peak onto the bald yellow expanse of our farm. You could hear but not see the fireworks that diehard patriots were drunkenly shooting off out on the Strait. Mary was waiting on the porch like this was just another vacant house she was trying to sell.

We found Mom out in the field with Dad, just how she always said *she* wanted to go: nestled against his affable bulk, mellified in that painterly sunset. We waited for her to wake up with a sharp rebuke on our tardiness and stood there for a long while before someone got the nerve to check her pulse. We moved a little faster when we discovered she was still alive.

Dad would have been hard to identify, were he found anywhere else. His cyanotic face and hands were swollen to the limit of their elasticity, every exposed inch of skin outraged with blisters larger than a child's fist. Some of them burst when we tried to move them, seeping creamy treacle that burned our eyes like onions and gasoline.

When they arrived—lights, but no siren—the paramedics took Mom to Mat-Su Regional's ER and Dad to the morgue. The Sheriff stopped by and offered his condolences, signed some papers, then left. There was no argument about an autopsy. There would be fights with the funeral home, but our parents' beliefs would be respected—Dad's body delivered unmutilated and intact, to the land he loved and served.

Joshua tinkered in the garage with Mom's old Husqvarna tractor. He was shaken, like all of us, but more so because of Eric. I promised him nothing would happen with all of us there, but last time Eric set foot on the farm—on the previous 4th—he'd tried to choke Josh out, and it took all of us to pull him off. Eric was banned from the farm except for high holidays because our parents felt it was unfair to punish Eric's kids for their dad's temper. Josh had no kids and nowhere else to go, so cutting Eric from the farm cut Josh off from everywhere *but* the farm.

I told him, if he couldn't deal, maybe he should go into town and get a beer or something. Scrubbing oil off his hands at the sink with eye-watering detergent, he shook his head. "It's our farm now. We have to get over it and give the land what it wants."

I didn't ask him what he meant. I assumed at the time Dad's death must have hit Josh the hardest, because he was the youngest, and had never left the farm.

He asked how my Honda was doing, and I admitted it was leaking oil, and the clutch was mushy. He chided me about not knowing my way around a stick and I retorted with a dirtier joke, and he said he'd look at it.

Eric went into the house and came out with a box of stuff he said Dad always wanted him to have, then we all went home to get drunk.

The funeral happened a week later.

Our town is only an hour out of Anchorage, but we are still the last frontier. Our men brave the wild and lethal elements to claw out a living, and are all too often killed by them, just as our women are all too often senselessly killed by their men. We are the people politicians invoke when they want to get elected. Salt of the earth, rock-ribbed, maverick stewards of nature's inexhaustible bounty. We don't believe their lies, but they remind us we exist. We listen to them describe our pride, our self-reliance, our mistrust for welfare, regulations, and know-it-all tree-huggers, and it helps us hide, for another four years, from what we really are.

Dad was as well-liked as any farmer in the valley—his death another inevitable casualty of pioneer life. The toxicology tests proved he had lethal levels of herbicides in his lungs and blood, and chemical burns on his hands and face from furocoumarin compounds in the weeds that had overrun the field.

Not that it stopped tongues wagging. Our family was ever a scapegoat and a scandal to those disappointed by their own sins and secrets. People no better than us came out to gather grist for the local rumor mill, and we didn't disappoint. But most of them were there to see Liz.

A gawky hockey phenom who led the U.S. Women's team to gold three Winter Olympics ago, Liz was the town's most famous citizen, and most infamous self-exile. She'd embodied everything they set their hearts against and achieved the one goal every man and boy in town wished for, and it seemed she'd pulled the ladder up behind her. Every last one of them hated her nearly as much as we did.

The rumors about how she secretly got pregnant in her senior year and had an abortion probably drove her as much as any inner ambition, to find a way out, the gossip about how she was gay— married to a Canadian real estate heiress, and rich enough to buy and sell the whole town ten times over kept her away, but always on the town's lips. After Father Dan's eulogy, a bunch of them cornered her for autographs.

Joshua rolled out the Ditch Witch and herded them out of the field, back to where they parked alongside the fallow patch Dad had been plowing under when he died. They must've talked about how the field had gone to weeds, how he must have been out of his mind, and how sad it was that his children weren't more of a help . . .

When they were all finally gone, Mary's husband, Doug, took

their brood home, and Eric's wife, Tammy, played with their and Liz's kids on our old swing-set out front.

The markers at the edge of the field give the names, but the bodies are elsewhere under our feet, many buried in secret by bereaved ancestors out of their minds with grief. Our great-great-grandparents and every one of us born and died since then (except for our paternal grandmother, who set fire to the house and field before she ran away to her parents). Beside the big markers are the humble crosses for Margaret and Daniel, the twins who died just shy of their first year, in an accident on the way to the hospital to deliver me. When I tried to understand why she hated me, which was often, I thought she blamed me for their deaths.

And beside them, the smaller, unmarked crosses for each of Mom's seven miscarriages. All of them beneath our feet, reclaimed by the soil, drawn up through the roots and into the hay and much of the food we eat.

Our farm prospered through four generations and continued, while so many of our neighbors who grew crops for export were foreclosed on or had to scale back. Our nearest neighbors, the Twombleys, abandoned their place after the father passed, and a bunch of townie squatters moved in. The Sheriff cleared them out after one took a potshot at Josh for confronting them about some stolen auto parts, but they returned in force the following spring, and we could hear their music, their fireworks going off in the gathering gloom, their laughter worse than screaming, as Eric passed around a flask.

We all pitched in to attach the winch and lower the body into the earth, shrouded, but not in any caskets. Josh filled the holes in less time than it takes to tell, and we retired to the fire pit at the back of the property, where the weeds grow unchecked around the derelict remains of all our old cars and trucks—a graveyard of failed and wrecked attempts to be free, to get away from here.

"We should talk," Eric growled around his cigarette, "about what's going to happen with the farm."

Eric was the fourth oldest, but the oldest *boy*. Dad always told him he'd be the one driving the tractor after they were gone. Eric never showed much interest in the family business, using the restraining order as an excuse to skip the harvest, when even I pitched in. He was a high school football star and bagged a fat scholarship, only to wreck his Trans Am on prom night, ruining those crazy legs and killing his date. He still walked with a limp, but even after a decade of drinking at the Witch's Tit with only periodic exercise, tuning up anyone who looked at him cockeyed, he still loomed over us and had almost fifty pounds on Joshua, some of it still muscle.

Josh flinched when Eric waved the flask at him. "Relax, I'm not gonna hurt you," Eric shouted, but the disgust in his voice made it clear Josh's fear was already driving him to rage. When Eric was a toddler, Dad had a dog, Blackie, a German shepherd, who relentlessly terrorized the chubby toddler. When Eric was seven and Joshua only a baby, the first time Dad let him drive the tractor, Eric ran over Blackie, adding him to the field.

Mary spoke up, saying we should turn the farm into a bed-and-breakfast with horses; turn the field into riding arenas and offer trail rides around Pioneer Peak and the Butte.

Eric snorted. "Who's gonna do that shit? Rich people don't come here. Nobody comes here."

"They will if we work together . . . "

"It's a stupid idea." Eric slurped from the flask, wiping his mouth on his sleeve.

Mary threw up her hands and strangled the air. "Well, what do you want to do?"

"Sell it."

"It's a farm," Joshua said. "We'll farm it."

"*You* want to? Really?" Eric laughed.

"I don't want anything to do with it," Liz said. "Sell it, if someone will buy it. Let it rot, otherwise. This place killed Dad, almost killed Mom. It's tried more than once to kill all of us."

"Did you see the field?" I put in. "It's half gone to weeds, and the bales in the barn are moldy . . . "

Eric took a long hard swallow, burped, and then spat. "I'm not the one who let it get all fucked up. If somebody wasn't such a pussy, I could've pitched in, and Dad might still be alive." His tone dripped with forced anger, but he couldn't hide his glee. The last person on earth who could tell Eric *No* was now underneath it.

When all you've got is a dick, every problem looks like a pussy. I must've been really feeling all the dope I smoked in my car. "I guess Mom's opinion doesn't carry much weight, either. Or were you gonna surprise her with all your big plans?"

"Maybe if she wakes up," Eric said morosely, "which she won't."

"Since when does the fourth oldest," Mary spat, "get to dictate a fucking thing?"

"Oldest with a dick," he snapped, pitching his cig in the fire and lighting a fresh one.

"Keep on smoking," Liz said, "you'll still die first."

"You don't know shit," he snarled. "Smoking *protects* your lungs. Folks near Chernobyl who got the first good dose of fallout, over eighty percent of them died. The non-smokers. But among the cohort of smokers, more like forty percent died, because the lining of phlegm and their coughing reflexes saved them."

We had all learned to hold our tongues until Eric ran out of bullshit. Arguing only fed the fire.

"Let's just see what the will says, is all I'm saying," he added. "There's a will, right?"

"You guys don't know shit about this farm," Josh said. "You never really did. It could do a hell of a lot more than earn out if we let it—"

"What the fuck, Josh?" Mary demanded. "We all grew up here. I was doing every job on this farm when *your* only job was planting shit in a diaper."

Eric laughed and killed the flask. "He's talking about weed, aren't you, little brother?" Josh blushed and shook his head, inviting Eric to push harder. "I know about your little secret garden out behind the barn. Half the kids in town are smoking what you grow."

"That's not what I'm talking about," Josh said. He took a big swig from an antique fruit jar and passed it to me.

We'd drunk whatever we could buy or steal out on the backside of the field since before we could drive. Once we were of age, we still tried to outdo each other with the shittiest liquor—Mad Dog 20/20, Everclear & Mountain Dew (a.k.a. Mountain Don't), etc. There is no greater sin than to spit out whatever you're offered at the bonfire. To complain about or refuse the booze is grounds for endless ball-busting.

My tongue went numb, the rest of my mouth tingling with the alarm bells of extremely rancid meat, but I choked it down. My bowels revolted, but I bravely smiled and passed the jar to Eric before it could force its way out of me.

Eric bolted a swallow from the jar and handed it off to Liz, took a step towards the bonfire, and then vomited into it.

Mary called him an asshole and shoved him. He shoved her back, without much anger and no coordination. The stench of his burning puke pushed us back, but nobody was going to be the first to give up. Liz took a sip of the awful stuff and gagged, passed it to Mary.

"Fuck all of you," our big sister said, but she swallowed the last of it and threw the jar in the fire.

You have to be pretty drunk to deal with my family at the best of times. But we were something more than drunk. Eric got a case of Michelob Ultra out of the back of his Camaro, and we killed it in half an hour, barely speaking as we drained cans and fed the fire. We watched the fire show us the faces of people we'd known all our lives, doing things we never would have dreamed they were capable of. We thought, at the time, we were just hallucinating.

Then Eric went off on a rant about the Eskimos all being child molesters or something, but Mary told him to shut up and then asked, "What was that shit you gave us?"

Josh shrugged. "Just some home-brew. You like it?"

"Where'd you get it? D'you make it?" Eric asked.

"No . . . I found it. Ripped up the worn-out floorboards in the back barn, and . . . "

It sounded like sarcasm, which was less likely from Josh than fluent French, but he solemnly nodded. "Our great-great-grandfather came up looking for gold in the Yukon and used his score to buy this land and settle here with his wife. His sons grew hay and raised horses, and during Prohibition, they ran moonshine."

We all knew the old gossip; it was the notorious bedrock of the Hulder family legend: some people went blind from drinking Grandpa Hulder's shine, and it was local vigilantes who burned his fields, but the *smart* gossip was that they burned him out because he stopped.

"So," Eric slurred, "this is hundred-year-old shit?"

"I feel like I'm tripping," Liz said, staring at her fingers as if they were brand new. "I can see . . . everything . . . " She didn't sound happy about it.

I felt dizzy and giddy and unspeakably good, but I didn't say anything. I never do, when I should.

"That's not what I meant," Mary snapped, throwing the last empty can into the fire. "What about this farm?"

"It's fed this family for four generations, and we've served it. Bled for it. Dad believed God talked to him in dreams, and he would've thrown us all on the grill if his God asked him to. But he didn't know what this land really needed. He exploited it without knowing its secret heart. We all did . . . but it's going hungry. That's why the weeds're taking over. Dad tried to fight it, and it killed him."

"What the fuck kind of talk is that?" Eric stirred the fire with a stick, sending cascades of sparks swirling up into the faded black sky. "Dad was more of a man than you'll ever be. He died working this farm, little brother."

"We all will, if we don't give it what it needs."

Eric stepped closer to Josh with the burning stick in his hand. I got between them to keep Eric back, to keep Josh from running, which would trigger Eric to run him down like a dog on a rabbit. "What does it need, Josh? Just talk plain."

He strode over to the edge of the partially reaped field, stubble crunching underfoot, then ripped out a hank of the looming weeds and brought it over to the fire, held it up in the light. I noticed he'd put on a glove.

The tox screening had flagged giant hogweed as the cause of his blisters. New invasive weeds crop up every season, tracked in by trucks and cargo containers from the lower forty-eight, from Asia, from elsewhere. The giant hogweed was making news because its sap causes chemical burns, even blindness, and the effected skin turns permanently photosensitive, liable to get second-degree burns in direct sunlight. We figured Dad had got the sap all over himself clearing the cutting blades, gotten turned around when his eyesight failed and drove into the cloud of weedkiller he'd been spraying.

But what Josh was holding bore only a passing resemblance to hogweed. The stalk was a deep, glossy red-black, like lacquered rhubarb, thicker than my wrist and segmented like an enlarged king crab leg. The leaves were elaborately crumpled, fleshy purple lobes, the flowers odd canopies of succulent blossom clusters, like cauliflower or brains.

"It feeds on secrets," Josh said, "and feeds dreams." By the way he was staring at it, I realized what we'd been drinking. "If you share a secret here, nobody will ever know it."

"Are you fucking crazy?" I asked, shoving him. "That's the shit that killed Dad."

"Relax, I filtered the poison out of it . . . I found great-grand's distillery rig down there, too; it's more or less fucked, but I can build a new one. It's not just liquor. It's not even regulated—"

"And you want to make wine out of it." I shook my head at the sheer cussed perversity of it.

"Tweakers next door would give a kidney to drink that shit," Eric said.

"Too bad they'll never get a chance," Mary cut in. "Tomorrow, we chop and roto-till the whole field."

"It'll come back," Josh said, "and keep coming back until you give up."

"I *won't* give up. This is our property, now."

"It's not ours. We belong to it." Josh produced a boda bag that was hanging from a cord around his neck, under his grimy overalls. Sheepishly, he held it out to us. "I made this batch, myself."

Eric took it from him before he could unscrew the lid and squirted a thick stream down his throat. He gasped. "Fuck me runnin—.'

"We could take up the plow like Mom and Dad," Josh went on, "and go the way they went, scraping by season to season, or we could let the land do as it pleases . . . "

"And what then, little brother?" Eric glowered bloodshot over the rim of the bag as he gulped it down.

"Profit. Like you said. We can sell this shit. Make a lot more than anyone ever did selling hay."

"How?" Mary asked. None of us were going to dignify his crazy assertion, not even Eric, until the firstborn spoke.

"Drink it."

"Fuck out of here, Josh," Mary scoffed, but she didn't refuse the booze.

"Telling you, it'll work. It's working right now. Feel it."

Mary took a steep drink and tilted her head back, eyes closed. Once the prom queen and captain of the cheerleading squad, our oldest sister had taken on heft and sensibility, dressed like she was running for local office. But now she looked to be floating a few inches out of her wedged heels. "Maybe it will," was all she said.

I took it next. The flavor was brighter than the vintage stuff in the jar—stringent, like biting into fresh rhubarb. This time, I felt transfixed by a mellow, cold glow and a sneaking sense that I almost knew everything there was to know—everything the world didn't even know it doesn't know, and all would be revealed with the next sip.

"We wouldn't be the first to do it," Josh said, so low, we all had to crowd in close to hear him over the crackling of the fire. "Great-granddad knew about the weed, and he cultivated it. Grandpa Hans knew about it, too, but his wife made him stop. Made him come over to the Catholic Church. But before that, we knew the truth. Before that, we didn't have to claw a living out of this land, we just took the fruit and lived. And all we had to give it," he paused, peering into each of our eyes until we each looked away, "was our secrets."

More than one of us laughed. "What the fuck kind of game is this?" Liz demanded.

"Ain't no game," Josh said, reclaiming the jar. "Mom and Dad paid the tithe, even if they didn't know what they were doing. Everything they kept to themselves, everything they never shared with us, went into this soil. Every miscarriage—Mom had seven—and every body. Hell, look at all our old cars. Every bad decision and secret hookup, laid to rest here along with all those mistakes that might've been our brothers and sisters."

He'd stunned us to silence. No mean achievement, in this family. Then he said, "I have a daughter."

"Get out of here," Mary said. "Who's the lucky girl?"

"Molly, the redhead from the trailer park who used to dance at the Kozy Kennel." Josh squinted into the fire as if picturing her there.

Eric cut in. "You put a baby in that bitch? Way to go . . . "

Josh let Eric's proffered high-five dangle. "She's in Juneau now. I send her money every month. I never told Mom."

I was thunderstruck. All you had to do in this family to be forgiven for the sin of being born was to bring in fresh babies. Mary had two sons and a daughter; Eric had three sons, and even Liz had a twin son and daughter by in vitro fertilization. Josh and I were the failures. Josh had withheld the baby from our parents not because he was ashamed, but the real reason eluded me. Now, I was the only one who'd failed to reproduce.

What the hell was *I* going to say?

Mary cleared her throat. "I cheated on Doug a few years ago. Guy from the office. Mike, you guys all knew Mike."

Nobody else remembered, but I did. "The one who—"

"Yeah. Right after I told him I was going to stay with Doug. Fucking coward did it right there in the office to send a message, but he didn't leave a note. Except . . . he did, but I took it." She nodded as if hearing someone else tell the story, knotted her fists, and then opened them before her, letting it go. She smiled, for the first time I can remember, without someone else suffering for it.

Eric took back the bag and gulped manfully from it. Wiping his mouth with the back of his hand, he stared at it as if he kept losing count of his fingers. "Roxanne was already dead when I wrecked the Mustang."

"Oh Christ," Liz said, turning away. "I don't need this."

Josh stopped her. Neither the meek kid brother nor the nervous, nasty terrier he could become when cornered, he quietly and authoritatively told her to stay put and hear what had to be said.

"Blood in, blood out," Eric said, chuckling. "We blew off the dance to get high and fuck, but she—"

"Fuck you all," Liz said. "He's *enjoying* this."

"And you're not?" Eric snorted. "I remember you eyeballing her when she used to come around."

"She was a person, and you fucking murdered her!"

"She was just a bitch with a big mouth. You should've heard the shit she and her cheerleader friends said about *you*." Finally noticing all of us staring at him, he passed the bag to Liz. "Let's hear yours."

"Fine." Liz shook her head, but she accepted the hogweed wine and drank from it, staring into the flames. "I know the stories they told in town. Most of them were bullshit, but . . . what kids used to say . . . it's true. I had a baby, too."

Oh fuck.

"One time after practice, we drank some peach schnapps, and I walked home late. I thought I was gonna get in trouble, you know? You guys were always high and smelling like booze and puke, but I was supposed to be the good one, so I wasn't allowed an inch. But I come home and nobody else is here, and he . . . he was drunk like I'd never seen before . . . and he took me . . . in the old stable . . . and he—"

"Who did?"

She threw the flaccid boda bag at Josh. "It was Dad."

"Bullshit!" Eric wheeled on her. "Is this some kind of repressed memory shit your rug-munching Quebecois therapist dug up? Because it's such fucking bullshit—"

I shoved him so hard he almost stumbled into the fire. "Leave her alone, fuck! Let her tell it."

"That's all there is to tell. He just did it once, and I don't remember him touching me; just laying me down in the dirt and . . . waiting. I don't know if he didn't remember, or if he blocked it out, or what. I didn't think about it until I missed my period.

"I told Mom, but I didn't tell her everything. I wanted to get it cut out, and you know how that conversation went. I had it at, like, a puppy farm for humans. I don't know what happened to it. Mom wouldn't talk about it. Dad just looked at me like I was crazy, so I stopped. But there's a kid somewhere out there, almost in high school, who doesn't know any of us, but he . . . or she's . . . mine."

She broke down sobbing.

And everyone was looking at me.

What the fuck was I supposed to say?

I hate you all.

I hate you because you all succeeded at this simple, animal thing that I failed at. Whatever else I might've done with my life, I pushed away or put it on hold so I could prove myself worthy by giving Mom another baby to fuss over. I chased every eligible man my age and then I fucked my way through the rest of them, seeking out the married ones who had children at home, until I'd assured myself something was wrong with me. I was raped twice by men I see on the street every day, but I never pressed charges, because I knew what they'd all say. I was smart about it—at least I never got anyone killed—but now, I'm getting old, and I live alone, and I always will, and I'm beginning to lose my mind. I think there's a ghost living in my apartment, and I've tried to seduce him, but once, one glorious night, he washed my hair, and that and my books and my cats and my family are my whole world, how's that for a big fat juicy secret?

I hate you because you're all I have.

I told them everything I could think of. Every secret shame and envy, until they gazed at me with utter disgust, and I didn't care. Until I floated out of my own shoes, unburdened by the million little secrets that had chained me down. I wasn't free of them, not even in my enhanced state, but in return for our secrets, we learned so many hidden, sordid secrets about our little valley and about the hidden face of Nature—that fickle, fecund bitch to whom we were enslaved by blood and soil. Laughing at the sublime awfulness of the grand design, we floated, we flew, and even if we forgot all we saw and heard, we knew such freedom that we became what Mom and Dad could never make us:

A family.

None of us believed Liz, but we had our reasons.

Over the years, we'd all shared the same stories of getting dunked in the bathtub by mom and held under as she "baptized" us, of being ditched by Dad on a lonesome road and sure we'd been left to die in exile, but it came to pass that each of us had our own Kodachrome-vivid memory nobody else could recall.

For me, it was the Soft-Serve Incident.

It was summer and Dad took us into Palmer for Dairy Queen after supper. It was one of those gorgeous, warm August nights when the sun never quite leaves and somehow, nobody had spoiled it by acting up. He ordered seven soft-serve cones and paid for them, then passed them back until we all had one. None of us dared taste it until Dad did. At one lick, he wiped his tongue off on a napkin and pronounced, "That's no good." He handed it back, then made all of us pass our cones back to the teenager working the window and demanded a refund. Then he jokingly asked if they were hiring; as we left, I counted our glum faces over and over and kept coming up one short.

They laughed at me when I brought it up, but Josh remembered a time when we were all in the Bronco on a boat landing at Seventeenmile Lake. Dad got out and the Bronco rolled into the frigid water. While we struggled over each other to escape, Dad just watched us. Mary, Eric, Liz, and I all got out, leaving Josh screaming in his car seat as the back compartment flooded. He swore up and down it had happened, but we'd never owned a boat.

Eric called us all liars, but once when he got blackout drunk, he'd told me a story about Christmas. He had snuck downstairs to peek and caught Santa Claus putting presents under the tree. Santa made him smoke Kools and drink peppermint schnapps until he got sick to his stomach, then dragged him outside to puke and shiver in the snow and then exited via the chimney. He woke up on Christmas morning in the field to Dad standing over him with a mug of hot chocolate and telling him that Santa gave his presents to the dog.

Likewise, Mary told only me about the time she went trick-or-treating with Dad and a few neighbors when Liz and I were just babies, and Mom was recovering from the car accident. Dressed as a witch, she remembered going to a neighbor's house in the woods behind our field, the door opening, and then a giant bloody paw reaching out to grab her. Dad shoved her over the threshold and slammed the door in her face when she tried to escape. She didn't remember anything after that, but for years, she had recurring nightmares of living as a slave in the house of a gigantic green witch called the Long Mama and her memories of life in the Hulder household were revealed to be hopeful daydreams.

I was the only one who saw a pattern in these false memories or thought to ask Mom or Dad about them. They would just stare at me, shake their heads, and say, "You were always the weird one." I'd asked Liz more than once about hers, she must have one, because we all did. She always insisted she didn't know what I was talking about, and I'd come to believe it was because she was the normal one. But she was just better at suppressing it than the rest of us.

Maybe that's why it let her leave.

We returned to our lives, as they were.

Mom came back from the hospital. They said she'd regained consciousness, but we didn't believe it. Wenda Chesebro, a retired nurse who lived up the road, was hired to care for her. I went back a couple times a week to sort through the finances of the farm and the tractor dealership Dad ran as a sideline. Mom had insisted on keeping all the books after firing Meg, the office manager of twenty years, out of suspicion she and Dad were having an affair. But really, the reason was to control something, to prove she was still useful even as her mind turned to mush.

The records were a mess. Invoices never sent spilled out of file cabinets in her office, and the accounting gradually became a shambles of non sequitur entries, doodles, and gibberish. Towards the end, she seemed to have created her own numbers, with marginal notes condemning both Latin and Arab digits, totaling up astronomical debts to "Long Mama," which gave me a chill as it seemed to point to Mom's advancing dementia, but also back into the past.

What was that song Dad used to sing, as he bounced us on his knee while driving the tractor? I only remembered a fragment of it, the end of a chorus. *"C'mon, long mama/Don't gimme no drama/Just grow my row, so I can go home . . . "*

I went outside to sneak a smoke and a beer from the garage fridge. Two figures worked in the field, chopping down the hogweed stalks with machetes. They wore crabbing gear and gloves and military surplus gas masks, but I could tell by the way they moved that it was Eric and Josh, working together for the first time in nearly ten years. It was after the accident we now knew was never an accident, when Josh was a D&D nerd nobody wanted to play with, and like so many mechanically inclined rural boys, decided to build a trebuchet. They got in a fight over who'd fire it first after it was done, and Eric tried to curb-stomp Josh on a boulder. Josh lost half his upper teeth and four lowers.

I thought about the last time I saw Liz before she went back home to Montreal. She came into the bookshop on her way to the airport in Anchorage.

I was planning to close in an hour, go home and kill a fifth of Reyka, cut myself all over my forearms and thighs, and read werewolf erotica until I passed out, so I might've been brisk.

After a few awkward swipes at small talk, she cut to the chase. "I can't do this anymore. I'm not coming back."

"It's just us dealing with grief. They'll realize they fucked up and scrape the field by next planting season."

"I don't mean this . . . scheme, I mean all of it. I can't do this. I've got my own family now, and this isn't how we . . . " Her throat closed.

I offered her a paper cup of water, which she used to wash down a handful of pills. "This is who we always were. Mom and Dad held it back as best they could, but . . . "

She saw me staring at her and said, "You don't believe me either, do you, Becky?"

"I don't know, what the fuck do you want me to say? I mean, you're talking about Dad."

"I don't remember what happened last night after we drank

that shit Josh is brewing, but I remember how it felt; it was just like I felt that night . . . that nobody believes."

"We were just drunk."

"No, I have the same fucked genes and addiction issues as you, and I've kicked pain pills twice. I don't know what it was, but after last night, I . . . I *hope* it really was Dad, does that make sense? Because what else . . . "

I just stared at her.

"You can talk to them; they'll listen to you. But I can't anymore." I didn't blink until she left the shop, then I went home and got puking drunk.

Now, Eric and Josh staggered out of the field arm in arm and hosed each other off with soapy water before stripping off the field gear and gas masks. The hogweed had begun to take over the portion of field Dad had harvested, and the purple king crab stalks jutted above the unmowed hay along the back forty. The canopy of fleshy flowers bobbed in the breeze, iridescent properties in their petals giving a weird rainbow sheen to the motion. I ran my fingers under my blouse where the few remaining blisters and welts I hadn't popped or cauterized with my lighter still bloomed from my scarred skin. I twisted one now and felt it burst under my fingers, trying to remember what had happened after we shared our secrets. I could remember everyone's but my own.

Did we take off our clothes and run through the fields, roll in the weeds? Did we . . . do something else?

I held my wet fingertips up to my nose, then licked the plasma off. It tasted of astringent licorice, like Josh's homebrew. I licked it clean.

Mary was the only one who attended church regularly, but I'd stopped going early. Our parents blamed books, but I stopped believing in the Church—if not in God—when they told me how much He hated masturbation.

Who could be lonelier than God? Who could blame Him for masturbating, and how could He blame us? We are only created in His image; we are only divine in our loneliness. I used to picture Him watching me get off on a hairbrush or a stuffed animal and imagined Him matching me stroke for stroke.

Later, I used to fantasize that when I cut or made myself come, the intensity of my sensations would spill out of me to assail the neighbors with alien ecstasy, phantom stigmata. I should've known better. Most of them couldn't even feel their own pain, and the closest to a real orgasm many of them felt was when they won a fistfight.

I was always the "weird one."

I won't add anything new to the most bloated corpus of cliches in American literature by berating the blank barrenness of small-town minds. Like every ugly trait in a species condemned to live in inhospitable climes, it's an adaptation without which they would emigrate or die. But I think in our valley, it approaches a diagnosable condition. Something like thirty percent of humans, researchers say, never converse with themselves in their heads, and never weigh their own motives or debate their actions. They walk among us and may soon outnumber us.

A related and seemingly worse, but perhaps even more liberating condition, aphantasia is the total absence of visual imagination. You cannot conceive of a meal you've never tasted or picture someone you love in your head without a photo. If they dream at all, it must seem like transmissions from an alien world. The APA says about three percent of humans "suffer" from this condition, though many do quite well, thank you, without daydreaming. I think the proportion here in my town is exactly the inverse. The unhappy three percent who can imagine any other life, any other meal, mate, or fate, either escape or make peace with living among people with their imaginations amputated, with no voice in their heads but the echo of what they heard on TV.

I know my father read books and sometimes wept over them in his office, and I know my mother at least mourned dreams she'd had of another life. Of my siblings, only Josh and perhaps one or two of Mary's kids were like me, and like most of you. These false memories of being abandoned were our parents' little dreams of rebelling against the flesh and the land that claimed their lives, somehow transmitted to us amid their gruff, scornful silences.

As the quiet middle child, I could usually escape by going unnoticed. Mom and Dad wore themselves out drilling Mary and Liz into perfect Catholic farmhands, athletes, and co-parenting machines, then indulged Eric and smothered Josh because they were the last babies until we blessed them with grandkids, so the land would continue to be protected and fed.

Mom only ever hinted at all the dreams she'd had to bury when she had us, and how deeply we'd disappointed her by just being ourselves, and not her unfulfilled fantasies incarnate. We failed her almost before we could speak. Liz came closest, and I fell furthest behind by never leaving town, by bringing her no grandchildren to hold and whisper her dreams to, hoping one of them would be the One.

That night, I really felt like someone was watching me from on high, and my secret, shameful act was the center of all creation— the origin of a new world, but I failed it. I rubbed myself raw but couldn't come. I drank until I vomited, but I couldn't get drunk. I was trapped at the bottom of a well, and I no longer wished for someone to pull me out and save me. I wanted someone who would dive in, take my hand, and drown with me.

That night, I had a dream.

Warm summer night, but the sky is dark velvet black, the moon full and ripe, and the aurora borealis undulates and lends a witchy glow to the moonlight. We come out of our homes, all of us skyclad and unashamed as the First Day in Eden, and silently fall into a long, orderly column. We file down the Old Glenn Highway, over the old bridge that spans the dry wash of the Matanuska River, now flooded to its highwater mark, but not with water.

Hundreds of us follow the highway to the Sandvik Family Trail that winds 'round the looming Butte that gives the nearby village its name. The ground beneath our feet shimmers with a muted but penetrating violet light that rivals the lightshow in the sky. As we climb the Butte, hogweed shoots erupt from the ground in a lush botanical fireworks display, until the tumorous stalks crowd the trail. Their touch doesn't burn so much as slough away the dead parts of us—the old shells. Reveling in our true forms, many couple and roll in the lush overgrowth, borne aloft by stalks like redwoods, growing so fast the sound of them fills our ears. When the moon comes out from behind a cloud, the hogweed flowers split open to regard the stars with opalescent eyes.

So many have been claimed by the hogweed forest, that only a handful remain by the time we reach the peak. We look down on the valley, on this fertile crescent between the rivers, and we see her clearly, her light shining through the dead earth. With her head in the Butte and tapering taproot limbs stretching from the banks of the Matanuska to the Knik, the tangled, luminous forests of hogweed are her hair. Our family farm, just a mile down the highway, rests upon her bosom, where she glows brightest.

A frigid wind lifts us up and bears us off on the polar winds like dandelion seeds. But not me—I gaze down and see the purple roots boring out of my feet and into the soil, at the last changes to my body, and I make, at last, my peace with it. To be here on this land, to share the bounty of her milk with all the valley's children, is a holy vocation.

I woke up weeping.

I lasted almost a week before I came crawling to Josh for another taste.

There were people in the road out front of the farm. I knew where they'd come from. Once or twice a year, the sheriff would raid the Twombley place and board it up, but the freaks would come back. Never much more than a nuisance once you remembered to lock your doors and leave nothing valuable in your car, they brought a taste of big city living to the country, and nobody really wanted the place burned down for good because every family in the area had at least one member it needed to get rid of.

This summer, a trailer park of sorts had sprung up around the old farmhouse; RV's and derelict campers up on blocks with cardboard curtains in the windows, and a horde of squatters spilled out into the road, so I almost ran them over.

They were wearing filthy sheets with eyeholes burned in them, layers of clothing covering every inch of skin, and cheap sunglasses or ski goggles over their eyes. They bunched up at the fence-line of the back field, hunkered down in the trees, waiting for dusk.

I honked at them, but they moved like deep-sea divers in iron-soled boots, wading across the road as if I was only another bad hallucination. Some of them wore flour sacks or grocery totes with no eyeholes at all, but a crudely painted sigil of a succulent blossom with a staring octopus eye at the heart of a tongue-petaled flower.

The field was not quite a jungle—the tallest stalks bobbing their bulbous bulbs over the roof of the long barn. Josh was loading hogweed cuttings into the still in one of the old hay barns. A shaggy green haystack perched on the roof of the barn. Eric, in a ghillie suit he ordered off a soldier-of-fortune website, sat with a scoped hunting rifle across his knees, watching the tree line through a pair of binoculars.

"They've been trying to get in all week," Josh said.

"No money, no fucking honey!" Eric shouted.

"What do you want?" Josh asked. The fumes coming off him made my eyes and my mouth water.

I glanced around, winced, and smiled crookedly. "I just wanted some . . . if there's any left."

Josh shook his head, but he went back into the barn and came out with an old Coleman cooler that jingled faintly with mason jars clinking inside. "This is all I can spare, but . . . "

"But what?" I was pissed he was being so stingy when we had a whole field of the shit outside.

"You got to look out for the side effects. I filtered it pretty good, but you drink too much of this shit, it does something to your skin. Regular sunlight gives you third-degree chemical burns. No shit."

Anyone but my kid brother could've made me hear what he was saying, could've made me understand why all the squatters lurking on the perimeter looked like racist scarecrows. But I wasn't going to listen to him.

I took my jars home and got loaded.

The cat came in to eat, swimming across the floor with his legs splayed out like four extra tails. I picked him up and immediately dropped him when I felt his boneless legs curl around my wrist. It was like holding a furry octopus, all his skeleton completely dissolved. None the worse for wear, he slithered to his bowl and dropped his face into it.

It got dark like the sun was snatched out of the sky, and the light from the lamps in my apartment were so dim, the light moving so slow, I could almost catch it in my hand and eat it. It got darker and darker, and when I went outside to look at the sky, I was back on the farm.

The perimeter of the field was lined with crosses—memorials to nameless babies.

The earth sighed and split open like a cyst. It came boiling out of the soil to speak with me. The Long Mama. She eclipsed the moon with her enormous head, which had five faces that rasped out commands in overlapping, whispering waves.

A procession of torchlights approached, but there was no one holding them. Floating, flaming fetuses, charred and glowing through cracks in their petrified flesh. With accusing eyes of lava, they converged on me, nibbled my skin with toothless gums like tiny beaks.

When I peered up at the mumbling god-thing, the Long Mama had eaten two of its faces. The three that remained spoke in one domineering voice, telling me what I must do.

I thought I knew what it meant, to want to die. Up until now, I was just kidding myself.

A tourist from LA told me something once, when I asked him how he liked working in television. *Kill someone, and you free up one parking space. Teach the world to kill itself, and you can park anywhere.*

I shouldn't have gone to work the next day, but I'm glad I did. The last day of summer passed quietly enough until around 3:00, when a salvo of gunshots and then an engine's roar and a squeal of tires echoed down the street. A man in a nice hand-knit sweater and corduroy slacks lay face-down in the street out front.

Nicole, the high school student part-timer, was changing our front display when it happened. She came out of the window with her hands over her head. "They shot the man in the street! They shot him!" She told the police she saw a silver extended-cab pickup truck like half the men in town drive, but she didn't see the plates or the driver.

The victim was Dr. Lingenfelter, who had run the local gynecologist practice for over twenty years. Mary, my mother, and I all saw him regularly. Joan, the store manager, just shook her head and said it was only a matter of time. Didn't I know he had impregnated thirteen women and molested who knows how many more? When I asked her where she heard this, she just polished her bifocals and told me to take the rest of the day off.

My house was two blocks away. I remember thinking about Dr. "call me T.J." Lingenfelter, he of the cold hands and hot cinnamon breath, who offhandedly told me once I'd never have a child. He never tried anything with me. I felt horrified by everything I'd seen, but really, also kind of slighted. He'd given thirteen women his babies, but not me.

He would come in once a week or so to buy the latest bestseller for his wife and a selection of magazines for the waiting room. When you asked him how he was doing, he would say, "Better than I deserve," which we all thought was cute. We didn't know.

To this day, nobody has ever been arrested for his murder.

Key in my hand, I noticed my front door was hanging by one hinge. Someone had ransacked my house.

The furniture was overturned, couch cushions slashed, mattress gutted, the fridge emptied onto the floor, my books—my fucking *books*! —tossed from their shelves, and that was how they found my last bottle of hogweed wine. They took my TV, some cash, and my coffee maker. My cat had, quite sensibly, run away.

They carved WHORE into the front door with my good knife.

I went outside and scanned up and down the street. Three people stood in a yard across the way wearing parkas, gloves, ski masks, and sunglasses in mid-September.

I've lived my whole life in this town. That was the scariest part; scarier than knowing they'd been in my house, was that I could stare at these people I'd grown up with and have no idea who they were.

I packed a bag with some clothes and my favorite books and drove to the farm by muscle memory. I was shaking and crying so bad, I couldn't have driven, if I had to see to find my way there. Josh helped me inside, then drove into town to get the rest of my stuff. "Don't go back there," he said. "You're safer at home."

I slept that night in my old bed, the one I'd prayed every night to escape from. The smell of tuna casseroles and dead mice in the ductwork was more soothing than suffocating, as it had always been. If it hurt to be sent whimpering back to childhood, I fought back by becoming my mother every day, burying myself in the byzantine ruins of her business records and guzzling fortified coffee before changing Mom's bedding. Wenda Chesebro saw the way the wind was blowing and quit, which was just as well; was impossible to look at her face and not see her fucking her stepson, or her husband watching through a peephole in the adjoining bathroom.

Hour after hour, call after call, I pursued delinquent accounts for hay deliveries from last season while fending off calls for delinquent hay deliveries from this season, because we were no longer in the hay business. Then I switched things up by becoming my mother's mother—changing diapers, treating bedsores, dispensing medications, and pureed peas and carrots. Then I drank myself into a stupor, left my body, and swam in the primordial sewer of my town's collective id.

I knew who killed Dr. Lingenfelter. I knew who broke into my house. I knew everything everyone in town tried to hide, and everything they wished they could do, but never had the nerve. All the petty secrets of people who can't dream or dare to be what they are. And with every sip and slurp of hogweed wine, they knew mine.

What must that be like? For someone who's never been able to imagine anything without looking at it, to be flooded with someone else's all-singing, all-dancing perversity in Technicolor and Odorama? Because the wildest and worst of what I'd done was nothing to all the things I dreamed of all my unlived lives and unfulfilled desires.

When life gives you leprosy, make leprosade.

We prospered as never before. Eric bought two new long-bed Chevy pickups, a new harrow, four AKM rifles, three Mossberg 500's with banana clips, and an actual fucking flamethrower. He and Josh strung up a new fence around the entire property and electrified it.

Every other morning, Eric drove one of the new trucks into Palmer, Sutton, and Wasilla, and once a week into Anchorage. He said we couldn't trust anyone else to do the driving.

At the end of each day, he brought bowling bags and shoeboxes filled with cash for me to count. He said we had to bury it until he could find a stable connection in Anchorage to launder it.

"So, we're a crime family now."

"What we're doing isn't even illegal—"

"Not yet . . . "

"Maybe not ever. We'll figure that out come tax time, I guess." He didn't want to have this conversation. He didn't want to think of us as criminals. Somehow, he'd managed not to. "Look, we're selling something that grows wild on the farm. Folks want it. That ain't our fault. Someday, sure, they'll catch up to us and see how good it makes people feel, and they'll clamp down on it like they always do, and then in a few years, some big pharmaceutical company will come out with a pill with the active ingredients in it that gives a few percent of the buzz, for fifty times the cost, and nobody will say boo."

"But what about that buzz, Josh? What the hell is it doing to us? Don't you care?"

He shook his head but not in negation, so much as trying to

empty it. "I know what it's doing. So do you. It's setting them free. Everything they locked up inside is in the air now. Everybody knows everything."

But do we, though?

We know we have always been lied to. We are not free; we are slaves to our freedom. Life is not short; it is unbearably long and empty. We fill it, wherever we can, with death. Eating, hunting, drinking, smoking, fucking, and occasionally, murder. Lies and secrets.

We do these things to ourselves to fill the void that only love could properly heal. We punish each other and ourselves for lack of it, and we take out all our anger on this land we're loving to death. But what if we could be made to feel, again, what we lost? What if we were shaken awake and taken in hand by our long-lost true mother, who was always right behind us? What if the land loved us back?

I made Josh take me back to the bookstore to quit and collect my paycheck. Joan didn't try to talk me out of it. I rummaged through the shelf of books I'd put on hold. I bought a self-published chronicle of Palmer by an amateur historian. Grainy reproductions of photographs taken of Main Street in the 1920's, presented to make the case the Ku Klux Klan was active in our town. What else to make of those men and women with mud-spattered sheets over their heads, like wayward ghosts trick-or-treating in the dog days of summer? Those crude wards painted on barns that looked like flowers with eyes?

We're not like the rest of you. We don't cry and call a lawyer when we fall. We harden the fuck up and carry on. We never learn.

Our family name is a bit of a mystery. I never got up the nerve to send in my swab for one of those tests, but I did some genealogical research on our family, up to when they immigrated from Norway in 1873. The Hulder family had no traceable roots, but the word itself has some history.

Hulder (or *huldra*) maidens were forest creatures partaking of equal parts human and cow, and prettier than that sounds, for they seduced young shepherds away from their flocks and down through a door under a hill into a gray netherworld, where they lived out their shortened lives awash in sex and shame, or escaped back to home and hearth, only to wither and die of longing.

I told Mary about it at the next holiday get-together when she joined me outside to sneak a smoke. She laughed and we both said, "That's us," and laughed some more.

"Ride 'em, cowgirl," I said, and our laughter went somewhere else.

I remember how her eyes became far away, and now I know she must've been thinking about that guy at the office who couldn't live without her. Maybe she was saddened by the story because it proved there was something wrong with us, something we could never overcome, even if we wanted to.

None of your fucking business what *I* was thinking about.

A month went by. Things that never would've seemed imaginable swiftly became normal.

Eric thought we should throw a harvest barbecue like Mom and Dad used to. Eric's wife and three kids came. Mom was up and intermittently lucid, so we brought her outside in her favorite rocking chair. Mary had said she'd try to make it, but when Eric fired up the grill, she still wasn't answering her phone.

Eric wanted to share another secret.

"Hey Becca, you're into chicks, right?" Before I could answer, he whipped out his phone. "No judging, but I just thought you could maybe appreciate this."

The last time I talked to our dad, I tried to call him out about Eric. Dad was catching up on invoices at the time, and he took off his bifocals and stared at me as if deciding whether to trust me with a sizable loan. As he talked, his hand absently went on totting up figures on the old paper-fed adding machine on his desk. "You have to understand how hard it is for Eric. He knows he's not the smartest or the oldest, so he goes with what he's got. He's always had this, I guess they call it a learning disability now, but he does everything half-ass the first time and when it blows up in his face, he gets so mad the second time, that he breaks something." Looking back at the tape spiraling out of the adding machine, he cursed, ripped out the spool, and flung it across the room in disgust. "I don't know where he gets it," he added with a wry twinkle in his eye.

I remembered the time I told him I had PTSD from being raped. He told me to "walk it off."

I don't know how long I watched the thing on his phone. I like to think the moment I saw what it was, what they were doing to the girl in the video, that I went away, and none of its stain got into me.

I couldn't recognize her. Her face was bloated fit to burst, her eyes swollen shut, mouth almost turned inside out from hogweed exposure. Her breasts were marbled with blisters and inflammation in the shape of pawing hands. When someone mounted her, wearing a gas mask and rawhide gloves but no condom, she started convulsively bucking. His friends counted the seconds as he fought to stay on.

Eric was talking to me, to himself, I don't know. "You know why I hated that dog? Really hated him. He bit me, but I can respect that. But you'd give that fucking dog a bone, he wouldn't just sit down and chew it. He'd fret over it, carrying it around trying to find a safe place to bury it. Wasn't smart enough to find it again, but he needed to feel like he had a bone in the bank so bad, he couldn't just enjoy the one he had in his goddamn mouth. You tell me anything that lives like that isn't better off in the ground."

I threw his phone as far as I could into the field.

I went into the kitchen to mix a drink. The phone rang. It was Mary. She asked about Mom.

"Why didn't you come to the barbecue, sister?"

She hesitated, but her breathing was like a freight train humping up a steep grade. "We—Doug and I argued, and he went out, I don't know where. Have you seen him?"

I tried to find the right words, but she brushed them aside with more than her usual big-sister impatience. Doug would never come here without Mary dragging him. She wasn't just angry and upset. She wasn't sobbing, she was hyperventilating. She was terrified. "You have to know, Becca. I didn't mean to, but I found out . . . "

I was the invisible middle kid, and quite thankful for that, but Dad always privately called me the smart one. I read books nobody had heard of, and I knew the difference between a stalagmite and a stalactite, and I corrected people (Snakes are venomous, toadstools are poisonous), and months before kindergarten, I carved the words in the underside of my bunk bed: MARY IS DUM. BECCA IS GUD.

But I was only a dreamer—a talent worse than useless, out here. Mary was always the smart one. I thought I understood the wider world because I read all those books that fed characters into plots like wood into a chipper, but she was the one who had to *know*.

"I sent samples to Jim at the U of A—"

"Samples of *what*?" I asked, but I knew.

"*It*, goddamnit. I asked him . . . and he had me send them again because he thought the first batch got corrupted, because he couldn't . . . "

Eric was shouting outside. I had to ask her to repeat herself.

"They couldn't identify it because it's not a fucking plant. Becca, it's not—"

"Fire!" Josh bolted into the kitchen. "The field's on fire!"

I told Mary I had to go. I dropped the old phone, and it clattered on the floor, dangling by its curly pigtail cord. I ran outside just as Josh fired up one of our Terr-X off-road vehicles. I jumped in beside him.

The flames licked up the back side of the field, ten feet high, feasting on the dry hogweed stalks. Josh pulled a ski mask and goggles on as he drove, pointed to the glove box, where I found another mask and gloves, and a 9mm automatic.

We stopped at the back shed and jumped out when we heard the gunshots. Josh shouted, "Stay here!" and took off into the field. I ran over to the irrigation pumps and turned them on. I wasn't going any closer to the field. The smoke smelled wrong, like burning hair. I stood by and lit a cigarette.

Eric came out of the dark. Smoke rolled off him, making my eyes tear up. He had a rifle carelessly thrown over one shoulder. In his other hand, he held a charred windbreaker for the Palmer Pirates hockey team. It was a coach's jacket. "All traitors must fucking hang." Eric held his hand out for a high-five. "Oh hey, you got my phone?"

I put my cigarette out in his palm.

The valley was unseasonably warm, that winter. By December, we usually get four feet of snow, but this year, none of it stuck, at least not to our farm. The ground steamed, filling the valley with sour fog. Mist gushed out of yawning holes in the soil like an animal's breath.

Eric moved back into the house right after Election Day when his wife took off with their kids. We hunkered down through November, taking turns watching the road and tending the still until the last straggling hogweed stalks had been plowed under. We all thought Josh would pitch a fit, but he relocated from the room they once shared to the fifth wheel on the back forty. "Somebody oughta watch our six, anyway," was all he said.

Eric had stopped making deliveries alone after he got robbed on Halloween. A dozen of the squatters barricaded the road and pointed shotguns at my brother like he was a fucking stranger. They took the delivery and Eric's guns. He said he would've shot his way out if he didn't recognize so many of them. "Tell your daddy why I ain't shopping at your store no more, Justin!"

After that, he hired a couple of local goons from the Witch's Tit to ride in the back with the deliveries and our new shotguns. Josh didn't like the carloads of hooded customers coming up to the tractor shop or skulking in the woods either, so he started delivering, too. I heard shooting like cheap fireworks for about a minute the first time he went out, but it was quiet after that.

Josh didn't tell me what they were going to do. He didn't have to.

I woke up from a nightmare I couldn't remember, to hear an ungodly racket coming from the field immediately behind the house. Staring out the window, I saw the old hay-hauler spinning its wheels in the mud, driving away from the house, towing back the flinging arm of Josh's old trebuchet.

Eric dropped an orange five-gallon plastic bucket in the sling cradle, lit a wick sticking out of the lid, and then kicked the release lever. The huge throwing arm flexed, accelerating to hurl the projectile high into the 11 PM twilight sky.

"What the fuck are you doing!"

Eric stage-whispered, "Shut up!" I ran to the windows at the other end of my bedroom. I could just see over the trees that lined the edge of the property. I got there just in time to see a little sun bloom in the distance, about two hundred yards away.

I broke the latch trying to open it, but even before I got it open, I heard gunfire. Volleys and salvos, buckets of bullets.

And it all came slamming back.

The nightmare I'd forcibly forgotten upon waking . . . or had I dreamt it just before it happened?

I never get out of bed. Don't have to. Don't want to . . .

The men come in a never-ending line, and they stick their things in me and fill me with their seed. It's not as bad as it sounds. The parts of me that used to hurt are long gone, and the parts they use are making something way better than babies.

The sleeping loft in the old camper shell gets cold at night, but I wouldn't trade it for what I had before. I wouldn't be so quick to leave if it was on fire.

I don't know how long I've been here . . . but it's bliss. Compared to everything I know, anything I could've imagined. They feed me all I need. I don't need to eat the gas station corn dogs or drink myself stupid anymore. I get all I need from the purple-black tendrils curling out of my flesh to anchor me to the rotting mattress, the crumbling camper shell, the soil, and the men who fill me with their protein and their need, and their secrets, and in return, I give magic milk. I am a prize cow.

Until now.

The man on top of me grunts and chews at the coarse fabric of his ill-fitting hood. I think he's trying to say, "You smell smoke?"

The dirty yellow light from the plastic dome light squirms with gray curlicue worms, and I hear screaming from outside.

And from down below.

The web of vines connecting us jingles like telephone wires. Pain and panic and terror in waves so strong I can't find my own body, can barely feel the man climbing off me and going to the door, barely hear him crying out, "Fire!"

I try to get up, but my body is woven into the bed. It feels like fistfuls of hair being ripped out all down my back, my arms, my legs. I haven't carried my own weight in weeks. I have no bones. Falling, calling for help, rolling across the grimy linoleum towards the door.

People fly past outside, spilling out of the old farmhouse and the sheds and derelict cars, and it's raining fire. Someone takes me by the hands, drags me out of the camper, and leans me against a stump, cooing, "There, Lil' Mama, you're safe," then they wander away and I only notice then that they're engulfed in flames from the waist up.

I lay there as my people—my tribe, my family—fire guns into the dark, throw buckets of mud on the flames, or dig in the half-frozen earth, trying to plant the wounded. I hear my sisters roasting and something like popcorn popping. A sister creeps up to me, stroking my hair and licking the milk off my skin and I can't recognize her because her face, her hands, every exposed inch of skin, is covered in snails and slugs writhing and fucking drunkenly in the milk and blood weeping from her wounds.

She drags me under an old postal jeep, but my honeypot is too swollen to fit. She whispers in my ear, "We are daughters of the earth. We are—"

Someone drags me out from under the postal jeep by my legs, then plants a boot on my belly, pinning me to the mud. My milk sluices back up my esophagus to gout out my mouth. Leans down in my face, so I can smell the vodka and Red Bull on his breath, the wet wool of his ski mask. "Hey there, wrong mama. How much for the bizness?"

The butt of his rifle comes down on my head before I can beg.

I vomited out the window and cried out for Eric and Josh, but they were gone. I went back to bed and buried my head in the pillows, but I still heard sirens and gunfire echoing through the valley until just before dawn.

Next morning, the Sheriff came by and talked to Josh, who slipped him a case of wine and shared what little he knew about the tragic fire that wiped out the Twombley farm.

Nobody was arrested, nothing on the local news.

I stopped drinking our product after that—went back to sucking down whiskey like the paperboy's dick—but the dreams kept coming.

The worst part of it wasn't even the dreams. The worst part was knowing everyone in the valley was dreaming the same dream. Everyone knew what we'd done. And nobody cared.

Eric only delivered once a week, with four armed guys in tow. Demand was fiercer than ever, but everybody wanted credit. No money, no honey.

Perhaps She was pleased with our sacrifice. Things got quiet. Normal. It was like She was waiting until after Thanksgiving to start shit again.

We were all hungover and passed out in our beds that Friday afternoon when Josh shouted that Liz was on the news.

I woke up swimming in sweat and wracked with cramps, but I

put it off as PMS (walk it off!) and the previous night's feast. I stumbled downstairs and found Eric passed out in Dad's recliner. Someone had written DICKS GO HERE in permanent marker on his chin.

A prominent Toronto real estate heiress was found murdered, and her wife and children were missing, feared kidnaped. Police were searching for the victim's estranged American wife.

"Jesus, Liz," I said. Josh woke up Eric and filled him in. At first, he didn't believe it, but then he switched gears in classic Eric fashion. "I hope that dyke doesn't think she's coming here, we don't need that kind of heat."

I got in his face. "Who the fuck are *we*?"

For a moment, I thought he was going to punch me in the face, but then he remembered I wasn't his wife. "Same team, Becca," he snapped. "Fuck, I've got such a headache. Go get me a beer, would you, doll?"

A knife in my belly, then a set of Ginsu steak knives, then a whole garden shed. I moaned and bent over the sideboard, but nobody noticed. The baby monitor beside the recliner was making a noise, and for the first time in four months, we heard her voice. "I can't die here," she said. "I'm not one of you, it hates my blood, that's why . . . I can't . . . "

Josh elbowed me aside and ran upstairs with Eric in tow. I staggered out of the room, clinging to the walls. It was sweltering, I was melting, and I had to get outside. Mom might be dying, but I couldn't see past my own agony. I was never allowed a minute to be the one in pain, I always had to put it aside. Now, it felt like it was all coming out at once.

I bulldozed the kitchen to the back door, knocking boots over in the mud room and stumbling barefoot out into red slush. It squished up between my toes, the consistency of dogshit. The cold hit me, turning the sweat in my nightgown to frost. I crossed the yard, tripping on a rhubarb patch, and kept going on all fours. I had no way of knowing what it was, but I knew I didn't want what was coming out of me anywhere near where I had to live.

I got to the edge of the steaming field before my legs gave out. I squatted, then fell forward with my head in the furrowed earth. It was warmer than my body. Something in the innermost cavities of my abdomen ripped and burst. It came out all at once. The pain was so all-encompassing, I blacked out. I came to crawling away, my nightgown plastered to my legs with bloody mud, and Josh lifted me up and took me in his arms.

I pushed him away. Fell again, but I crawled back to see what I'd given birth to.

It looked like a clutch of dinosaur eggs—lumpy, ovoid things of a yellowish, crystalized texture.

"What the hell's wrong with you, Becca?"

I'd thought I had no babies, but I was wrong. They were lithopedes, petrified miscarriages I'd been carrying inside me for who-knows-how-many years. Wizened, unfinished faces, brittle limbs. I hefted each one and held it close to my eyes, silently naming it before covering it up in the soil.

Five of them.

"Becca." Josh shook me and pulled me to my feet. "Mom's gone."

Never a minute. *Quit being a selfish bitch, Becca. Walk it off.* I hugged him and let him cry into my chest. "Come on," I said. "Let's go take care of her."

We carried each other back to the house. Eric was pounding vodka out of the bottle, pacing the living room in his boxer shorts. "Where the hell were you?" he screamed.

"Fuck off, Eric," I managed through gritted teeth.

"We should tell Mary. She should know. You do it."

I took the vodka from him and killed it in three swallows. Somehow, I didn't club him with the empty bottle. "Sure. Hi Sister, Mom's dead, and guess who killed your husband?"

He slapped me, but no harder than I wanted to be slapped. I hit him across the temple with the bottle. It shattered and he tumbled backward into the coffee table. He came bellowing after me, but he stopped in his tracks at the sound of the front door slamming.

Liz came in, towing her twins, with a duffel bag on one arm. "What'd I miss?" she said, looking like nothing was wrong here or anywhere, why do you ask? "And who are all those people outside?"

Eric went outside. We heard a couple of shots, and a few minutes later he came back and confirmed that the farm was surrounded. Maybe fifty or sixty of them out there, all hardcore winos from town. The hardline was down and after a while, the lights went out, but Eric got the generator going. I called Mary and told her about Mom and the blockade. We didn't talk about the other thing. She said she was coming over.

I tried one more time to reason with Eric. "What do they want?"

"What do you think they want?"

"So, give it to them!"

"Hell no. They're all fucking broke."

Josh stuck his head in, as usual, at the worst possible time. "Been thinking," he said, looking at his boots. "We can't keep charging them for it. It's wrong—"

"Fuck 'em," Eric shot back.

"They're outside with guns."

"We got guns, too. Look. We're down to the last dozen cases, if we let them have that, what's the rest of winter gonna be like? Fuck, we'll run dry before New Year's, even if we throw in our private stock!"

Not much could've surprised me, right then. "Private stock? You're still drinking that shit?'

"Of course! What the fuck else is there to do around here?" Eric stormed out and slammed the door.

Liz's eyes were slits, but they grew wide now. "I want some more."

"Are you fucking crazy?" One sip had set Liz on the path to murdering her wife. But I knew that was bullshit. It hadn't put anything in us that wasn't always there. Maybe she saw inside her wife's head, saw how little Liz really meant to her. Liz was more like the rest of the town than us; she never dreamed, never finished reading a book. To suddenly see pictures inside her head, to see inside her partner's head, and realize what a festering snake pit she'd tried to build a life in. Slept next to it until it contaminated her dreams, until her inner world was invaded and infested with someone else's contempt for her.

I tried to explain something I'd been afraid to think in my own head. "The first time we drank it, I don't know. I thought we—"

"We didn't fuck each other," Josh said. "We . . . fucked it. And it fucked us. That's what it means, to belong . . . "

"Yeah, that doesn't put my mind at ease."

Liz took a mason jar from Josh. I tried to stop her, but she smacked my hand away. "What is it?"

Josh said, "Don't you remember that old song Dad used to sing? It's the milk of our true mother."

Liz drank the whole jar down. She didn't offer, and we didn't try to take it. Maybe it would set her free of the memory of what she'd done, but more likely, it would throw fresh fuel on the fire we'd started.

"She was going to kill me," Liz said. "And the twins. I saw her doing it, over and over, every time she smiled at me."

This thing was supposed to be good. Bring us together. The family, and the community. No secrets, every good thought and feeling shared. That's what it did for the people who came before us. That's what it could have done for us, if we weren't all wrong inside.

We don't think. We don't really feel. It hurts too much, even more than all the ways we hurt ourselves and each other. You're always told there are no secrets in a small town, but no. All we have are secrets—little sicknesses we nurture, selfish things we do to ease the pain of being ordinary. There's nothing else. And lancing the boil to let them out didn't bring us together. It made us all sick, but we can't stop glutting ourselves on it.

The ones out there weren't angry at us for what we did to them. They knew what they were becoming, and they wanted to go the rest of the way.

Liz put her kids to bed and went to sit with Mom in the master bedroom, to get her ready to go into the earth. Josh doused all but the most indirect lights, drew all the curtains, then went from room to room, and watched out the windows. After killing another bottle of vodka, Eric shot up out of Dad's chair and said he knew what to do. "Watch the house and keep an eye out for Mary." He and Josh went out to the barn. I saw Eric spraying down the dooryard with the pressure hose, then he came out with four cases of hogweed wine and set it out in the middle of the dooryard.

Eric came up onto the porch. "You fucks are welcome to this little sample of our gratitude, but if I see anyone on my property after it's gone, I'm gonna have to go World War Three on your asses."

You could hear them rustling out of the long grass on the edge of the property, where we parked all our dead cars and trucks. But you could hardly see them, because none of them reminded you of a person. Swaddled in rags, bulging where a body shouldn't and bent where limbs have no right to bend, they came shambling out into the moonlight, twitching with eagerness and descended on the cases of wine.

Eric popped open a beer and guzzled it, then took a road flare out of his back pocket. "Take all you want, losers . . . and pay for it."

Before we could stop him, he struck the cap off the igniter and tossed the road flare out into the dooryard. Where the spark-spitting flare landed, a roiling plume of flame shot up, streaking across the yard to engulf the townsfolk. Some stumbled away wreathed in fire, while others seemed to sink into it almost greedily, welcoming its embrace, pouring the wine down their throats as they burned.

Did I say, 'before we could stop him'? I lie. None of us tried.

When it got dark again, we went inside. I made it to my room and collapsed on my bed. Thinking about Mom. Liz. All of us. We had been given some kind of gift. In other hands but ours, something wonderful might have been done with it. A new golden age. We wasted that gift. Now, like my brother said, it was time to pay for it.

I could hear voices outside—moans, shouts, and curses prominently featuring our family name. There was no point in calling 911. I recognized the voices of two local cops I had dated out there, calling *my* name.

The fire had claimed maybe a dozen. The rest came out of the shadows to surround the house. Hoods lopsided and much too large for human heads, they wobbled like top-heavy toddlers, gloves swelled, and coats bulging like each was smuggling a secret Siamese twin.

Rocks began to rain down on the roof. A shotgun blast took out the kitchen window. We all hit the floor and crawled inside, kicking the door shut. Josh hit the lights. Eric called out their names as he shot at them. "Rusty Neiditch, you out there? I got you, bro! I got something for all of you."

Liz came into my room. Her breath preceded her in ripping gasps, presaging a panic attack. "I didn't mean to do any of it."

"I know." I hugged her, feeling the quivering, lean muscles of her back and waiting for her to come down before suggesting we take her kids and hide in the cellar.

"I was wrong about Dad. But he . . . he and Mom, they gave me to it, and the baby. When it came . . . they fed it to the field. Dad said he was protecting us."

I said, "I know."

She let go and pushed me back to where our eyes could meet. She started to say something. I could tell it was something she'd always wanted to say and there wasn't time, but she had to. I nodded at her to go ahead.

She opened her mouth, choked up, then just choked. Her eyes bulged, pleading for help, for someone to rescue her from what was coming out of her body. Her lips parted and fingers came out of her mouth, the perfect little fingers of a baby's hand tugging her upper lip and scrabbling up her face to crush her nose and gouge her eyes.

I held onto her, but I couldn't touch it, couldn't look away. Liz stumbled backward, clutching at the hand, trying to pull it out, but it must have been rooted to the rest of her, because all she managed to do was hurt herself.

All I managed to do was watch.

This was my sister. I didn't care what she did in Canada, didn't even care that she got to leave, got to live in the world. But I couldn't help her. I didn't want to. I couldn't get over the bitter satisfaction of seeing her like this; she who'd pulled off the ultimate hat trick that eluded me all my life. Without ever catching a dick, she had twins. To see her burn it all down and come back here for a drink out of our dirty jar should've been like two Thanksgiving feasts. This was the late summer flood that spoils the bumper crop. This was chocolate on top of cheese, and I'd never realized until now how bitter I'd been, how much I'd wanted this. Everybody else got what they thought they wished for. Was this my turn? Was this my wish come true?

I watched until she flopped in the corner, legs kicking a few times, then fell still. The plump, purple arm jutted out of her mouth up to the elbow. I got closer, but then recoiled at a galvanic twitch and a gurgling cry that came from deep inside her. The unborn thing in her throat kept trying, with desperate violence, to escape from her the wrong way. Whatever else it was, it had the Hulder genes.

My ears were ringing from all the shooting, but I heard Eric shouting, and then screaming. I went into Liz and Mary's old bedroom. Her set of Hermes luggage was there, but not the children. I went to the master bedroom.

Mom lay on the bed with a twin cradled in either arm, snuggled against her in their matching pajamas. Mom's face was a waxen mask, her eyes half-lidded, her mouth smeared with sticky hogweed wine. The empty jar sat on the nightstand. A noise came from deep inside Mom when I picked up the twins, but I told myself it wasn't her, just what the wine put inside her, trying to come to life. What would it make of people with more to offer?

I resolved right then, to stop beating myself up. I would be better and give back more; I would love this land as it was trying to love us. All this time I felt like garbage, I was the one throwing away my life.

I carried the sleeping twins downstairs in my arms. The living room was being looted by hooded townsfolk who hissed at me to get out. A man I might've dated until his wife found out threw a torch into the seat of my father's recliner, ripped a twelve-point buck's head off the wall, and ran out a step ahead of the flames. I remembered last Christmas morning when he out-of-nowhere said his wife was coming home, and at the liquor store, I found all our used condoms stuffed into my purse. Another one carrying an armload of old bowling trophies tripped on the stairs and fell on his torch. The canvas sack on his head caught fire and he rolled around at my feet.

Outside, Eric was screaming, and the rest of the town was cheering rhythmically like they were urging someone on in a contest.

I had to push them out of the way to see. It took eight of them to hold Eric suspended between them, two at each limb, while two more worked his torso with baseball bats. One of them, in the least surprising turn of the evening, was Josh.

"You want more of that shit?" I shouted. I had to repeat myself, but by the time I was done, I had their undivided attention.

One of them rushed me, hands out to grab the twins. Josh swung the bat and knocked his teeth out his ears. The rest of them backed off. Eric lay on the grass, panting. You could hear his broken ribs grating against each other as he, God bless him, still tried to get up.

"We were always hers, but we forgot. We remember now, and if you want to make it through winter, you'd better remember who we are, and who She is. You want what She brings, give her what She wants."

There used to be a ritual, but it was just for us. She didn't care, so long as She got what She wanted.

They gathered round Eric and picked him up. They carried him into the field and laid him in the slushy furrows. They stabbed him with every tool in our shed, and stood back to let the soil drink it in. Tendrils and vines sprouted like green fire to enfold our brother. He somehow still found the breath to curse us as She dragged him headfirst down into the earth. His body thrashed frantically, hands clawing at snow and soil, legs kicking in the air like an incredibly slow dive, until the soles of his boots disappeared into the churning earth.

Lurid purple-green light seeped out of the hole long after he was swallowed up. It was like the Northern Lights shining up through the soil, a corona of secret fire shrouding something that slept beneath our feet, stretching as deep beneath us as snowy Pioneer Peak loomed above us.

They gave a cheer and then peered around and realized for the first time what they'd done. These little people with their ugly little secrets, their sordid, sad desires, had always thought they were good because they kept their animal natures in check. Now there was nowhere to hide from what they really were.

"See you in church," Josh said to them as they lurched off. He gave each of them a jar to take home. We can be generous, even if She isn't.

He put his arm around me when they were gone, and only one stood between us and the burning house we grew up in. Mary pointed a Glock at us. She had an assault rifle slung on her shoulder. "I tried to tell you," she started, then she screamed and emptied the gun into the ground.

We knew. I'd erased the answering machine message she left about what the plant samples really were. I knew more about it than any asshole with a microscope. They weren't plants. They were hair. Her hair. The samples were more animal than plant cells. And they had more in common with us than either of our parents.

She knew it, too, but couldn't accept it. Maybe she would've killed us all if the town wasn't already trying to, just to prove to herself that she wasn't one of us.

That she wasn't Hers.

We held each other until we all started to shiver. Josh went into the barn and made us a place. They took or trashed our generators, but he had a couple of car batteries on a trickle charger and wired them to the lights.

That first winter was hard, but new sprouts broke through the new snow the very next morning, and we were harvesting the week after Christmas. Little gifts—blankets, coats, boots, home-cooked food, toys for the twins—turned up every morning. The town had to change more than we did, and they were the better for it.

In the midst of all of it, I found something I never could have hoped for. My dreams are not a brand of shame, but a cherished mythology. I am now the eye of this valley, the doorway to other lives. With every sip of Her milk, we grow closer and engulf and accept all that we are not.

I won't say it's perfect now, because what is? But almost everything is better. Every day, in every small way, we are working to be worthy of Her love. And every day, in ways small and sometimes great, She is turning the cold, secret seeds inside us into miraculous new fruit.

Black Rings

ED KURTZ

Whisht! lads, haad yor gobs,
An' aa'll tell ye aall an aaful story,
Whisht! lads, haad yor gobs,
An' aa'll tell ye 'boot the worm.
—Clarence M. Leumane, "The Lambton Worm," 1867

"It is shaped like a sausage . . . and it is so poisonous that merely to touch it means instant death. It lives in the most desolate parts of the Gobi Desert."
—The Jalkhanz Khutagt Sodnomyn Damdinbazar,
Prime Minister of Mongolia, 1922

1993
Central Connecticut

I t all began with a fractured shoulder. Allie was out with some of the old squad, Char and Sophie and them, popping from bar to bar, the group metamorphosing some as one person slipped away and one or two more joined in. There hadn't been any particular cause for celebration; it was just one of those things that happened when they started having a good time and nobody wanted the good time to end. Everybody drank Zimas at the first place, Nag's on Main, but by the time it was just Allie, Sophie, Luce Fitzsimmons and some guy she knew called Stanley, the group had graduated to Wild Turkey 151 shooters with beer backs and not a one of them could stand on two legs for more than a few seconds at a time. Fitz climbed into a cab with Stanley after that and Allie joined Sophie for the short jaunt up the street to the only 24-hour filling station around so that Soph could pick up a pack of menthols before using the payphone outside to score a ride home.

Trouble was it was 23 degrees and falling, dead of winter in old New England, and the very second Allie's right sneaker met with a small patch of ice on the crumbling sidewalk, she went down in a thrashing whirlwind of pinwheeling arms and legs before the preponderance of her body weight slammed her left shoulder right into the concrete. It was all laughs while the girls were still tight, but when Allie woke up on Sophie's couch the next morning, she discovered she couldn't so much as lift her left arm without it feeling like somebody was taking a power drill to her shoulder. She'd managed to hurt herself worse than she thought, and after

Sophie finally convinced her to see the doc about it, Allie was x-rayed and the worst was confirmed: the shoulder was indeed fractured. Worse yet, she had managed to fracture it in such a way that there was no surgery capable of repairing the break.

PT and pills. That was all they could offer her.

It took her five weeks to become addicted to Percocet. By mid-spring, she switched to a new doc who was much more liberal with the script pad. By the following summer, Allie Garrido found herself in desperate need of something more, something stronger, just to keep herself together. Something no doctor could help her with.

The road from Zimas with the girls to copping junk at a dilapidated no-tell motel on the Berlin Turnpike, had only taken six months, and all it needed to happen was a little slip on the ice. The next time there was ice on the sidewalks, Allie was in far worse shape. Junk wasn't cheap, not when you needed it as badly or as frequently as she did. Half a gram a day was no small thing, and to maintain that pace was no small cost. In the beginning, Allie only went down to the Turnpike to cop. Come Thanksgiving, she never left.

First, the Allie Garrido her sister Kat knew, disappeared, seemingly replaced by the bone-weary creature on the Turnpike with the gnarly network of scars from collapsed veins in both arms. Then, two weeks before Easter, Allie simply disappeared altogether.

It was as though the Turnpike had gobbled her up.

2

K at absently plucked at the strings of her unplugged bass, fingering her way through the only song of hers that the band ever played. She'd written "Black Rings" in high school, treating it largely as a poem that she constantly tweaked, reshaped, and refined throughout the entirety of her senior year until she was satisfied with it. Mostly satisfied, at any rate.

The bass was well-worn, cheap as hell. She'd picked it up at a pawn shop in Waterbury for eighty bucks cash six years back and never thought seriously about upgrading. It got the job done, as far as she was concerned, and she figured if the Bloody Merries ever made it, *then* she'd look into getting something flashy. But the old pearl black Rogue would always be her first love, the one on which she's learned to play. The one with which she turned "Black Rings" into a song. Her song. In many ways, that bass was just about the only thing Kat felt she could really depend on.

She knew perfectly well they were never going to make it. They weren't serious enough. Most of them fantasized about leaving Connecticut, heading out west where things really *happened*, but none of them ever would. It was like every other small town in every other state in America: you either got out early or you got stuck for life. And as far as Kat was concerned, she was dead stuck. She never heard from old friends who went away to college, or to the city, or anyplace but BFE in the Naugatuck Valley, because she knew they wanted to cut all ties lest they, too, end up boomeranged right back to Nowheresville, drinking nippers in the packie parking lot before pumping out half a dozen kids, all their names beginning with J. It was a trap and only those who figured that out before the trap clamped down on them forever ever had a chance. Kat's chance was long gone, and though she was beginning to accept it for what it was, that didn't mean she had to like it.

The Bloody Merries played the Sting up in hard hittin' New Britain once a month, and Kat was delighted to have once scored a gig at Toad's Place in New Haven, though only as an opening act and only for three songs, all of which were covers and none of which was "Black Rings." Still, after seven years, she never finished another original song, never so much as landed a manager, and the rest of the band were aging at the same pace as everybody else, which meant it was only a matter of time before they all went their own ways, to their boring day gigs, their boring marriages, their boring families and boring weekend barbeques and tag sales and boring fucking lives.

And one dumb song she wrote in high school was never going to change any of that, no matter how desperately she wanted it to.

Kat set the bass back on its stand and fished the soft pack of Marlboro Lights out of her bag, along with the mini Bic she'd copped off Joan, her rhythm guitarist, and never given back. Last one in the pack, the "lucky smoke" she always slid out and put back in upside down with each fresh pack, though she couldn't say why. It never seemed to bring any detectable luck, but she'd been doing it since she started smoking at fifteen and had no plans to stop now. Habits were weird that way. People were weird, too.

Weird and sad and broken. Case in point was her older sister, the junkie, who Kat hadn't spoken to for over a year, and who—according to her mother—was now "missing," a designation Kat couldn't quite buy. Junkies didn't go missing, they just went underground, into that underworld most people never thought about or even knew existed, right under their feet. The *real* Allie, the girl she grew up with and wanted so badly to be like, had vanished a long time ago, well before this latest crisis. The key difference between Kat and her mother was hope; Mom still had some, and Kat pitied her for it.

Still, she pitied Allie, too. Nobody chose to wreck their own life—it was just something that happened when things went south. Sometimes, the only decisions available to somebody were all bad ones. Sometimes, people just fell through the cracks. *There but for the grace of God . . .*

Kat glanced out the sole bedroom window, down to the street below. She lived in a studio apartment above a vacuum cleaner repair shop with irregular hours and few customers, that she suspected was a front for something not quite legal, but as long as they didn't bother her, she didn't worry too much about it. Occasionally, her mother stopped by with extra groceries or homemade tamales, but for the large part she lived a fairly solitary life. She liked her own company, and on the rare occasion that she craved human contact, there was an Irish bar called The Riddle up the street, where the bartenders were friendly and the pours generous. She may have felt stuck, but she knew perfectly well that things could be much worse.

Some kids were skateboarding up and down the street, to the dismay of every driver that came along, but otherwise it was a quiet afternoon and Kat had no immediate plans for the evening ahead. For a second, she considered hitting The Riddle, but she wasn't feeling particularly sociable or thirsty, so she dropped her still-smoldering cigarette butt into a mostly empty can of 'Gansett on her dresser and flipped on the TV she had precariously balanced on a plastic milk crate she'd swiped from behind the Shop and Stop on Rubber Avenue. Cartoons and talk shows. She flipped it back off, lay back on her bare mattress (she always kicked all the blankets onto the floor in her sleep), and heaved a sigh as the phone in the kitchenette began to ring.

"Fuck."

One nice thing about living in such a small place was she didn't have to go far to get the phone, but she still wasn't thrilled about the prospect of having to deal with whoever was calling. It could have been her mother, or possibly a bandmate, but if Kat had any money to wager she'd have guessed it was just somebody trying to sell her something. *Nice try,* she thought, *but I couldn't buy whatever it is even if I needed it to live.* She was flat broke, like most musicians, and almost never had an extra dollar for anything remotely frivolous, except for smokes, but that was different. She *needed* those.

The phone—the same transparent one with all the colorful circuitry inside she'd had since tenth grade—hung from the wall beside the circuit breaker and above the whole ten inches of counter space the studio afforded her. Kat hauled herself off the bed and padded over to answer it, prepared to tell whoever was on the line to fuck right off and let her be.

Instead, she got the shock of her life.

"Hel—"

"Kat? Kat, help me—help me, Kat. *Please.* I don't have long, they—"

A scuffle, some static, and a click that signified the line was dead.

It was Allie, her sister, with a tinge of genuine terror in her croaky voice that Kat had never heard before. There and gone again, before Kat could so much as take a breath. The first time she'd heard from Allie in what seemed like forever, and her fear was infectious. Something was seriously, deeply wrong.

Or was it? If she was being honest with herself, Allie's entire life was one ongoing crisis, which was about what she would have expected from anybody living the way she did. Last she heard, Allie was a permanent resident at one of those godawful no-tell motels down on the Berlin Turnpike, which was little more than a long stretch of packies, titty bars, sex shops, and truck stops. Allie was likely in one of those seedy places with hourly rates.

It gave Kat the creeps just driving along the Turnpike, never mind stopping to get ogled by the sleazebags that crawled all over it like ants on spilled ice cream. She even dumped a guy, a couple years out of high school, just because she found out he used to hang out on the 'Pike, and she hadn't bothered to ask why or what he was doing before she cut things off. What was the point? She knew what he'd been doing. There were only a handful of reasons to spend any time on that stretch, and none of them were good.

"Damn," she said. "I don't need this shit. I really don't."

Missing, according to their mother. And yet, there was Allie begging for help from probably the last person alive she would ever ask for anything. It didn't seem normal, even for how deeply abnormal her sister's life had become since that one little accident had sent her on her journey down the well. And the more Kat replayed that brief call in her mind, poring over each word Allie had said to her, the more her focus was drawn to that last word before the line had gone dead.

They.

She'd said she didn't have long, *they*—who? And what were they going to do when time ran out? Kat couldn't imagine. She didn't dare. But she knew damn well that if she didn't find out, and soon, nobody would ever know what became of Allie Garrido. Girls who vanished into the world of the Berlin Turnpike didn't get found, didn't get rehabbed, didn't get their lives and families and happiness back. The 'Pike was a predator, and it was never sated, and very few people lost a second's sleep over it.

The Turnpike didn't just swallow people whole; it erased them, and Kat couldn't let that happen to Allie. She just couldn't, not if there was the tiniest iota of hope that there was something she could do about it.

She glanced at the kitschy cat clock she had hanging askance on the wall above what used to be a fireplace but was now bricked up and unusable. Ten to four in the afternoon. She was out the door, behind the wheel of her second-hand Subaru, and on her way to the last place in Connecticut she ever wanted to be before rush hour got underway. She didn't realize she was driving in utter silence, the radio off, until halfway through her drive, but she didn't bother to remedy the situation. Her brain was loud enough without more noise to fill her skull.

3

Brewster Ames sat on a creaky wicker chair directly in front of a humming fan by the window, chewing his fingernails and sweating through his clothes. The front office air conditioning had gone out by the end of the previous summer, but despite repeated promises to get it either replaced or repaired before the heat set in again, nothing had been done. Brewster would have been shocked if anything had, given the way things were, the way they always were. Nobody ever said what they meant, they just said whatever got them off the hook in the moment. He got it; he wasn't any different. All the same, he was so goddamned hot he wanted to strangle his boss, Todd, for dragging his feet on this one—if only he had the energy to do it. The heat made him too lethargic, and the clonazepam he was constantly popping like M&Ms didn't help much, either.

He was a big man, Brewster Ames, six-foot-one in his stocking feet and regularly hovering around three hundred fifty pounds, which was bound to compromise the structural integrity of the old wicker chair holding him up night after night, day after day. Some weeks he sat at that desk for twelve hours straight, but he lived rent free in the adjoining room—101—so it was hard to muster anything resembling complaint. Besides, he spent at least a quarter of those hours asleep at the switch, as it were, with only a rusty old desk bell to wake him should anyone wander in. Someone always did, but Brewster didn't have much trouble drifting right back off where he sat, snoring away into the fan blades so that he sounded like some kind of monster from outer space.

The Welcome Inn wasn't the worst motel on the 'Pike, but it wasn't exactly a lush resort, either. They had their share of weary travelers, typically traveling salesmen with paper thin travel

172

budgets, but their age was coming to an end and there were fewer of them year after year. Brewster was old enough, and had been at the Welcome Inn long enough, that he recalled a Fuller Brush salesman called Ike, who had come through every year and tipped generously for a good lead on who was the best in the game that year and the means to get in touch with her. One year he even gave Brewster fifty bucks just to point him at a VD clinic that would get him clear of whatever he'd picked up and keep it off his medical record, but that was the last time he'd ever come through. Maybe the VD got him. Brewster didn't honestly care—he just missed the tips.

Nowadays, it was almost all johns and junkies, and they never tipped at all. Hell, half the time they trashed the rooms and skipped out before they could be held to account for the damage. Everything in every room had to be bolted or chained in place, from the old two-knob TVs to the lamp, phone, and radio. If they could have figured out a way to chain up the soap and towels, they'd have done that, too. Folks would steal anything, regardless of whether they needed it or even really wanted it, and for some reason that went double for motel rooms and literally everything found inside of them. Brewster couldn't say why, apart from the simple, age-old fact of life that human beings were the absolute worst. He didn't trust his own mother as far as he could throw a Volkswagen, and she was a saint compared to the crowd that hung around the old Welcome Inn.

Around two o'clock, the desk bell startled him out of a sound sleep and a pleasant dream about Ravyn, one of the working girls who operated between the motel and Rascals, the strip joint next door. He'd propositioned her more than once, but all she'd had to say to that was, "You can't afford me." Which didn't mean he wouldn't try again, and it definitely didn't indicate he would stop having torrid, borderline pathological dreams about her and all the things he wished he could do to her. Nevertheless, getting dragged from the dream into the miserable reality of his actual life did little for Brewster's mood, which was why he responded to the bell the way he did.

"Fucking hell—*what?*"

The figure on the other side of the counter from him gradually came into focus as Brewster wiped the drool from his lips and blinked the sleep from his eyes. It was, he discovered to his tremendous dismay, Turk Tolliver. Turk worked the door at Rascal's most nights and acted as a nanny to Todd Foligno's ever-rotating stable of whores who graduated from the pole to the motel room at the same rate they moved from blow to horse. As far as Brewster knew, it wasn't Todd who got them hooked on the shit, but like the scavenger he was, he swept in and circled down on them as soon as they were under its spell. Junk cost money, and turnpike strip club regulars were notoriously tight-fisted with their crumpled-up singles. A girl had to make do.

"I didn't know they let you out during the day," Brewster said.

"Fuck you, fat ass," Turk growled back. "I'm lookin' for Allison."

"Who?"

"*Velvet*," the bouncer/pimp corrected himself. "Her real name's Allison."

"Shit, I thought that *was* her real name."

"The fuck kinda parents you think name their baby Velvet?"

"The kind whose kids end up on the 'Pike, I guess. And I don't know where the fuck your whores are, man. That's why they're *your* whores. That shit's above my pay grade."

"I don't like it when people call 'em that."

"I don't really give a shit what you like, Turk. You asked me where's Velvet, and I told you I don't know. Is there anything else, or are we done here?"

In lieu of response, Turk grabbed the bell off the desk and threw it as hard as he could at the wall just to the right of Brewster's head, where it went straight through the drywall and dropped down on the other side.

"Jesus!" Brewster cried out. "You gonna pay for that?"

"Say another word, fat man," Turk said, drilling holes into Brewster's skull with his furious eyes. "One more fuckin' word. *Please*. I want you to." He punctuated the threat by cracking all the knuckles on both hands, which to Brewster sounded like walnuts exploding.

Brewster elected to remain silent, and Turk Tolliver left the front office in a huff, angrier than he'd been when he came in. Which was fine and dandy with the big man behind the desk, who couldn't stand Turk and hoped it ate him up inside. Velvet, on the other hand—or Allison, or whatever her name was—Brewster actually liked her. She was a nice girl, too nice for the life she was living, and somehow hadn't yet grown as jaded and cynical as most of her peers, which to him made her kind of special. Always a twinkle in her eyes, almost as though she didn't realize how bad things were or could be. Velvet was like a wildflower in a landfill.

Despite his deep animosity for damned near everything and everyone around him, Brewster Ames sincerely hoped she was all right. He hoped she'd *escaped*. But in his gut, like a suppurating ulcer, he knew she hadn't.

4

Kat pulled her Subaru into the expansive lot of the Luv's truckstop at the border of Newington and Berlin, where she found a pump to fill her tank with unleaded while she headed inside for something vaguely resembling lunch. Pot-bellied truckers, lot lizards, and greasy ne'er-do-wells eyeballed her every inch of the way, but she deftly ignored them in favor of focusing hard on the aisles of stale snacks she could see through the glass before she got inside. Ultimately, her one meal of the day consisted of salt and vinegar potato chips, a Twinkie, and a bottle of Diet Pepsi, which she purchased along with a fresh pack of Marlboro Lights and a scratch-off, because why the hell not? She didn't win anything, but she felt a lot better once she finished her snacks, which she ate in her car after pulling it away from the pumps and up to the side of the store.

There, leaning up against the propane tanks and smoking a cigarette in defiance of the plentiful signage warning her not to, was a young woman with a jet-black bob and a septum piercing that gleamed in the sunlight when she wasn't blowing smoke through her nostrils. While she did this, she stared right through Kat's windshield at her, like she was trying to figure out the meaning behind a particularly obscure example of abstract art.

Kat opened her soft pack, removed two cigarettes from it, replaced one upside down, and lit the other. She drew in a deep drag to the bottom of her lungs and, rolling the window down with the crank at her knee, leaned out and said, "You got a problem?"

"I got a lot of fuckin' problems," the young woman said with a grin. "Which ones you wanna know about?"

"I wanna know about why you're staring at me like I got two heads and five tits."

The girl laughed. "I just never seen a girl park here like that. Usually, it's guys old enough to be my dad, but hey—you do you. It's all green and it all spends the same, right?"

Kat sneered. "I'm not trying to get *laid*, if that's what you're thinking."

"That right?" She shook her head and dropped the smoke, only halfway burned down, to the pavement where she stepped on it. "Then you're about to get some bad news, sister, because that's not how shit works around here. There's a system."

"A system?" Kat said. She was growing tired of the conversation she never wanted in the first place, but at the same time, she didn't really want to let it go when she felt like somebody was having fun with her. "The hell are you even talking about?"

"You want to work the 'Pike, you don't just *show up*. There's lots of girls around here worked hard and long to get their spots, and you're asking for a blade between your ribs you try and fuck with that."

"You think—?" Kat cut herself off, gawping with disbelief. "Oh, hell no. I'm not here for *that*, neither. *Jesus*, no. Just—no." She laughed it off, stabbed her smoke out in the overflowing ashtray beneath the tape deck, and rolled the window up. She was done with all that.

She turned the key in the ignition and switched on the radio, which was playing Mudhoney at the moment. She dug the song and had the tape at home, but Kat found it hard to enjoy a good song when there was a lot lizard knocking on the driver's side window.

"Chrissakes," she hissed. "I'm going, all right?"

"Some free advice," the girl shouted through the glass, over the music and the engine. "Go see Todd at Rascal's. He'll get you started faster than anybody. Just don't tell him I said nothing, a'ight?"

"I don't even know who you are or what the fuck you're talking about," Kat shouted back, shifting in reverse. "But hey, good luck." *I'm sure you need it*, she thought, and with that, she backed out and got back on the turnpike before anybody else accosted her for just sitting and having a goddamned snack.

Only on the 'Pike.

Her key problem now was that she had no clear idea of where she was heading or what she was doing. As far as she knew, Allie wasn't even necessarily around the area anymore, had maybe hitched a ride out West someplace or ended up in stir, the call Kat got from her the one they let you have before they locked you in a cell. She had no way of knowing, and the prospect of just hanging around to talk to people like that woman back at Luv's seemed deeply unpleasant at best, seriously dangerous at worst. She'd jumped in feet first with nothing so much as resembling a plan, and now she was just aimlessly cruising south, past more than a dozen sleazy motels, any one of which could very well house her supposedly missing sister. But it wasn't like she could just spend the day knocking on every door. For starters, there had to be a thousand rooms on the Berlin Turnpike. Moreover, she knew perfectly well many, if not most of them contained people she absolutely did not want to meet, even for a second.

It was hopeless. She wasn't a detective. She was a bassist, and a failed one at that. All Kat could do now was admonish herself for thinking she could just head on down to the 'Pike and, *voila*, there would be Allie, standing on the side of the road and waving her down. *Here I am!*

"Stupid," she said aloud. "Goddamn stupid idi—"

Then she saw it, bold as brass. Hot pink neon with a blue border that flashed on and off, impossible to miss.

RASCAL'S, read the sign. Kat tapped the brakes at the next red light, realizing with a sinking sense of dread that she did, in fact, know of one person who might be able to help her, no matter how much she wished she didn't. *Todd at Rascal's.*

"This is a bad idea," Kat told herself as she waited for the light to change. "This is really a bad fucking idea, Katherine."

The light turned green, and Kat turned left into the Rascal's parking lot, her lousy lunch doing somersaults in her stomach.

5

By four o'clock in the afternoon, Turk had already broken two fingers on the right hand of a would-be groper when he went to see what needed to be done about the guy who had tried out his Van Damme impression on the cigarette machine next to the ATM. It was a touchy machine, to be sure, particularly for any poor bastard hoping to get his hands on whatever went in slot A8, which was why they always kept the Virginia Slims in there. Guys almost never smoked them, and all the dancers knew the machine wouldn't fart that brand out no matter how much you punched or kicked the goddamn thing. Of course, every once in a while, some drunk came along who pulled the wrong knob and before he knew it, Turk had to deal with the problem. Dealing with problems was what he got paid for, after all, but this was nighttime shit, not day shift shit. He expected assholes on their lunch breaks from their bullshit corporate insurance jobs when the sun was still up, willing to get a little buzzed but not so much that they couldn't go back to the office. The dude playing Kumite with the cigarette machine, conversely, was well sauced, three sheets to the wind, and most definitely cruising for a bruising once Turk got his hands on him.

Turk moved slowly, which in this case meant he didn't quite make it to the area before the drunk managed to crack the glass with the heel of his shoe, splintering it from one corner to the other like an intricate spider web. Turk stopped when he saw this. "Shit. Okay."

Behind the nearby bar, Trisha—"Diamond" when she was working—glared wide-eyed at Turk, lifting her shoulders and waving her hands as if to say, *You gonna do something about this?*

"Yeah," he said. "I got it."

With a heavy sigh, he reached his right hand between the guy's legs and his left around his torso, where they met somewhere in the middle and he hefted the drunk up into the air like a bag of rice. The drunk tried to kick his legs and flail his arms, but it was no use; he was just too small and too inebriated to free himself from the big man's formidable grasp.

"Look—hey! I'm sorry, all right? I just wanted some fuckin' smokes!"

"Get 'em someplace else," was all Turk had to say about that, and he used the guy's forehead to ram open the door before hauling him out into the blinding midday sunlight. Both bouncer and bouncee squinted in the searing light after so long inside the dim cave of the titty bar. Turk hurled the guy bodily into the air and onto the macadam, where he landed with a dull thud and stayed put, groaning.

He waited a moment to make sure the drunk didn't get back up and come at him, as they sometimes did, but all the guy did was spit out a bloody tooth.

The tooth landed about a foot and a half from the toe of Kat's left shoe, where she stopped and looked down at the comet tail of blood and mucus trailing after it. The guy whose mouth it used to belong to moaned on the pavement, and when she looked up from him to the huge guy who had put him there, the two of them locked eyes for an uncomfortable moment.

Turk shrugged. Kat turned on her heel and headed back to where she parked her Subaru.

"Wait," he called out. She stopped, back to him. Turk was as surprised as Kat was, and once he said it, he wasn't sure what he was supposed to do next. He improvised. "He was wigging out. You're fine. It's not such a bad place."

Kat turned slowly back. "They should hire you to do the commercials."

"They hired me to toss out drunks and crazies."

"Who else goes in there?"

"You'd be surprised."

"Yeah," Kat said. "I guess I probably would."

She turned her attention from Turk to the guy on the pavement, who was just starting to heave himself up. A long string of bloody spit dangled from his lower lip like a pendulum, swinging in time with his blinking eyes. More than anything else, he just looked to Kat like he couldn't believe this was how his day had ended up. She empathized.

Turk kicked at the pebbles around his boots and said, "Anyway." Then he went back inside.

Kat said, "Well, this is already fucking weird."

And she went inside, too.

* * *

Beth hunched over the makeup table and checked her eye shadow—the bottle said it was *amethyst* but she knew lilac when she saw it—and satisfied with that, she sat back and lit a Virginia Slim that was longer than her middle finger. She drew in a long, pleasant drag, held it in for several seconds, and exhaled a blue-gray cloud that masked her reflection for a blessed moment. Some days, she wished no one could see her, not even herself. But everybody had to eat, and getting looked at was how Beth earned her daily bread.

Only two hours into her shift—a day shift, at that—but she really wasn't doing too badly. Of the $120 in cash she had splayed out on the table in front of her, she was going to take home $85 after tipping out to the house and bar, and she was relatively confident she could double that before five o'clock rolled around. The pickings were slim when the sun was still up, and the lunchtime crowd consisted mostly of notoriously bad tippers, but at ten bucks a lap dance all she really needed to do was work the floor, cajole the cheap suits a bit until they agreed that, yes, it was a good idea to pay a stranger to shake her tits in their faces before heading back for that afternoon presentation in the boardroom. Couple more days like that and she'd get caught up on rent down at the Welcome Inn, which was about to welcome her broke ass to the curb. Beth could hardly wait to see the disappointment in that fat fuck Brewster's face when she squared up with him, thus denying him his little control fantasy of evicting tenants and feeling like a Big Man.

Still, it was as cheap a place to live on the 'Pike as one could get without the cockroaches outright sitting on your face while you slept, and even if worse came to worst, Beth had a sneaking suspicion Turk Tolliver could make Brewster see his way clear to giving the girl an extra few days to come up with something. Of course, it would be a damn sight easier to just work nights, where the real money was, but since Velvet had vanished, Beth hadn't been all too eager to be seen by anybody on the Turnpike, clothed or not.

She was a nice kid, that Velvet. A little in over her head, but everybody was when they first started out. It was a weird and sometimes disturbing transition to make, unlearning half of everything everyone ever told you about your body and what you were allowed to do with it, not to mention double-learning everything you ever assumed to be true about men and what they believed they were allowed to do with your body. Some of the guys were perfectly nice, sure, and a few of the regulars were even downright pleasant to be around, if a little odd for spending all of their free time and money in a titty bar on the 'Pike. But quite a lot of the guys who found themselves at Rascal's, particularly at the end of a night of carousing and raising all kinds of hell, were—well, they were *guys*. And *guys* tended to think if they put up the tenner to get in and another for a four-and-a-half-minute lap dance to the tune of H-Town's "Knockin' da Boots," they were goddamned *owed* something. For twenty lousy bucks, they thought they were owed *everything*.

Of course, that was life. That was *men*. But what happened to Velvet, that was something else.

That was something *special*. And whatever—or whomever—it was, Beth wasn't interested in anybody thinking she had anything to do with it. A lot of the time, at least in her experience, when girls disappeared, they ended up right there on the 'Pike, or someplace just like it. It was when they disappeared *from* the 'Pike that things got truly gnarly. For one thing, nobody lifted a finger, and most times, everyone just acted as though they'd never even known the chick. Everyone liked Velvet, but asking questions led to turning over rocks nobody wanted turned over, so no one asked the questions that needed asking. One night she was right there on the stage, spinning around the pole to Jodeci, sipping a cranberry and vodka at the bar, showing the other girls in the dressing room photos of her cats, Mittens and Sheba. The next night, she was gone. Nobody knew anything. Nobody saw anything.

Hell, when Beth wondered aloud if anybody had checked on the cats, everybody looked at her like she was nuts. *Leave it alone*, or so the unspoken message seemed to be. *Nothing can be done about it now, anyway*. Which, to Beth's mind, was for the best.

"Coming up to the stage right now," boomed the voice of the MC, Terry, over the sound system. "Please put your hands together for *Odyssey!*"

She hated the stage name but having never thought one up prior to her initial audition, it was the only thing that popped into her mind when asked. Unfortunately for Beth, it stuck. Odyssey it was, and it was her time in the limelight. The opening keys to Hi-Five's "She's Playing Hard to Get" seeped through the walls, signaling her imminent appearance on stage, so she went to give them what they paid for.

Kat wasn't expecting it to be so dark inside. After she paid the cover and ducked through the beaded curtain to the club itself, she had to stop for a moment to let her eyes adjust. It seemed to her that the entire point was to *look* at what was on display, and yet it was dim enough that she had to squint to see the performer presently gyrating on the main stage. She was a tall, lithe woman, maybe mid-20s, with fire-red hair that Kat suspected was a wig. Beneath her left breast was a tattoo of a small blue butterfly; upon noticing it, Kat decided her eyes had indeed made the transition. The dancer noticed Kat back and winked at her. Embarrassed, Kat averted her eyes and hustled to the bar.

The bartender, a broad-shouldered woman with short, spiky bleach-blonde hair and a crimson halter-top, looked surprised when she saw her next customer. She gave Kat the once-over and said, "Auditions are by appointment only. You gotta call."

"Aud—no, I'm not—ha, no," Kat stammered.

"Ah, okay," the bartender said, smirking. "Didn't realize you were family. What ya having?"

"Just a beer." Kat glanced at the bottles on the glass shelf behind the blonde woman, grasping a moment too late what she'd meant by "family"; the bartender thought she was gay, come to ogle the girls. She considered correcting the misunderstanding for a fraction of a second before deciding it really didn't matter in the least. The blonde cracked open a Miller High Life and set it down in front of Kat, who traded a fin for it. "No change."

"Thanks."

"Got a question, though."

"Thanks, but I'm taken."

Kat laughed. "No, I'm not—listen, you ever know a girl named Allie, maybe danced or hung out here? Looks a lot like me, only taller with shorter hair. Kinda like yours, actually, but black."

"Kid," the bartender began, despite looking the same age as Kat, "I don't know nobody's name around here. Ain't nobody's Christian names are *Cinnamon, Odyssey,* or *Jinx,* you know what I mean? Whoever Allie is on the outside, if she comes in here? She's somebody else."

Kat hadn't considered that. If nobody on the Turnpike knew Allie's real name, and Kat didn't know what name she was using, her objective was going to be a hell of a lot harder than she'd initially imagined. Grabbing a matchbook off the bar with RASCAL'S crookedly stenciled on the front, she lit a cigarette and took a swig of the barely cool beer in front of her. *Good fucking job, Nancy Drew*, she thought bitterly.

When she finished the beer, she extended a forefinger to signal for another. Giving up was the last thing she wanted to do, but Kat already felt like she had failed. She'd failed Mom, but much worse than that, she'd failed Allie. A full beer replaced the empty one, and she took half of it down in one go as someone dropped down onto a stool two seats over. Kat looked over, and she immediately reddened at the sight of the girl who'd winked at her from the stage. *Odyssey* was the name, she remembered. And Odyssey wasn't wearing anything but a g-string and a pair of hot pink lace-up platform shoes with opaque heels, her bare breasts practically resting atop the bar when she leaned over it.

Kat snuck another look at the butterfly tattoo. She wondered how bad it had hurt.

"Dewar's," the girl told the bartender. "Neat."

"Comin' up."

Odyssey sat back, waiting on her drink, and craned her neck to look first at Kat, then at the pack of smokes in front of her. "Mind if I bum one of those off you?"

"Go right ahead," Kat said, nodding. "Just don't take my lucky one."

"I wouldn't dare."

Odyssey slid a cigarette out of the pack and, in lieu of the matches, simply leaned toward Kat with the square between her lips until she got the picture and touched the end of her cherry to the tip of the dancer's smoke.

"Thanks, doll."

"Don't mention it."

"Next time I won't," said Odyssey with a grin.

The women drank and smoked in silence for another couple of minutes before Kat summoned the courage to try the same tactic again, but this time with a new person. "Listen, you ever know any of these girls' real names?"

"All names are real, honey," the dancer came back cryptically. "Or equally made up, however you want to look at it."

"Okay," Kat said. "How about Allie? Anybody with that name ever cross your path?"

All at once, Odyssey's face sagged, her skin gone milky white beneath the heavy makeup. She stabbed out her smoke, downed what remained of her scotch in one gulp, and shot up from her stool like it was on fire. "Come on," she said in a way that made it clear it wasn't a suggestion. "Come *on*. With me. Now."

The woman curled a hand around Kat's upper arm and gave it a yank, slightly digging in with her obscenely long nails, hot pink to match the shoes.

"Wait, I don't—"

"Look, either you come with me now, or we don't talk about Allie."

Kat opened her mouth for another retort, but the look she got from Odyssey told her it was now or never.

She chose now.

The women went together, quickly, from the bar, past the main stage, to a tacky, upholstered door toward the back of the club marked PRIVATE. Every step of the way, Turk Tolliver watched them from his station by the beaded curtain.

$$6$$

The moment the door to the dressing room closed all the way, Kat said, "Odyssey . . ."

"*Please* don't call me that. It's Beth."

"Beth," she corrected herself. "Okay. I'm here. I'm listening."

"Sit down," Beth said, gesturing at the ragged loveseat crammed between a filing cabinet and one of the makeup tables. Above it hung a poster for the movie *Faster, Pussycat! Kill! Kill!* Kat had never seen it, but like half the hip kids she knew, she usually lied and said she had whenever it came up. She half-wondered whether Beth had.

To Kat's immense relief, Beth pulled a tank top down over her boobs and sat down on a wooden stool across the cramped room. From the club, they could still hear the thumping bass beating like a gigantic heart behind Bel Biv Devoe's "Poison." The MC announced the impending entrance of a girl called Ravyn.

"She went by Velvet around here," Beth said at some length. "I'm guessing you're her sister. Katie?"

"Kat."

"Right. Sorry. She mentioned you a few times."

"That—that's nice to hear, actually," Kat said. Her eyes misted a little bit, but she fought back the tears. "But what happened . . ."

"I'm getting to that. She started here—I don't know—like, maybe three months ago? Three and a half? Todd didn't want to bring her in. Said she had 'sad eyes,' like this is supposed to be fuckin' Disneyland or some shit. Anyway, she was shy, but she was good. She looked good. The dumbass customers liked her, anyway, which is all it really comes down to, right?"

"Sad eyes," Kat said, casting her own to the ragged, cigarette-burned rug at her feet. "Yeah, that sounds like Allie."

"It's her," Beth said. "We talked. Real talk, not just stripper bullshit. For what it's worth, I tried to give her the lay of the land, you know what I mean? What to do, what not to do, who to avoid. She got her a room next to mine, right over there at the Welcome Inn. I mean, it's a shit-heap, but there's worse places on the 'Pike, believe me."

"I appreciate you helping her out, but . . . "

"I know, I hear you. I talk too much, say too little. Least that's what my old man always told me, but he's in prison down in Bridgeport anyhow, so what the fuck does he know?"

"Allie," Kat reminded her.

"Yeah," Beth said. "Allie. Last she worked here was Wednesday night. Slow night, right? I guess guys actually go home to their wives on Wednesdays, I don't know. Sometimes we do theme nights, special events, that type of shit. Get a visiting porn star to dance. One time we had a midget. A midget! You believe that? She was good, too. Probably made a fuckin' grand in two hours."

"Beth, please."

Beth smirked. "Guess the old bastard was right about me, after all. Sorry. It was just a regular Wednesday night. No porn stars, no midgets. Just me and Velvet—*Allie*—oh, and Chastity, but she went home early, 'round eight, eight-thirty. Ridin' the cotton pony, you know what I mean?"

Kat tried not to audibly sigh. The woman was doing her a favor, talking to her like this, and so candidly, but Kat just wished she'd get to the point.

"So after that, by nine definitely, it was just her and me dancing up 'til last call. One of us on the main stage, the other at the backstage, then we'd swap every two songs. It would've killed me, only there were long stretches where nobody was really around, so we just sat around and bullshitted until some jagoff stumbled in again. I don't think I ended up with seventy-five bucks when it was all said and done, tell you the truth.

"Turk was working, I remember that. Bartender left early— Todd figured Turk could pour drinks if he was just standing around anyhow. So, closing time? Yeah, just the three of us. I got cleaned up, cashed out, and waited at the bar for Allie; see, we always walked over to the motel together, ever since I got her the room. Except she never came back out of the dressing room. I went to check on her and she wasn't there. Turk turned the fuckin' place upside down, but nothing. One minute she was back there getting ready to go home, next minute gone like a fart in the wind." Beth snapped her fingers, startling Kat a little.

"What do you mean, gone?"

"I'll put it this way," Beth said, lighting another cigarette. The woman smoked like they paid her to do it. "Take a look around—how many doors you see?"

Kat looked up for a second, wondering if it was a riddle, but when she did look around, the meaning was clear. There was, in fact, only the one door in and out of the dressing room. Which meant if someone went in, there was only the same way out again.

"She disappeared," Kat said, "in this room?"

"I mean, she *couldn't* have. Right? But she went in, and—well, hell. She never came back out again."

"No, that can't—wait. Either she did come back out and you just missed it, or there is another way out of here. That's all there is to it. She didn't fucking *teleport* out of here, did she?"

"I didn't miss it," Beth insisted. "She would have had to get past Turk at the door, too. We sure as shit didn't both miss her. Plus, why would she sneak past us?"

"If she did, she would've had a good reason."

"I'm telling you, she couldn't have. She was in *here*—and then she wasn't."

Kat drew in a long breath and, smelling Beth's smoke, decided she'd have one of her own while she pondered what she'd been told so far. Mötley Crüe was blasting in the club and some fool was hooting and hollering at whomever happened to be on stage. It was next to impossible for Kat to imagine Allie—*her* Allie—up there, spinning around that pole with her tits out and hair teased up to heaven the way Beth's was. When she was a kid, Allie always had her hair hanging in her face like she was trying to hide, which she had been. She was always hiding, and now that Kat thought about it, she supposed that becoming Velvet was a way of hiding, too.

Question was, where was she hiding now?

"There's another way out of here," she said, mostly to herself.

"Come again?"

"If she didn't get past you and Turk, then that's the only answer. There's another way out of this room."

"Honey," Beth said matronly, "I've spent more time in this fuckin' room than almost anyone alive, and I'm telling you, there ain't."

Kat frowned and drew in another lungful of her cigarette. As she began to exhale, she watched with interest as the smoke pillared from her lips and gradually drifted toward the far corner, where a banged-up metal filing cabinet stood. She squinted, sucked in more smoke, and blew a cloud right at the filing cabinet. Again, some of the smoke broke away from the rising haze and drifted right down behind the big, black metal tower, seeping into the floor.

"Don't be so sure," Kat said, stabbing her smoke out in the ashtray.

"What are you . . . "

Beth fell silent and watched Kat cross the room, take the potted plant down from atop the filing cabinet, and then commence working it away from the corner inch by inch. The front right corner of the cabinet caught a snag in the rug and tore it open as she went, but neither woman much cared. A cockroach the size of a strawberry scattered once exposed to the light, which made Beth gasp, but Kat kept on until she managed to move the cumbersome thing a few feet away from the wall, exposing the corner where the rug was curled up and frayed at the edges. She cast a brief look back at Beth, then knelt to gingerly pinch the edge of the rug to peel it back.

A small cloud of dust kicked up from the filthy rug, which the two women ignored as they peered down to see what was underneath. Along with the dust and dirt, desiccated insect carcasses and mouse shit, was a pair of rusty metal hinges nailed into the floorboard. Kat pulled the rug further back to reveal what the hinges were for: a square hatch cut into the floor, hidden only by the carpet and filing cabinet. The hatch was maybe two and a half square feet, made of thick cedar, and so worn down by handling that the surface was smooth as though lacquered. It looked to Kat like it had been there for quite a long time, and that it had seen quite a lot of use.

Kat looked up at her new acquaintance and asked, "How about that?"

"Well," Beth said, "I'll be fucked in the ass."

Terry announced Odyssey twice before shrugging at Turk, who gave him the signal to move on to whomever came next in rotation, which happened to be Ravyn, who groused and grumbled all the way back to the stage because she'd just started her lunch break. Rascal's had two-dollar steaks most weekdays until five o'clock, and Ravyn's was going cold beneath a pond of store-brand steak sauce while she eyed it mournfully from behind the pole. As for Turk, he was considerably less concerned about the steak than he was about Odyssey. Ravyn ground it out for a pair of weekend warriors with their Harley Davidson t-shirts tucked into their jean shorts and fistfuls of crumpled dollar bills to the tune of "Joyride" by Roxette. Meanwhile, Turk scanned the room through narrowed eyes for any sign of Odyssey—or the other girl he'd nearly scared off in the parking lot. The two had latched onto each other like starving leeches, and he'd watched them sneak off together to the dressing room. *Odyssey's dealer,* he figured at the time, or else she played for the other team and he'd just never noticed. Neither seemed quite sufficient to make her miss her stage time though, so now Turk was growing suspicious.

Last time he'd seen someone go into that room and fail to come back out, nobody'd ever seen her again. The longer Ravyn's dance went on and the dressing room door stayed shut, the more concerned Turk got. He glanced around the club again, double-checking for any potential issues like handsy drunks or plain-clothes pigs hanging around, and when he was satisfied that things were under control, the bouncer made his way behind the main stage to the dressing room door. Velvet's sad eyes blinked wetly at him in his mind's eye, which made his chest feel too tight as he reached for the door handle.

It was locked. They weren't supposed to do that—house rules—except in the case of an emergency. If it weren't for that last clause, Todd would have had the deadbolt taken out altogether, but maybe the man wasn't *completely* inhuman. Still, if there was an emergency in or around Rascal's, Turk Tolliver figured he ought to be the first one to know about it, and nobody had told him shit.

"Goddamnit," he said. He tried the handle again, just in case, and when he found it was still locked, Turk made a face. "Goddamnit it all to hell."

The song ended, which brought Ravyn's dance to an end, so she gingerly made her way down the two steps from the stage to the floor in her four-inch heels to see if there was anyone in the place with twenty bucks to spend on a private dance. Instead, she found the bouncer walking backward, away from the dressing room door but still facing it, whereupon she said, "What are you—?"

The rest of her question got swallowed up by the noise and chaos of the huge man barreling back at the door, leading with his right shoulder, which he bashed against the door as hard as he could. The result, predictably, was the utter destruction of the door, all but smashed to splinters, not to mention a severely damaged frame from which bent nails and hinges hung at wild angles. Ravyn yelped, and somebody shouted over the music (wisely turned up by Terry, the MC), but Turk ignored it all. His focus was squarely centered on the little flap of frayed carpet he saw fall down over the far corner of the floor, where the filing cabinet was supposed to be.

"Aw, shit," he growled. "That ain't good. That *really* ain't good."

7

K at counted the iron rungs bolted into the wall as she climbed down, just in case it was information she might later need to know. There were in total thirteen of them, which struck her as ominous, though she conceded it was likely just coincidence. At the bottom, quite a lot of dirt and grit had collected on the floor, but the rungs were smooth and clean. She waited for Beth to join her, and while she waited she looked around with the pocket torch Beth had given her before they'd made the descent. To her left, with the ladder to her back, there was a series of steel shelves pushed up against the wall and laden with canned and jarred food, the ancient labels faded and peeling away. Soups, vegetables, condensed milk, alongside blankets, tools, soap, and enough toilet paper to last a decade. Further investigation revealed a first aid kit, a fire bucket full of sand, and a stack of moldering newspapers dating back to the 60s. Kat shook her head and said, "Huh."

"The hell is all this crap?" Beth said when she joined Kat at the bottom.

"Supplies. I think we're in an old bomb shelter."

"No shit? Oh, hey—some of these cans are older than I am."

"They all are. See?" Kat pointed down at the newspapers. The headline from the paper at the top of the stack read: DEATHS OF 3 APOLLO ASTRONAUTS SEVERE BLOW TO MOON PROGRAM. Beth whistled.

"Guess a lot of people had these back then."

"Sure," Kat agreed, "but under a strip bar?"

"Probably a regular bar back then. There's an apartment upstairs, above the club. It's just storage now, but it used to be people lived up there. Could be the owner was freaked out about the Russians, and all this shit just got left behind."

That much made sense enough, as far as Kat was concerned, but still did nothing to answer the question of Allie's whereabouts. It looked to her like the way down to the shelter was not completely forgotten. Somebody had been down there, and fairly recently. Could have been Allie, she supposed, but *then* what?

"Maybe," she thought out loud, "she just came down here to hide, then snuck back out later, after everyone was gone?"

"Hide from who?" Beth countered. "It was just me and Turk."

"You trust that guy?"

Beth barked a short laugh. "Baby," she said, "I don't trust nobody."

"Smart," Kat said. She figured a woman like her either got smart fast or ended up—she cut the thought short, following the weak light from the pocket torch as it vaguely illumined the rest of the room. There was an old metal desk, a couple of wooden chairs, and a Murphy bed that pulled down from the wall. On top of the desk was an emergency radio with a hand crank and an empty box marked .30-06—ammunition. Bullets.

"That's some serious ammo," Beth said.

Kat walked up to the desk. The box the bullets came out of looked as old as the cans on the shelves. She wondered if bullets expired. She also wondered why she was suddenly cold enough that a shiver rocked up her spine out of nowhere. The air seemed to bite at her exposed arms and neck, where before she'd felt perfectly warm. She glanced all around the tight space, leading with the flashlight and following with her eyes, and when that didn't yield any immediate answers, Kat dug out her Marlboros and fired one up.

"I thought *I* smoked like a chimney," Beth said.

"Hang on." Kat drew in slow, long drags and exhaled them into broad clouds of smoke and then shone her light on them. Drag after drag, cloud after cloud, in short time she filled the entire shelter with more smoke than a bowling alley on Saturday night.

Beth coughed and said, "You know, it's not real well-ventilated down here."

"Yeah, it is," Kat came back. "Look." She whipped the torch around to light up the Murphy bed in the wall; whatever smoke drifted near to its edges was blown back, as if by an invisible person fanning it away. Just like with the filing cabinet before, a little cigarette smoke went a long way toward progressing her little investigation. "Give me a hand."

She dropped the smoke to the concrete floor and ground it out with her shoe. The two women then stationed themselves on either side of the Murphy bed and pulled. At first, it appeared that it was nothing more than it appeared to be, a simple pull-down bed. But it didn't take much for Kat to see that there was indeed more to it—the frame that hugged the bed into the wall was itself built into a larger frame, and the entire contraption swung out on one side, just like a door.

"Holy shit," Beth said. "A secret goddamn passage? This is like an old Dracula movie."

"Too bad we don't got any garlic," Kat said. She paused for a moment to steel her nerves, then pushed beyond the bed-door to shine the pocket torch around what looked like a roughly hewn, utterly dark corridor. It seemed to have been tunneled right through the bedrock underneath Rascal's, as though by some massive machine. Then again, a massive machine drilling gigantic tunnels underneath a busy expressway wouldn't exactly go unnoticed, so Kat didn't really know what to think.

All the same, she went into the tunnel.

"Hey, wait—no, hold on," Beth stammered. "You can't go *in* there."

"Why not?"

"Because it's dangerous is why not! We don't know where that goes, or if it'll fall in on top of us. Christ, we don't even know what might *live* in there." She made a show of shivering all over. "Gives me the fuckin' creeps."

"If it was that fragile," Kat said, "it would have collapsed by now. And if Allie came this way, voluntarily or not, I'm checking it out. Beth, she's my sister."

"Yeah, I know."

"You don't have to come. You've done enough already, and I really appreciate it."

"Aw, shit," Beth growled. She pulled a face and sighed dramatically.

"What?"

"You know I can't let you do this alone."

Kat smiled. "Thanks."

"*Shit*," Beth reiterated.

Together, with Kat in the lead, they went into the cold, dark tunnel.

8

The clock radio bolted to the nightstand jumped to life at precisely 5:20pm, startling Brewster Ames awake with a squealing arena rock guitar solo. He supposed it was Foreigner or Boston or Journey or something like that; the man really didn't care for the stuff, which was why he'd chosen that station for his alarm. As soon as it went off, he couldn't wait to leap up and shut it off.

Once he restored blessed silence to his room, Brewster sat up on the edge of the bed and groaned. The fitted sheet was pulled halfway off and mostly soaked through with sweat, which meant another fitful, restless day of sleep. It seemed to him that every week his sleep got worse, his dreams uglier and more upsetting; ungodly things moving in the dark, his feet lodged in thick, sucking mud. A part of him was incredibly relieved whenever he woke up in the late afternoon to be done with all that, while another part was just disappointed that he'd woken up at all. But the predominant part of Brewster was really just hungover and thirstier than hell, so he killed off the can of Miller High Life he'd started before he'd fallen asleep and released a satisfying belch before hauling himself up to go piss.

His was the room directly adjacent to the front office at the Welcome Inn, included as part of his salary, and it was the only place Brewster had called home for going on three years. He could have counted the number of times he'd ventured beyond the Turnpike in the previous year on one hand if he wanted to, only he didn't want to. Truth was, there really wasn't much of anything he wanted or needed that he couldn't get within a half-mile radius, and anything else could most likely get delivered in a pinch. Most nights he subsisted on pizza from a New Haven style joint a couple

195

of traffic lights down the 'Pike, or else he had someone run some chicken wings or a two-dollar steak over to him from Rascal's. When he felt like a little company, he was already in the right place to find it. And when Brewster felt like a drink or three, he had only to cross the expressway to the packie next to the jack shack that masqueraded as a massage parlor.

Life, to Brewster Ames' eyes, was a pretty sweet fruit.

At least until he went from his room to the back office and heard the unmistakable sound of voices beneath him. Human voices. *Female* voices.

Someone was in the tunnel. He was certain of it.

"Aw, Christ."

Brewster poured himself a Styrofoam cup of the sludge that had been cooking in the coffee pot for days, and he went up to the front desk where Cal, one of the day-shifters, sat and yawned and scratched his balls.

"You look beat to shit," he told Cal.

"Probably hit it a little hard last night is all."

"Hair of the dog, my man," Brewster said. "It'll never fail ya." He gulped down some of the sludge and made a face.

"I don't know how you drink that shit."

"It's prescription," said the big man. "Say, why don't you go ahead and take off for the night. I got it here."

"No kidding?"

"Sure. You can owe me one next time I'm as bad off as you."

"Shit, Brewster," Cal said. "You're always worse off than me."

To that, Brewster shrugged. Maybe the kid was right. He didn't much care one way or the other. All he cared about in that moment was getting Cal out of there as quickly as possible so he could look into what was beginning to feel like a minor crisis. Nobody ever went down into the tunnel without Todd's explicit say-so, and Todd never said so without giving Brewster a heads up.

Cal didn't waste any time or wait around for Brewster to change his mind. He grabbed his Walkman, his car keys, and the book he was reading (a Western with a scowling gunslinger on the cover), and twenty-five seconds later, Brewster watched him pilot his little brown Dodge out of the parking lot and onto the 'Pike. And no sooner was Cal gone than Brewster picked up the phone and dialed the only number he had memorized, and yet went out of his way to avoid calling.

"Todd? Yeah, it's Brewster at the motel. Listen, man—I think maybe we got a problem."

The deeper into the corridor they went, the colder and wetter the air felt on their faces and arms. Kat wished she had her hoodie, which was crumpled up somewhere in her apartment, the weather having warmed in recent weeks. Behind her, Beth shivered and moaned about what a terrible, stupid thing it was they were doing. Her voice wasn't especially loud, but it echoed throughout the underground chamber, like reverb through concert speakers. Kat wished she'd be quieter but didn't want to say anything; she was lucky Beth was helping her at all. Indeed, without Beth's help so far, Kat wouldn't have been any better off than she'd been when she first headed down to the Turnpike.

Neither of them expected the tunnel to be quite as long as it was turning out to be. They were walking slowly, careful not to trip or get surprised by anything that might be down there, with Kat turning the light down to their feet and back up again in a measured rotation, covering as much space as she could with such a small flashlight. Still, it was sufficient to reveal the rebar rungs punched into the rocky wall to their left, some 100 feet or so in. They were just like the rungs they had climbed down to get into the bomb shelter, except these were rustier and appeared far less used. Kat very nearly missed them entirely, and even when she stopped to double-check, Beth goaded her to continue on.

"Come on, I don't want to hang out in here."

"Look."

The weak, diffused light fell on the rungs, which were eye-level to the women. Kat followed them up with the flashlight, to the top, where the last one hung about a foot below what looked to her like a round hatch of some sort, like in a submarine or maybe a sewer. Another way down.

Or up.

"What do you think?" Kat asked.

"What do I think? I think we should get the hell out of here and forget we ever found this fucking place."

Kat turned the light on Beth.

"Are you kidding me? You're telling me this is the only way my sister could possibly have gone, and you think I'm just going to give up now?"

"Not give up, exactly," Beth said, holding up a hand to shield her eyes from the light. "Just maybe think this through before jumping in headfirst, you know what I mean?"

"You mean call the cops?"

"Cops! Christ, no. You know what cops'll do? Turn Rascal's upside down, run in anybody they feel like, maybe close the place down and put a lot of people out of work. You think the motels around here give a girl a chance when she's behind on rent? 'Cause they don't. Jesus, no. Cops just make everything worse."

"Yeah," Kat reluctantly agreed. "I guess so."

"Trust me," Beth continued. "Maybe the police protect and serve where you live, but here on the 'Pike?" The dancer just raised her eyebrows to punctuate her point.

Kat nodded. "All right. But that just leaves us right back where we started. I'm *not* going to just walk away, Beth. If you need to, I understand. But I'm keeping on. I have to find Allie."

Beth looked from Kat's face to the dark corridor still stretching on in front of them, then back again. Her brow compressed into a network of worry lines and she seemed to deflate a little.

"I'm sorry, Kat, but . . . "

"It's okay. You don't—you don't owe me nothing, Beth. But you sure did a lot anyway. Thanks." She gently rested a hand on the dancer's shoulder. "Oh, and if I don't come back up again?"

"I'll be waiting," Beth said.

Kat wasn't sure if it was appropriate to hug the woman, but she went ahead and did so anyway. Beth hugged her back, and whispered into Kat's ear, "Be careful, for Christ's sake."

Kat began to answer that she would but fell silent at the sound of a thump coming from the entrance they'd come down. The thump was followed by a low voice, too far away to understand but loud enough to hear. Both women went rigid.

Beth said, "Shit—Turk."

"The bouncer?"

"We gotta go."

"But I thought—"

Pulling away from Kat's embrace, Beth bolted for the rungs on the corridor's wall and leapt up to the second from the bottom before commencing her climb up to the hatch. She only made it another three or four rungs before that, too, thumped, followed by the earsplitting squeal of metal on metal as the hatch began to open above them.

Beth jumped back down, grabbed Kat by the upper arm, and yanked hard.

"Let's go. Hurry!"

Her heart suddenly hammering against her ribs, Kat's blood turned hot as she fought the panic rising inside her. She fell in step with Beth, who was already sprinting headlong into the darkness. She could only think of one thing: that they'd already been found out, or else they wouldn't be coming in from two different directions at the same time. They were already found, and it was only a matter of time before they caught up to them, whoever *they* were and whatever *they* wanted. Her only hope lay in whatever awaited them in the pitch black ahead, the end of the corridor, and that did very little to comfort Kat's frayed nerves.

The lyrics to "Black Rings" involuntarily reverberated inside her head, an unwanted soundtrack to accompany the noises of men climbing down into the subterranean filth and shadows to come after them.

"Don't let anyone tell you
When enough gets to be enough
We're more than just their things
We scream into black rings . . ."

Listening to her own song in her mind was all she could do *not* to scream, whether she was in a black ring or not. It didn't much help matters that she wondered whether she'd ever sing the song again, or if her last gig really was the last one. For all Kat knew, she had only moments left to live, which would mean dying without ever knowing what happened to her sister.

"Fuck that," she said aloud. Beth hushed her. Kat winced at her own stupidity, making noise like that, but shook it off and went deeper into the corridor with Beth.

Someone hollered, "Hello?" Kat figured it was probably Turk, though she wasn't sure. Keeping the light low, she spotted a pile of old wooden crates, half-toppled over, against the wall to their right. They were all busted up and the slats were rotting through, but it was the only place to hide she'd found so far, so she hurried to crouch down behind it. Beth quickly followed suit.

Once they were hidden, Kat switched off the pocket torch. Her shoe knocked against one of the old crates; a couple of bottles within loudly clinked against one another. Beth hissed at her. "*Shh!*"

"Anybody there?"

Almost too quietly to hear, Beth whispered into Kat's ear, "Gimme one of them bottles."

Without waiting around to find out why she wanted one, Kat grabbed the first one she touched and passed it over. The glass was coated with dust, like it had been down there for years; as soon as Beth had the bottle, Kat wiped her hands on her jeans.

A cloud of dusty yellow light, much brighter than the light from the pocket torch Kat had been using, drifted over the crates. Footsteps and heavy breathing accompanied the light as it grew brighter, closer. Kat felt like she could hear her own heartbeat pounding and almost worried that Turk could hear it, too. Half a second later, she had bigger things to worry about.

Beth launched to her feet and cried out, "Hey, Turk!"

Turk said, "Who—" But he was cut short when Beth hurled the bottle at him, which collided with the side of his head and smashed to pieces, knocking the huge man to the ground with a surprisingly high-pitched wail. The tangy odor of stale booze filled the stagnant air as Turk rolled over a hundred shards of broken glass, which crunched beneath his weight.

"Jesus!" Kat said.

Once again, she was grabbed and yanked by Beth, only not in the direction Kat expected. Rather than hurrying past the stunned bouncer on the ground and rushing for the ladder back up to the Rascal's dressing room, Beth pulled them both still deeper into the underground corridor. With her flashlight off, Kat was running blind. She tried to keep her hands out in front of her, lest she run face-first into a wall, but it wasn't a wall she needed to worry about. Instead, the floor disappeared from underneath her.

She simply took a step that wasn't there and dropped like a stone into open air. The fall only took about three and a half seconds, but to Kat it seemed like much longer. And when she landed, it was much softer than she expected. Still, pain radiated through her. In short order her shoulders, back, tailbone and knees began barking at her from the pain of the impact, but she hadn't splatted like a watermelon the way she expected she would. Rather,

Kat was still very much alive, and as far as she could tell, she hadn't even broken anything.

A minor miracle, but not one she had time to enjoy. Somewhere above her, light started to glow faintly, and somebody was coughing.

No—*laughing.*

"Buh—Beth?" Her voice was barely above a hushed croak, her head swimming from the disorientation of falling into a place she couldn't even see. "Beth!"

"I'm here, honey."

"I fell—I fell . . . someplace. I don't know. Shit, where's the light?"

"Here's one," Beth said, her tone oddly merry.

Above Kat, the light grew brighter, more focused, as it was shone down onto her. She squeezed her eyes shut from the sudden brightness, but quickly adjusted and took a quick look around her. What she'd fallen onto was a pile of old mattresses—very old, by the look and smell of them, and spotted with dark stains she didn't want to think about. It was nauseating, but she had to admit it had saved her life.

The drop-off in front of her wasn't sheer and didn't look to Kat like it had been carved out by a machine the way the corridor had. It was rugged and craggy, dripping opaque water the way it did in caverns she'd seen, like Twin Lakes in Salisbury. Only this wasn't any tourist trap; it was just a big, cold, dark chamber she didn't want to be in and didn't know how to get out of.

"Can you see if there's anything to drop down to me? Like a rope, or maybe the sheets from that Murphy bed?"

"Oh, I don't think I can do that, Kat," Beth called back.

"Why? Is it Turk? Oh, no . . . "

"No, Turk's out cold. I think that bottle really fucked the poor bastard up. I wouldn't be surprised if he wakes up even dumber than he was before I hit the stupid son of a bitch. 'Course, I haven't checked his pulse—maybe he won't wake up at all. Couldn't tell ya. Anyway . . . " The light moved away from Kat, drifted up and out of the massive pit she was in, and settled on the heads and shoulders of two figures peering down at her—Beth, and an obese man Kat had never seen before. "It's been fun, *chica,* but I still got work to do before the night's done, so I'm gonna leave you to Brewster, here."

The fat man grinned and wiggled his fingers in a creepy, childlike wave.

"Hiya," he said.

"Oh my God," said Kat.

"No," Brewster said. "Not here. God can't see down here. Sorry."

Beth chuckled lightly at that and, handing the flashlight back to the big guy, turned on her heel and went back the way she'd come. Brewster was still grinning like an idiot, having the time of his life seeing a complete stranger so frightened and helpless before him. Kat couldn't tell if she was more scared or angry, but she was plenty of both.

The man licked his lips and said, "You hungry, darlin'?"

Caught off-guard by that, she said, "What?"

"Shut up," Brewster shot back. "I wasn't talking to *you*."

"You weren't . . . " she began, but stopped as she grasped the implication of what he'd said.

She wasn't alone down there. And something was beginning to stir in the darkness.

9.

Big Todd Foligno sat behind the wheel of his lime-green convertible Mazda MX-5, a Camel in his mouth, the radio tuned to the country station, and a lot lizard who called herself Randee working over his cock from the passenger seat. He'd picked her up outside the Luv's where Newington ended and Berlin began, right off the 'Pike, with a vague assurance that he'd take her off the street if she was willing to impart a favor or two for the trouble. This was her first favor, and by Todd's reckoning, she wasn't half bad. Then again, she didn't exactly look to him like this was her first rodeo, so he presumed his was merely one in a long line of pricks that had been so satisfactorily serviced in the shadow of the truckstop. He figured there probably wouldn't be any harm in putting her on the second stage on the day shift for a while, throw her the occasional free drink and keep her on the string until he grew tired of her. Of course, if she kept up this pace, he might not tire for a while, yet. The lady was a pro.

When Randee finished—or, rather, Todd did—she rinsed her mouth with a travel bottle of Scope from her purse and spit it out in the parking lot. After that, the two of them sat together for a moment in silence, smoking and listening to Patty Loveless expressing her incredulousness at falling in love. Neither of them knew that they were both thinking what a crock of shit that was. Neither of them said anything or moved to change the station, either. Just a quiet moment of afterglow for him, and for her, a silent anxiety about when she was going to get to leave.

The moment was interrupted, however, when Todd's car phone began to chirp obnoxiously. A bag phone he'd gotten for a song from a fence he knew up in Torrington, Todd only really kept it in the car for show, but once in a while one of his employees rang him

203

up when the idiots couldn't figure something out on their own. It always irritated him, but then again, he was the one who gave them the number—strictly for emergencies. He picked it up and said, "This better be good."

"Todd?" said the strained voice on the other end. "Yeah, it's Brewster at the motel. Listen, man—I think maybe we got a problem."

"Talk to me."

"It's—well, I think there's somebody down there. In the tunnel, I mean."

"Somebody? Who?"

"I don't know. I just heard voices is all."

"You're hearing voices now?"

"I'm serious, Todd. There's somebody in there, and I don't think anybody's supposed to be."

"Jesus Christ," Todd groused. "I can't get my goddamn piston polished without some fucker ruining the party, can I? Look into it. I'll be there in five."

"On it, boss."

The line went dead, and Todd put the phone back in the bag. Beside him, Randee flicked the remains of her smoke into the grass growing up through the cracks in the pavement and said, "Who ruined your blowie, baby?"

"Somebody who's gonna wish to hell they didn't," Todd said.

A fraction of a second after Turk opened his eyes, he practically slammed them shut again. The harsh fluorescent light from the ceiling drilled into his skull like steel screws, which in turn made his stomach lurch. He tried to roll over onto his side so that he could vomit, but his muscles refused to obey. Instead, he fought it back, swallowing the upchuck before it made it all the way into his mouth. The acidy bile burned his throat, but he figured it might take his mind off the agony everywhere else in his body, so it wasn't all bad.

After a few more minutes, he was able to gradually open his eyes again. When his hazy vision cleared enough, Turk determined that he was laid out on the loveseat in the dancers' dressing room, his legs hanging down over one of the arms. The last thing he remembered was seeing that Odyssey had discovered the old nuke bunker under the club, which was more or less top secret according to his boss, Todd. The thing had been built under there back in the 60s when Rascal's was just a regular singles bar called Marcy May's, before Todd bought the place sometime in the late 70s or early 80s. The boss used to store booze down there but at some point decided it was off limits. Turk didn't know of anyone other than him who'd ever even seen it, so when he saw the hatch standing wide open, he was alarmed. Odyssey shouldn't have even been aware of its existence, never mind climbed down into the goddamned thing.

He was worried she'd get in trouble, or worse, hurt. But no—it wasn't her who got hurt, was it? It was him. Turk's head throbbed and he felt hot, sharp pain in his neck and arms. He tried to sit up, but it was no good. Not yet. Instead, he raised his head a few inches and took a look at his arms, which were sliced to shit and punched through with tiny bits of green glass that sparkled in the harsh fluorescent light.

The bottle.

Somebody hit him with a bottle, a big one, like a magnum of champagne or something. Enough to knock him out.

"Odyssey," he croaked. But why?

And how the hell had she hauled his ass back up those rungs to the dressing room? Clearly, she hadn't. She couldn't have; she clocked in at maybe half his weight, tops. No, that girl had help.

"Brewster," Turk growled. Now he was getting mad.

Getting mad got him thrown out of the service. Getting mad got him divorced, as well as zero contact with his son. Getting mad was why the only job he could hold down was throwing drunks and creeps out of a T&A bar on the Turnpike.

But for all the grief his own anger had brought down on him over the years, getting mad was exactly what Turk Tolliver needed in that moment. It got him up from the loveseat, and in short time, it got him on his feet. He stomped over to the nearest makeup table and bent down to see his face and scalp, much of which was littered with small slivers of glass that sparkled in the lights that framed the mirror. One by one, he plucked the shards out, dropping them onto the table in a widening puddle of his own blood. After that, he gingerly shrugged out of his shirt and went to work on the glass in his shoulder, arm, and side. When he was satisfied that he'd gotten out all of it that he could without medical intervention, Turk busted open the first aid kit and set to pouring stinging alcohol all over the hundred tiny wounds that plagued him, after which he bandaged up with every last inch of gauze in the kit. Digging through some drawers, he found a bottle of Percocet, knowing full well at least two of the regular dancers never went on stage without it. Turk dry-swallowed a handful of them and put the bottle back where he'd found it.

He felt substantially better than he had when first he woke, but he was still mad. Plenty mad.

And if he was being honest with himself, that felt pretty goddamned good, too.

"Brewster," Turk said again. He stormed back out of the dressing room, slamming the door behind him, and didn't let anything or anyone get in his way en route to the Welcome Inn.

* * *

To celebrate his unexpected bounty, Brewster Ames put in a couple of calls to arrange for a pair of chicks to meet him at Room 101 of the Welcome Inn at precisely midnight, whereupon he intended to put up the sign (CLERK AWAY TEMPORARILY—BE RIGHT BACK!) and direct his new friends to freely explore one another while he watched with keen interest from his chair in the corner. This was always how he handled that sort of thing, watching but never touching, and he supposed it was always going to be his modus operandi. Fact was, the first time Brewster heard about AIDS a decade earlier was the last time he ever put his prick in a stranger. That shit terrified him to no end, and he wasn't about to end up the way all those homos down in the City did, wasting away in hospital hallways for the price of getting off. He was just as happy to watch and pull his pud as he ever was pumping away on top of some broad he picked up at the truckstop. In some ways, it was even better.

Life was a pretty sweet fruit, all right. Yet as much as he was looking forward to that little slice of heaven, Brewster was almost more excited to see the look on Todd's face when he found out everything was already taken care of. The girl, whoever the hell she was, wouldn't be bothering anybody anymore, and Brewster had a sneaking suspicion that if Turk woke up at all, he'd be brain-damaged for the rest of his life from the clobbering Odyssey had given the big bastard. If he'd had his 'druthers, he would have dragged Turk to the pit and rolled him over to join Kathy or Katie or whatever the fuck her name was. Two for one. But that was against the rules. Todd's rules.

Women only. Brewster never knew why, and until today, he'd never cared much anyway. Seemed a shame, though. Todd would take care of Turk, to be sure, but it sure would've been sweet to give him that medicine down there. He never got to see it, but he heard it a time or two, and though he'd never admit it to anyone including himself, he sometimes had nightmares about it. Sometimes it gave him the creeps just walking around the motel and knowing it was down there, practically right beneath his feet. But if it was Tolliver? He was sure he'd have the sweetest dreams of his life if he'd had *that* chance.

The MX-5 squealed into the Welcome Inn parking lot at a quarter to seven, its boss stereo system bumping as Todd turned a wide arc on the macadam and came to a screeching stop right in front of the office. He had a honey in the passenger seat, to whom he tossed a key on a plastic fob for whichever room he was going to let her use, and once she was on her way, Todd made for the lobby.

The moment he was through the front door, he said, "Talk."

"It's taken care of," the fat man said with a self-satisfied grin. "Not a thing to worry about."

"You stupid fuck," Todd spat. "Nothing gets *taken care of* 'til I take care of it, you get me?"

"Well, sure, but . . ."

"Is there somebody in the pit?"

"I—well, yeah, there's somebody in the pit. This nosy broad, came 'round asking questions, and you know . . ."

Todd bum-rushed the front desk, picked up the guestbook, and hurled it at Brewster, who caught it by the spine against his left eye. Pages ripped free and flew everywhere as the big man went down like he'd been shot. The book opened up the skin beneath his eyebrow, which spilled blood directly into the eye below it. Brewster howled, clawing at the wound and his stinging eyeball.

"Nothing gets taken care of 'til I take care of it!" Todd roared down at him.

Brewster made a whining sound and stayed put. The blood was beginning to seep between his fingers.

The boss walked around the desk, stepped over his bleeding employee, and went through the door to the back office. When he reached the refrigerator up against the back wall, he rolled it out of the way and peeled back the rug to reveal the hatch in the floor— identical in all respects to the one in the Rascal's dressing room. There, he paused and listened. The idiot on the floor out there said he'd heard voices, but Todd didn't hear a thing apart from the occasional low moan or groan from Brewster.

"Shut up!" Todd shouted.

Still nothing. It didn't matter. Whether he liked it or not, the dumb fat bastard had forced his hand. Him and whoever the hell the girl down there was. There just wasn't any getting around it.

Todd was going to have to perform the ritual, and he was going to have to do it right away.

10

Whenever she thought she'd surely dried up, run out of tears to shed, Kat learned that the wellspring was eternal and she would always start weeping all over again. She thought about the phrasing of that—shedding tears—which made her think of snakes shedding their scales or spiders shedding their exoskeletons. Maybe people needed to shed their tears in the same way, in order to grow and go on living. It was a sweet thought, but inapplicable. Kat knew perfectly well she wasn't going to go on living. She was going to die in this pit, same as her sister undoubtedly did; it was merely a question of when.

Having crawled onto the soiled, stinking mattresses to the closest wall, she pressed herself up against the craggy, seeping rock like she was trying to melt into it. The hollow sound of water dripping somewhere rang loudly throughout the pit, as did vague scuttling that may have accounted for any number of subterranean creatures Kat didn't want to think about. But it was whatever occasionally moved at the farthest end of the massive hole that concerned her most. Unlike the rats or bats or whatever else was down there, it neither scuttled nor skittered about; it remained largely still and silent, except for when it shifted its weight or released a wheezy, whistle-like exhalation. Whatever in hell it was, she was close to certain that it was bigger than a rat. A *lot* bigger.

"There was a man from Wisconsin," came a voice in the darkness—it startled Kat into a mewling yelp that embarrassed her almost as much as the voice frightened her. She made herself flatter still against the rugged stone wall and breathed shallowly, lest she give away her position. "He was what they used to call a *naturalist*. Went all over Asia, found the first dinosaur egg fossils anybody ever dug up. Pretty famous in his day." The owner of the voice cleared his throat, which was followed by the familiar sound of a lighter flicking to life. Kat glanced straight up and caught the faint edge of the glow directly above her. The speaker stood at the edge of the precipice, where Kat had been pushed by Beth.

"Anyway, our boy headed into Mongolia—this was back in the 1920s, you understand—and became the first person from the outside to hear all about something every man, woman, and child in the country had known about all their lives. A goddamn monster, living in the Gobi Desert, that killed anything—and *anybody*—that came anywhere near the fuckin' thing. The goddamned prime minister of the country told him about the monster, and he never talked to anybody in Mongolia that didn't believe it. Several folks had seen it with their own eyes. And you know something? *He* believed it. To his dying day, he knew those people weren't just fucking with the foreigner, telling bullshit stories. It was *real*."

Kat couldn't identify the voice. It didn't sound like the fat man who had been up there before, and she was sure it wasn't Turk. This was somebody new, somebody she'd never met before. And based on what little nuggets of truth must have been mixed up with the horseshit Beth had fed her, Kat had a pretty good idea of just who he was, too.

"Todd?" she called up from the pit.

He just snickered, but she took it as verification. It was him, all right.

"England, Ireland, Scotland, much of Northern Europe . . . there's been stories just like it for *millennia,* my dear. The worm of Linton, the Sockburn, the Lambton worm, the Laidley worm, the Stoor worm. Accounts, fairy tales, poems, fuckin' songs. Some said they were actually dragons, but the truth, the honest to goddamned fuck reality of the thing, is that they were all the same damned thing. More or less. Same thing Ctesias describes in India fifteen hundred years ago, which he said was seven cubits long. That's more than ten feet, and he said there were much bigger ones, too. I'm telling you, kiddo, there's just no escaping these fucking things once you start looking!"

"What in the blue *fuck* are you talking about, *Todd?*" She spat out his name like it was an especially obscene expletive. It even tasted obscene in her mouth.

"I didn't know about *any* of this shit until this place, of course.

That's all my own research, by the way. Libraries really are the goddamn best. Christ, I didn't know *what* to think first time I saw it! But then, nobody ever does."

The keening wheeze of the thing across the pit from her returned, almost a whine, followed by wet, plopping noises like rotten fruit falling from branches and bursting against the ground. With that, the thing began to move, a slow, sloughing that sounded to Kat like it was dragging itself over the ground with no small effort. She had barely processed any of the ravings emanating from the madman lingering above her, but some of it was beginning to alight in her mind as the terror gradually began to take hold, a cold hand closing around her heart.

"What did you do, Todd?"

"I think it's waking up," he said, his tone giddy.

"What did you *do?*"

"They tried to kill it. Do you know that? Some of them did. But never me. I don't know how old it is, but I know it's at least a hundred, maybe more. It could be a thousand years old, for all I know. I got to respect that, girlie. I got to *respect* it. Because I know they were here first. Before us. Before the world *we* made. I don't think there's many left, but they're still here, baby. Still here, and still as by-God hungry as they ever were."

"God damn you," Kat wailed into the tightening darkness, "what the fuck *is it?*"

Todd snickered. "See for yourself."

She could hear him walking away, and before she had much of a chance to puzzle over what he meant, a loud crunch echoed out through the tunnel and a series of floodlights exploded to life around the periphery of the pit's edge. In an instant, the world went stark white, blinding Kat, who squeezed her eyes shut but nonetheless saw bursting stars going supernova on the insides of her eyelids. Still, she didn't dare keep them closed long, so she forced herself to face the light until her eyes began to clear— whereupon she found herself focusing in on a pile of gray bones not three yards from her feet.

The bones were worn, broken, some more black than gray, but there was no mistaking them. They were bones, all right, and worse still, almost definitely human. They rose up from a heap of black sludge like the dead rising from the soil, but Kat knew that wasn't soil, not exactly. It was shit. A gigantic mound of shit, which meant that the bones had to have been eaten before they were excreted. Bones that she freely and horrifyingly assumed were still inside the people who owned them whenever that happened. Eaten by Todd's bizarre obsession, the nonsense he was babbling about Mongolia and India and . . .

Her vision further restored, Kat's mind blanked upon noticing a second pile of shit and bones. And then a third. It was a goddamned ossuary. And she wasn't alone in it.

At the opposite side of the pit, the direction from which she had heard that awful shuffling, sloughing noise, a hole gaped from the rocky side wall—a tunnel within a pit within a tunnel. Her nostrils filled with the earthy odor of petrichor and something far less pleasant; tangy and rotten, the stench of death. Fear gripped her, and she began to feel dizzy, faint. It was coming. Whatever it was, it was coming. And nobody even knew where she was.

Above her, Todd began chanting, his voice cracking.

"Skōlex! Minhocão! Olgoi-khorkhoi! Wake and feast! Skōlex! Minhocão! Olgoi-khorkhoi! Wake and feast!"

11

Turk never did care much for Todd, and he would have a hard time believing anybody really did. He was a smarmy, slippery little son of a bitch with zero self-awareness and even less regard for anybody who didn't happen to be himself. In other words, he was perfect for the 'Pike, and the 'Pike was the best place for a scumfuck like Todd to thrive.

Still, whatever the hell was going on underneath Rascal's seemed beneath even the likes of him, and Turk knew for a fact that the bastard eyed every single girl who auditioned for him as future motel bed fodder for his side hustle across the way, at the Welcome Inn. Though he was sure the nasty little motor lodge got its share of actual travelers just looking for a few winks before they got back on the road, the place was little more than a low rent brothel where half the dancers at Rascal's ended up when they burned out.

Now, he reckoned both the club and the motel were used for much, much worse than that. And nobody but Todd could be behind it all.

But why the fuck didn't they just kill me?

It was a solid question, and one he planned on asking Todd— and Odyssey—personally. But first, he had a pretty good idea of who he was going to have to deal with before any of that, and if Turk Tolliver was being honest with himself, he was sincerely looking forward to it.

Brewster Ames was laid back in his wicker chair as far back as it would go without upending him, crushing a blood-infused wad of paper napkins against the gash above his eye and groaning like a sorrowful ghost. He was so wrapped up in himself and his anguish, that he didn't even notice someone walk through the front door from the darkening, blue-black evening outside and approach the front desk with purpose, nor that it was probably the last person on Earth he'd ever want to see. Fact was, Tolliver reminded Brewster of every lunkhead jock in high school who'd ever kicked his ass or humiliated him in front of a gaggle of girls. That was enough in and of itself for the fat man to loathe the bouncer on principal, despite Turk having nothing whatsoever to do with any of that. Tolliver felt just as warmly about Ames, and there was never a time when either of them was happy to see the other. With his head throbbing and eyebrow still gushing blood into a wad of brown napkins, Brewster was even less happy than usual about the situation, once he bothered to notice the intrusion.

"The *fuck* do you want, Turk?"

A small, cheap, white and pink ceramic vase stood on the front desk between them, with a single, wilting tulip leaning out of it. Turk picked it up, regarded it for a fleeting moment, and then hurled it with his full strength at Brewster's head. The vase exploded into a thousand tiny shards at the point of impact, which happened to be an inch or two above his left eye. The tulip's head snapped from the stem and dropped to the floor, after which Brewster collapsed on top of the flower, both hands to his bleeding forehead and howling like a coyote caught in a bear trap.

"You sumbitch!" he hollered. "You goddamned big sumbitch motherfu—"

It only took Turk a few quick strides to move around the desk and over to Brewster, who he seized by the front of his shirt and lifted up from the floor. The injured man rapidly blinked his eyes, which filled with blood from both sides, clearly terrified.

"Listen to me, Ames," Turk boomed. "And listen good, or I'll make you wish you had. Where is the girl that came into my bar tonight? Where's Odyssey? What the fuck is going on in that bomb shelter? Open your mouth and start giving me answers or I'll open it for you and start taking teeth."

Brewster sputtered. Turk slapped him with an open hand, then squeezed his jaw so that his mouth was forced open. It was enough.

"No—wait. Wait! They're underground. The girl, anyway. And Todd. They're in the pit, man—they're in the pit!"

Turk didn't like the sound of that, and he assumed a disgusted expression to show it. "What," he said slowly and clearly, "is the *pit?*"

He didn't know much, just what Todd had told him over the years, but it was more than enough to make the hair on Turk's neck stand up, even if he wasn't altogether sure he believed a word he was hearing.

"I dunno what the fuckin' thing is, man," Brewster whined, his brow crumpled beneath the huge bandages he'd stuck to his matching wounds. "I only ever caught like a little glance at it one time, but I'll tell you one thing for sure: it's *huge.* And to hear Todd tell it, it's been down there for a long, long time. Like a hundred, two hundred years. I dunno."

"In the pit."

Brewster nodded. "Yeah. I mean, the 'Pike's been here a long time, and folks got to building, and somebody or 'other musta found it down there, built up on top of it. Todd got this place and the club from his uncle, and I think it was the uncle built the bomb shelter, to sorta hide it, like."

"Hide *what*, Ames?"

Turk loomed over him, threatening in his body language. Brewster recoiled in his chair.

"Todd says it's a worm, man! A big fuckin' worm! Jesus Christ, Turk, he practically *prays* to the goddamned thing!"

Tolliver stepped back, his mouth trying to ask more questions but his mind spiraling at the bizarre answers he'd received so far. A secret underground pit? A giant, ancient worm? And a second-rate titty bar owner and pimp who worshipped it . . .

All he could think to say now was, "What the fuck."

"Man," Ames said, "somebody's been feeding that monster for a lot of years. Long before any of us was here. I was you, I'd just walk away, Turk. I mean it, just walk—"

Turk lunged, pushed Brewster so that the chair tipped back and spilled him out onto the floor again. The clerk yelped, fearful of the beating to follow, but Tolliver had other plans. From where he now stood, he had a direct line of sight through the cracked door to the back office, where Ames hadn't bothered to cover up the hatch in the concrete floor underneath the pulled-up carpet. Just like in the dressing room back at Rascal's.

Only this time, he wasn't going to get caught with his drawers down. This time, Turk was climbing down with his eyes wide open—but not before taking the break-action, sawed-off shotgun he also spied, suspended by hooks drilled into the underside of the desk beside the hatch. The gun looked older than he was, and he could only hope the two shells already loaded into it were better than birdshot, but at least he wasn't going to make that descent empty-handed again.

Turk just hoped two shells would be enough.

12

"Wake and feast!**"** Almost more than anything, Kat Garrido sincerely wished Todd would just shut the complete and absolute fuck up. The situation was maddening enough without his eerie chanting up there at the lip of the pit, which she suspected was at least a tiny bit more than just one lunatic's personal brand of insanity. Whether or not he thought he was invoking some kind of ritual magic, one thing all that shouting was sure to do was alert—and possibly agitate—the creature stirring from the far side of the light-flooded hole. Though she had no way of knowing if it knew she was in here yet, it was only a matter of time. Minutes, Kat reckoned, or maybe just seconds.

"It's here," Todd bellowed, his voice cracking with pleasure. "It was *always* here. Before us, before the fucking Turnpike. It'll be here long after all of us are dead—well, you'll be dead in a few minutes, but you know what I mean."

He broke into a fit of girlish giggles.

Kat fought back tears. A part of her wanted to just curl up on one of those filthy mattresses, weep, and wait for the end. Instead, she desperately scanned the walls of the pit, looking for any way up and out. Finding none, she felt the blackness of despair creep over her like a cold wind. It only grew colder when she finally admitted to herself that she did, finally, know what had happened to Allie. Some of the bones piled up around the periphery of the pit were undoubtedly hers; all that remained of an imperfect, frustrating, beautiful sister to whom Kat would never speak again, with whom she would never commiserate or celebrate again. She felt torn in half, left to bleed out underneath the world that would never understand the fate of the Garrido sisters. Disappeared. Lost. Sad, but what can you do?

"No," she rasped. "Fuck that. Fuck *that*."

She stood up, ramrod straight, and stepped away from the wall, away from the stinking mattresses. Whatever it was that was coming for her, Kat meant to stand up to it. She meant to die fighting, not cowering. She was not going to go down easy.

"Come on, you motherfucker," she growled. "*COME ON!*"

With both hands squeezed into dense fists at her sides, Kat steeled herself and kept her wide, unblinking eyes on the tunnel in the wall of the pit.

An instant later, the thing began to writhe its way out, into the light.

The worm—if one could accurately call it that—was gargantuan, bigger even than Kat's terrified imagination had suggested. The head of the beast had the diameter of a traffic circle at its widest juncture, narrowing down to a cone-like maw that twitched and trembled as it worked its way out of the burrow. At least five yellow and black antennae jabbed and probed around the mouth of the burrow from the top and sides of the creature's head, picking up the slack for an apparent lack of any eyes by feeling out the immediate environment. Once the enormous head was out in the open, the tip of the cone began to split open in three equal parts, hooked prongs from which two sets of pale mandibles sprang, spilling an opaque gunge onto the pit floor as they unfurled and began snapping at the air. All around the base of the head were hundreds, if not thousands, of spiny protrusions that wiggled anxiously like a living collar. In the wake of this came the segmented body of the tremendous worm, each yellowish section oozing still more mucus as the beast writhed out into the open, snapping its massive mandibles at the humid subterranean air.

Kat said, "Oh my fucking God."

"You're goddamned right it's a god," Todd shouted back at her. "Now get on your knees."

"Eat shit, Todd."

"Whatever," the maniac pimp pouted. "You're going to die, either way."

From the undulating craw of the impossible monster before her, a squealing hiss erupted, which was accompanied by a jet of yellow liquid that sprayed the wall. The liquid filled the stagnant air with a fetid odor, a rotting stink that made Kat gag and try to hold her breath to no avail. She was just going to have to breathe and hope she didn't vomit.

To that end, she steeled her focus and, to a lesser extent, her nerves, and cast her eyes about the bright, filthy, reeking arena—because what else could it be, but a spectator sport for a single, demonic spectator?—for something, *anything*, she might use to defend herself. She hoped for hefty rocks she could launch at the worm, but there were none. She considered trying to pry springs from one of the mattresses, but the notion was impractical at best. In fact, all that Kat could really see anywhere around her were bones, bones, and more gray, stripped bones.

So, Kat seized a bone. A femur, if she had to guess. Maybe eighteen inches long, not much more than half a pound. It was a poor weapon, but it was all she had at hand. She practiced swinging it, then smacked the head of it against her palm. Dissatisfied with its heft, the panic began to well up in her chest again. *Drop the bone, Kat*, the panic pleaded with her. *Give up. It's over.*

Tears spilled from her eyes, cutting gutters through the dirt and grime caking her cheeks. She began to release her grip on the femur, but then thought better of it. Instead of dropping it, she held it by the knobby head and batted it, hard, against the rocky wall beside her. The bone cracked, so she did it again, and then again after that, lengthening the break. Kat then raised her right knee and, holding the femur by both ends, brought it down against her patella. It took three tries for this, too, but on the third the thing finally split, turning one blunt weapon into two sharp ones with jagged spikes from the uneven break protruding from each half.

The monstrous worm had crawled on its belly until more than ten feet of it protruded from its dark warren. Kat suspected there was still more of it in there. Much more.

It lifted its head, mostly closing the tri-form beak, then split its face open again to release another earsplitting squeal and another spray of bilious foam into the air. Most of the fluid splashed down away from Kat, but a few errant drops landed on her arms and neck. Her skin tingled unpleasantly wherever it touched her, and her gorge rose again in her throat. To keep herself from puking, she screamed as loud and as long as she could in response.

The head turned, mandibles mushrooming out again as the

antennae jerked anxiously in Kat's direction. She didn't think it could see her, but she was certain it knew she was there.

Her scream had been its dinner bell.

* * *

Beneath the hatch in the floor of the Welcome Inn's back office, there was no bomb shelter, real or otherwise, but rather a dark shaft with iron steps that faded into shadows before a bottom was visible. For all Turk knew, there was no bottom, or it ended in some kind of trap, or something still worse he couldn't even think of, but he doubted it. Odyssey hadn't carried him up to the dressing room alone, and nobody but him, her, and the girl he'd met in the parking lot had come down that way. There had to be a secondary way down to that tunnel, and this had to be it.

Besides, the only thing he was really worried about running into down there was Todd, and Turk was more than amply prepared to meet that son of a bitch. He just hoped he wasn't too late for whatever the hell the sick bastard had going on down there—like he'd been too late to do anything about Velvet.

Such a sweet, sad girl, he mused as he descended into the shaft. *She didn't deserve this shit. Nobody does.*

It took him two and a half minutes to make his way down to the bottom, and it was only when his feet were flat on the ground that it occurred to him that he should have looked for a flashlight, too. For a moment, Turk considered the wisdom of climbing back up to find one, but he really wasn't sure the girl had that long. He was just going to have to make do.

He paused, holding his breath and listening to the darkness. His own heartbeat was like a drum solo inside his head, overpowering any little sounds that might give him clues about where to go, what to do. His skull began to feel like it was too tight, the muggy underground air too soupy to breathe. Grasping the shotgun with both hands by the forearm and grip, Turk led with the barrel and began to slowly walk forward, away from the ladder.

Turk's left shoulder found a wall when he all but crashed into it, so he kept along that as he went, alternately blinking and opening his eyes as wide as he could. His ears felt like they were plugged, as though he was underwater, because the air was so still and thick, the blackness seemingly swallowing up sound as well as light. An unexpected sensory deprivation tank, except he wasn't alone in it. That girl was down here, somewhere, and besides her, there was Todd. Apart from them, there was no telling who else—

Something cold touched his face, just to the side of his right eye, and pressed hard against the bone. It wasn't the first time somebody had put the muzzle of a handgun against his temple, so Turk knew somebody had gotten the drop on him, and good.

"Okay," he said, lowering the shotgun. "Okay."

"Pass it over," a feminine voice instructed. Turk recognized the voice as belonging to another one of the dancers, Ravyn with a Y, and he did as he was asked. *How many of Todd's fucking girls are in on this?* he quietly wondered. An instant later, the cold steel at his temple was replaced with the sawed-off's barrel against the small of his back. "Take this."

A white light erupted in the darkness and Turk found a plastic flashlight in his hand. He aimed it directly ahead, at wet, seeping rock coated in lichen and small, black, skittering things that sped away from the light. He didn't know what they were, but he suspected they were the friendliest things he was likely to run into down here. But at least he could see where he was going now. Sort of.

"Walk," the dancer said.

Turk said, "I never did like you, Ravyn."

"Don't fucking call me that," she barked. "My name is *Patricia*."

"Fuck you, Ravyn."

"*Walk.*"

He walked.

The passageway was narrow, and it only grew narrower as he slowly made his way forward, careful not to trip or fall. Ravyn prodded him in the back with the shotgun every so often, but it did nothing to increase his pace. Even with the flashlight, visibility was low and he wasn't too interested in breaking an ankle or dropping off a ledge he couldn't see.

It didn't take long before he reached what looked like a dead end, but another jab from the dancer suggested to him there was another way forward, so Turk swept the light around until he saw a steep drop-off to a continued path below, where he thought he detected a faint glow that wasn't emanating from the flashlight. He slid down, nearly losing his balance but still landing on his feet, and Ravyn dropped down gracefully behind him. She always had been a real talent around that pole, nimble like a cat and strong, to boot. Turk wasn't compelled to underestimate her. But he was interested in seeing whether he was right about the light ahead.

A few yards more, and he found that he was. The light grew brighter with each step he took until he found he no longer needed the flashlight. Turk switched it off with his thumb and dumped it in his pants pocket. The path ahead turned sharply left, and as soon as he rounded the bend, he was forced to squeeze his eyes to slits against the harsh glare of the floodlights in front of them. But as soon as he heard the strident, head-splitting squeal from somewhere within that blinding flood of light, his eyes popped wide.

Whatever it was he had just heard, it sure as shit wasn't Todd.

It was Todd, however, who responded to the horrendous shriek with a cry of his own: "Most people end up wasted—ashes, or sealed up in concrete. They give nothing *back*, the selfish cocksuckers. But you—*you!*—get to be part of something special. Something motherfucking *holy.* You get to be part of a *god!*"

"Jesus Christ," Turk muttered under his breath.

"Shut up," Ravyn snapped at him. She jabbed him again with the shotgun barrel. He was confident he'd have a nasty bruise there if he managed to live long enough for it to form. All the same, he went forward, closer to Todd and the retina-scarring floodlights.

"Who's this?" Todd said, turning. Turk's eyes were beginning to adjust to the brightness, and he could mostly make out his boss's pale, grinning face. The man always looked like a scumfuck to Turk, but in that instant he looked like a deeply crazy scumfuck, delighted with his own madness. "Turk? That you, Turk?" The smile melted away into a mock pout. "Oh, what a shame. What a goddamn shame. You turned a blind eye to so much, Turk. Why stop now?"

"Where's the girl?"

For a second, Todd looked puzzled by the question, but then he erupted into laughter. "The *girl?* Which girl? Oh, you think there was only the one?"

Velvet, Turk thought. And God knew who else, how many others. Turk's blood pressure spiked. He sucked in a breath he meant to turn into a screaming demand to know what was going on, interrupted by another, still louder shriek from somewhere below, underneath the three of them. He blinked most of the rest of the light spots from his eyes and, indifferent to Ravyn or Patricia or whatever her name was, he crept forward until he realized he was facing a massive, open hole in the floor of the cavern. The pit was easily big enough to swallow up most, if not all the Welcome Inn, and still have room for a Greyhound bus or two, with enormous floodlights on steel stands glaring down from three quarters of the periphery. Thick, worn cables ran from the lights to the back of the chamber, where they snaked up the wall and out of sight, to whatever power source Todd used to keep them juiced up.

"Velvet?" he bellowed down into the pit. "Velvet! You down there, girl?"

"Hello?" a voice cried back. "Somebody there? Help me! My name is Katherine Garrido and there's a big goddamned wor—"

Turk failed the make out the rest of what Kat said due to his own sudden shout of surprise when the butt of the shotgun slammed into his back, right between his shoulder blades, driving him forward and over the edge, down into the pit below.

13

Almost the instant the butt struck Turk, Ravyn lost her grip on the shotgun, which flew from her hands even as she grasped futilely at the air trying to get it back. The gun hit the ground before Turk did, whereupon it spun on part of a human mandible before sliding off toward the lumbering, stinking leviathan and disappearing somewhere beneath the creature's contracting and expanding setae. Unlike Kat before him, he did not enjoy the relative luxury of landing on one of the soiled mattresses, instead crashing directly into a mound of rib bones and worm shit. It was repulsive, but in all likelihood, it saved him from more serious injury and possibly saved his life. But nobody had the time to think about that sort of thing now; Todd's monster was not only awake, but very much aware of the bounty provided to it in the form of two fresh meals.

"What—the *fuck*—is *that?*" Turk hollered from where he knelt. He had been halfway through heaving himself up when he realized what was gradually moving toward his side of the pit.

"Todd's god," Kat said matter-of-factly, as though it explained everything.

Turk spun to look at her, crouching in an attack position with a makeshift bone-dagger in each hand. "You!"

"Was that gun loaded?"

Nodding, Turk said, "Two shells."

"We need it back."

He looked again at her meager weapons, then back to the approaching nightmare, its mandibles snapping eagerly at the smell and sound of the people on its dinner plate. Even with the sawed-off, he didn't believe for a second it would be a fair fight. With two halves of a broken bone, Turk reckoned neither of them had long left to live. *Six one way, half a dozen the other.*

"Shit," he hissed. "And you wanna know something funny?"

"Funny?" Kat said. "What the hell is funny about any of this?"

Turk grinned sardonically and shrugged his shoulders. "It's my birthday," he said.

And with that, he ran headlong for the worm and the shotgun somewhere underneath it, kicking most of a skull out of the way as he went.

"Skōlex! Minhocão! Olgoi-khorkhoi!" Todd started again.

Kat frowned deeply. "Oh, shut the *fuck* up, Todd." She hurried after Turk. When she got within a couple yards of him, she shouted, "Heads up!"

Turk turned his head in time to see one of the femur-daggers sailing through the air toward him. It landed in the dust at his feet, and he swept it up.

The worm reared its head back again, squealed, and sprayed an arc of yellow bile into the air like the Bellagio fountain in Vegas before slamming back down to the ground with enough weight and force to shake Kat right off her feet. She landed hard on her back and the bone flew from her grasp, disappearing into the upset dust and bone fragments that littered the pit floor. Above her, Todd cackled with glee.

Before her, the leviathan's forked mandibles bloomed like a ship's sails, dripping reeking bilge and curling rapidly toward her. The closer they loomed, the more clearly she made out the hundreds of thousands of finger-sized spines jutting out from the underside of each of the four forks, like a mechanical harvester for tearing and slicing its meal before stuffing it—*her*—into its waiting maw. The foul odor emanating from that orifice made Kat's head spin and blurred her vision as though she was huffing paint fumes, but she shook it off as best she could and dug her heels into the dirt to begin backing away in an awkward crabwalk as quickly as possible. But for every inch she gained, the worm matched her speed. She couldn't outrun it. She couldn't fight it.

It was the end of the road, and Kat knew it.

Just like her sister before her, Kat was about to die.

"Oh, Allie," she cried. "I'm sorry. I'm so fucking sorry. I tried."

She scrambled behind a mound of bones and dirt and shit and hugged her knees, face buried between them, to wait for the end.

When the worm let loose another bone-shaking shriek, Kat knew it was over. But then, after a few seconds came and went, she lifted her head and opened her eyes to find Todd's monstrosity pulling away from her, snapping and squalling not at her, but at Turk.

He had scaled the worm's side to mount its back, where he was strenuously fighting to stay on while digging gashes into the creature's gray flesh. Gouts of pinkish fluid Kat assumed to be blood spouted and spilled from the wounds Turk opened up with the jagged bone she'd given him, splashing all over him and forming puddles in the dust below. He roared like a maniac, screaming through the gruesome bloodletting in a way that sounded awfully close to laughter to Kat's ears. She couldn't tell if the man had lost his mind or if he was having the time of his life, but whatever the case, she was just grateful he'd managed to save her life.

For now.

"*Todd!*" he bellowed, the echo of his voice ricocheting across the pit. "After I finish with your goddamn pet, I'm gonna carve you up next!"

"Are you?" Todd shouted back down, laughing. "That'd be some trick, Turk. That would be some fuckin' trick!"

The worm curled its body so that the massive head was now facing the man attacking it at the middle, and then it lunged. Turk was moments from piercing the creature's hide again when he looked up, saw the mandible stretching open wide. He felt his own mouth spread wide into a broad, toothy grin.

"Abracadabra, motherfucker."

He stood up on the worm's back, bent at the knees, and as soon as the sucking craw was near enough, Turk Tolliver took two long strides and leapt headlong, past the unfurled jaws and directly into the monster's mouth.

Kat jumped to her feet, her skin buzzing with shock. "Turk!" she screamed.

But he was gone.

Beth Harbow checked her makeup in the little mirror she kept on the nightstand for the umpteenth time, then checked the time on the clock radio again. A quarter to nine, and the goddamned john was supposed to be there at eight. It annoyed her, but she didn't really mind all that much; ever since she graduated to appointment only, the schmucks had to pay when they booked her, which meant if they no-showed, Beth still got paid and didn't have to worry about some sweaty fat fuck pinning her to the bed for all of five minutes before he blew his wad or his heart exploded, whichever happened first. And since this sweaty fat fuck in particular, who must have made out at Foxwoods, paid for the full service cruise, she really had no complaints. Still, she hated the tediousness of just sitting around, smoking one cigarette after another, wondering how everything was going down there.

Brewster had agreed to tell the boss everything that went down with Kat, and she figured Turk would be out cold long enough for them to figure out what to do with him. She was involved, but not *involved*, which to her meant there was sufficient thrill to be had from the entire wild operation, so long as she didn't have to do any of the actual killing. Besides, the big guy had always been respectful—even kind—to her, enough so that she almost felt bad when she walloped him in the tunnel. Almost.

Of course, the girl was different from the usual livestock they corralled for Todd's little pet project. She wasn't some chick who fell through the cracks, off the grid and far from anyone troubling themselves too much about whatever happened to her. She was from the world, the real world, out there beyond the limits of the Turnpike and all it entailed. Those kinds of people were missed. Those kinds of people had friends, families, co-workers. Folks to worry about them. Folks who liked to call the cops any chance they got.

Still, Beth could never have guessed a bottom-scraping loser like Velvet—formerly Allie before Todd got a hold of her—could have had anyone like that, too. She knew about the sister, but like just about everybody else who'd ever come through looking for some stage time and a few bucks to keep them in fast food and junk for a few days, Beth never would have bet on anybody much caring anymore if she was even alive or dead. In short, Beth never counted on Kat.

At ten 'til, the phone rang. Beth groaned, expecting the john on the line with a litany of excuses and *can't we still have our date?* She answered on the second ring with, "Listen, dude . . ."

"I think we got a problem," Brewster Ames spat at her from the other end.

"The fuck you mean we got a problem?"

"Turk."

"Oh, shit," Beth said. "*Shit.*"

"And he got Todd's gun."

"The fuckin' *shotgun?*"

"What are we gonna do?"

Beth clamped her jaw and ground her molars. She should have had Brewster do the big bastard. *Made* him do it. Instead, she only made him lug the son of a bitch up the ladder, passing the buck to keep from getting too close to something she couldn't exactly walk away from. A stupid mistake, and one that was coming back to bite her on the ass.

"Is there another gun?" she asked.

"I dunno, maybe in one of his desk drawers but those are locked and I ain't got no key."

"Break them open until you find something. I'm on my way."

Beth slammed the phone down on the receiver and held her breath to stifle a scream. Todd would never have even told her anything about it if she wasn't so adept at everything he liked and a few things he never even imagined he'd like. Now she was a part of it, whether she killed anybody or not, and despite not believing the crazy fucker's religious spin on the whole affair. She was, in a manner of speaking, the right-hand woman to an unhinged would-be cult leader with a giant worm for a god, which wasn't something she thought she'd ever say, but here she was.

The phone rang again the moment she shrugged into her denim jacket, but Beth just let it ring. It was still ringing when she left the room, locked the door, and hustled for the front office to see what could be done about Turk Tolliver before everything blew up in all their faces.

14

With its meal so easily taken, the worm lifted its cumbersome, spiked head higher than ever before, some twenty or more feet off the ground, and shook its massive, segmented body with pleasure as it swallowed Turk whole.

"I know what you're thinkin', darlin'," Todd called down to her in a sing-song voice. "Maybe it's full now? Hate to tell you, but it's *never* full."

As soon as the worm finished its meal, the head slammed back down against the floor of the pit, kicking up choking brown clouds of dust on either side of it. Kat pulled her t-shirt up to cover her nose and mouth, and she sprinted to put more distance between herself and the still-hungry mouth that had just eaten a grown man in front of her. She felt as though she was trying to outrun a sandstorm, which would have been a preferable alternative to her actual predicament. As far as she could tell, she was faster than the worm, which lumbered and slithered at a glacial pace, but Kat knew she couldn't just keep running laps around the pit forever. Eventually, she would run out of steam. And when that happened, it was over.

"Keep running, girl!" Todd screamed with delight. "Keep running!"

She did, the dust beginning to settle all around her and all over her, stinging her eyes and irritating her throat. The stink of the yellow bile the worm spewed everywhere made her stomach roil and every joint in her body was hot with pain. The end was coming even faster than she imagined. Once again, Kat considered simply giving up. After all, wasn't that what Turk had done? And if a guy like that couldn't hack it down there, what chance did a five-foot-five bassist from Naugy have?

As the air cleared, the beast began to move again, its body pulsing as it dragged itself over the dirt and bones and shit. Kat rubbed the dust from her eyes and blinked hazily at the arena around her—and the startling gleam that came and went in half a second, somewhere near to the middle of the worm's undulating trunk.

The shotgun.

The glare of the floodlights hit the short barrel for a fraction of a second, but long enough for Kat to catch it. Now it all but glowed in her eyes, an unavoidable focal point to which she was instantly drawn. Her only chance.

She bolted for the gun, sweeping it up with her left hand as she banged a uey right back where she'd come from, getting a feel for the mysterious object now in her hands. She'd never held a gun before, any kind of gun, and the weight of it imbued her with equal parts power and fear. It wasn't a combination she enjoyed, but none of her day thus far was especially enjoyable, so why start now?

The beast retracted its mandibles and lugged its head to the left until it was facing Kat, who had stopped just a couple of feet away from the wall before turning around. She raised the twin barrels, aiming it more or less directly at the worm's mouth. Its beak snapped closed, then spread open again to permit the mandibles to inflate, while every antenna and spiky protuberance twitched and spasmed, collecting sensory data in order to locate its next meal—Kat.

"Eat this," she said, and her forefinger hooked around the double triggers to squeeze them simultaneously. Both barrels spat fire and the stock punched her shoulder hard, knocking her back against the wall. For an instant that felt like several minutes, her head spun as her ears screamed from the blast, and she dropped to her ass, the sawed-off shotgun falling from her hands to clatter against the ground beside her. She hadn't put it together at the time, but she realized now that by squeezing both triggers, she'd fired both shells, leaving the thing unloaded—and herself unarmed. But that wasn't even the worst of it.

Though she'd aimed as best she could, the recoil was so much more than she'd braced for that the barrel kicked up and to the side, sending most of the scattershot at the worm's trunk rather than at its head. From the distance she'd put between herself and the monster, the spread was significant too, peppering the worm's side rather than creating a focused—and more devastating—hole. Another lesson hard learned, and too late. Had she understood the ins and outs of the weapon at all, she might have avoided such simple errors, but as things stood, she feared all she had accomplished was making the goddamned thing even angrier than it already was.

For the briefest of moments, Kat thought she'd had a shot at getting out of this alive. Now, she was no better off than she'd been before she saw the gun, and arguably worse. Somewhere in the blinding glare of the floodlights above, Todd giggled like the complete maniac he was, though to Kat's ears it might as well have been life itself having its last laugh at her.

Life's last laugh and, in her mind, the final irony. *I should've saved a shot for myself.*

She scooted backward until her spine was flush against the wall, closed her eyes, and started singing; softly at first, but her voice rose as the song bloomed out of her.

"Don't let anyone tell you
When enough gets to be enough
We're more than just their things
We scream into black rings."

Her fingers almost involuntarily found the strings on the bass she wished she was holding, plucking the chords as she did her level best to transport her consciousness elsewhere, anywhere else, for these final moments of her short life. Kat only hoped Allie had been able to do the same.

"There's a bridge in the darkness
There's a raft on your lake of tears
There's a balm for all the stings
We scream into black rings
We SCREEEEEEEAM into BLACK RINGS."

Kat had no idea she had stood up until she opened her eyes again, fully expecting to find herself inside the repellent leviathan's gob, en route to its digestive tract. Instead, she remained against the wall, facing the worm, which whipped its head *away* from her just as it ejected another revolting geyser of stinking bile into the air.

She fell silent, wondering how and why her song repelled the worm. Kat then saw it had nothing at all to do with her singing, but rather the pulsing, hemorrhaging wound around the middle of the creature's long body, where Turk had gone to work digging its flesh open with the split bone fragment. He must have done worse damage than she originally thought, though she couldn't quite suss out why the wounds throbbed and undulated the way they did. At least, she couldn't until something popped through the surface from the inside, something pink and dripping with slime. Something that was beginning to look very much like a human arm to Kat Garrido.

"No fucking way," she said. "*Turk?*"

As soon as Beth hit the ground at the bottom of the ladder, she switched on her flashlight and spun around to find someone standing directly in front of her. She yelped, dropped the flashlight, and scrambled for the switch she always kept in her boot.

"Settle down, dipshit," Ravyn hissed at her. "It's just me."

"The fuck are you doing down here?" Beth hissed back, swiping the light back up into her hand and composing herself.

"Boss needed a hand, and you had a date. Over that quick?"

"Never showed." Beth spoke through gritted teeth, deeply annoyed that Todd would so easily fill her position with someone like *Ravyn.*

The two women had never liked one another, not from the first moment they met, but as soon as Beth began to sense Ravyn was working hard to take her position at the top of the food chain, she'd begun to outright despise the woman. More than once she had fantasized about "accidentally" shoving Ravyn down into the pit, whoopsie daisy, oh well, easy come and easy go. But if there was one thing you didn't fuck around with, it was Todd's god-worm. Nothing and nobody went down there without Todd saying so, and Beth was legitimately afraid that if she did Ravyn that way, she would be next in line. Accordingly, she did her level best to grin and bear it, but inside she seethed at the mere sight of Ravyn.

"Really?" Ravyn said, laughing. "Never had *that* happen. You get dissed like that a lot, or . . . ?"

"Listen, *cunt—*" Beth began, but before she could continue or Ravyn could react, a skull-splitting squall erupted from the other end of the tunnel, causing them both to wince.

"The hell was that?" Ravyn said, still grimacing.

"It was the fuckin' worm, dumbfuck. Come on—hurry!"

Together, the women raced down the tunnel for the pit. By the time they reached it, the worm-god's shriek was replaced by Todd's panicked wail. He was on his knees, right at the edge of the pit, pulling at his own hair with both fists and screaming at the scene below.

"No!" he screeched. "*No!* You fucks! You motherfucks! Who do you think you are? *Who do you think you fucking are?*"

Beth sprinted to the rim of the pit, smelling the foul odor of the creature's ejecta before her eyes could make sense of what she was looking at below. She saw the worm, the bones, and poor, gullible Kat with a shotgun dangling from one hand.

"Where the hell did she get—" Her words got stuck in her throat when next she realized it wasn't the gun Todd was so upset about. It was the man literally tearing his way out from inside the worm-god. It was goddamned Turk Tolliver. "Oh my *God.*"

The minutes Turk spent inside the largest and by far, most disgusting creature he had ever encountered, ranked among the very worst minutes of his entire life, and that counted every minute he'd ever spent in stir and even the year and a half he was married to Big Teresa up in Holyoke. The only reason he'd dived headfirst into the awful thing was to avoid the mandibles or any other part of the mouth liable to snap him in half or reduce him to pulp, and even so, Turk was surprised to find himself still alive and in one piece after being squeezed through the tight, slimy aperture. After that, he could only breathe shallowly and barely move at all, having become Jonah but with no room to maneuver. The digestive sludge that covered him from head to toe was beginning to make his skin burn and he was fighting as hard to avoid vomiting as he was to breathe.

But he still had the femur, the improvised dagger Kat had given him, and he wasted no time going straight to work with it. His right arm was pinned to his side, but he was able to move his wrist, and in so doing, find purchase on the inside of the enormous intestine with the jagged points of the bone. Turk scraped at it until he'd worn it down enough to punch through a layer, widening the space he was in and permitting him to redouble his attack. Before too long, he found he could move his legs, so he curled into a fetal position in order to kick at the torn flesh with his boots while continuing to slash at it anywhere he could. When the worm squealed in agony, a vile and clammy wind poured over Turk, seemingly from all directions, whereupon he lost his battle against the impending upchuck and spilled his lunch right down the front of his shirt. But since he was already sodden with the repulsive mire of the monster's digestive fluids, it really didn't seem to make much of a difference to the situation overall.

Still, he was quickly running out of air, so he quickened the pace and ripped his way through one layer after another until he breached the intestine and reached the outer epidermal cuticle. Even if he didn't make it, Turk was relatively confident the worm wouldn't, either. It would be a Pyrrhic victory, but it was better than total failure. Sometimes a man had to take what he could get.

To his surprise and relief, however, Turk had only to keep at it for another two or three minutes of sustained stabbing, slashing, and digging at the thick epidermal wall before he realized he'd found the injuries he previously inflicted to the outside of the worm. And had he heard gunshots? And *singing*? From there, it was only a matter of punching and tearing his way through to relative freedom. Eventually, he spilled out of the perforated gut of the atrocity that had swallowed him. He collapsed into a reeking, dripping heap on the dirt, spitting and coughing and determined to suck in as much oxygen as his lungs could hold. He was exhausted, disgusted, and in a lot of pain, but he was alive.

"Turk!" Kat called to him.

He blinked the slime from his eyes and squinted at the woman limping up to him. "Oh," he said, "hi, there."

"I thought . . . "

"Me, too."

"It's hurt bad."

"Not bad enough."

"Then let's finish it."

"Yeah," Turk said, heaving himself up to one knee. "Let's."

15

The worm-god squealed and Todd squealed with it, almost feeling his god's pain. He reached behind his back and withdrew the pistol he had stuffed into his waistband, a 9mm semiautomatic he never went anyplace without. Often brandished, rarely fired. Todd raised the gun and took aim first at the girl, then at Turk, who was preparing to rush the worm-god for a fresh attack with the bone he'd used to dig his way out of the beast. Todd squeezed one eye shut, both hands on the grip, and fired—a miss. The second shot he squeezed off struck the worm on the back, changing the timbre of its anguished shrieks.

"Fuck!" he screamed.

The worm retracted its mandibles, slammed its beak closed, and whipped its head around to the right to begin surging back from whence it had come, U-turning toward the warren that served as its lair. The meals it had been offered were no longer worth the trouble, not with a ragged, suppurating hole in its side and now even the one who typically fed it attacking from above. Todd fired a third round, the bullet striking the ground a foot and a half to the left of Turk's left boot. Kat wished for just one more shell so she could return fire, but barring that, she searched for her half of the split femur as Turk fell into a sprint to resume his attack on the creature that had swallowed him whole.

Unable to see where she'd dropped the bone fragment, Kat gave up on it and scanned the nearest mound of bone-filled worm castings for a replacement. To her surprise, she almost immediately found a long, already-broken and jagged bone that served her purpose perfectly. But to her horror, something beneath the mound shifted, gleaming in the bright glare from the floodlights as the shotgun had before—something she instantaneously recognized. It was a silver locket, in the shape of a heart. Kat picked it up, her eyes welling up with hot tears as she opened the tiny latch on the side with her thumbnail to reveal a small, black-and-white photograph of her mother.

It was Allie's locket. It was the final proof that her sister was indeed gone. The final insult from Todd and his goddamned monster from hell.

Kat tightened her grip on the bone in her hand, half-hoping and half-believing it belonged to Allie so that they could hurt that nightmare together. She raised it aloft and screamed until her voice broke. Another bullet from above split the air, striking the wall. Kat ignored it and ran to join Turk, who was already picking up where he had left off, digging at the worm's hide as hard and as fast as he could.

* * *

A strange mixture of dread and arousal filled Ravyn's chest and made her skin tingle. This wasn't exactly the way any of this was supposed to go down, and it was the first she'd ever even heard of Todd's pet getting injured by its own food. As things stood, he was clearly panicked and even Odyssey (*the big bitch*) was starting to look pretty pale. But Ravyn wasn't one to get too wigged out over chaos; in fact, she thrived on it.

She was reminded of the guy from Torrington she used to date, Jake Howell, whose bones she so eagerly jumped a few minutes after she watched him strangle a guy to death over a meth deal that went south. The guy had lain dead on the floor of Jake's trailer, not six feet from the bed where she rode his killer like a government mule, hornier than a rabbit on ecstasy from all the screaming and the violence and the light going out in that poor dumb bastard's eyes. If Todd had so much as made eye contact with her then and there, she wouldn't have been able to control herself. But the boss was much too wrapped up in the plight of his slimy, invertebrate god to acknowledge much of anything else.

Ravyn figured she could get his attention, though. She waltzed right up behind him, wrapped her arm around Todd's waist, and grabbed a handful of his package while she whispered in his ear, "Make 'em die, daddy. Make 'em *die*."

By way of response, the agitated pimp pivoted, seized Ravyn

by the waist, and hurled her over the edge. The dancer screamed, but only for the short period between the start of her descent and the worm launching itself up to catch her in its opening maw. Even then, the creature did not stop, crashing against the wall, continuing its ascent, snaking its way up the rugged, high wall to the top with astonishing speed. Crazed by hunger, rage, and pain, the beast reached the edge in seconds, mandibles flying open and a fresh jet of bile tinged with blood aimed directly at a terrified, retreating Todd.

The muculent jet struck him square in the back and knocked him down on his face, whereupon he skidded and slid in a vain, almost comical attempt to stand back up in all the slime that now surrounded him. Forgoing that, Todd turned onto his ass and tried to crab-walk his way out of the worm-god's range, but it was too late—the mandibles, fully unfurled with every spike, turned in the man's direction and snapped together with a thunderous clap that cut Todd in half just beneath his ribcage. Victorious, the worm lashed its massive tail against the pit wall, caving it in and creating a minor avalanche of rock and dirt and debris from which Kat and Turk had to run to avoid being buried alive.

As the life drained out of Todd Foligno, his greatest love and achievement in life commenced feasting on his severed bottom half and he found himself pondering the end he'd never seen coming and wondered what rewards awaited him after so many years of murderous loyalty to the polychaete deity he'd served. What he got was a smoky sort of darkness that closed in on his vision and his mind until he blinked out of existence, after which there was nothing. Nothing at all.

Diamond heaved a sigh and decided to pour herself a couple of fingers of well bourbon since nobody else was drinking. She threw it back, lit a Newport, and shot a glance at the new girl on the second stage twirling lazily around the pole for an audience of zero to the tune of Night Ranger's "When You Close Your Eyes." The kid had both nipples pierced and a tattoo on her thigh of her boyfriend's name, Zeke, who was doing a nickel at MacDougall-Walker for knocking over a packie with a water pistol he'd painted black. Diamond recalled her real name was Sarah, but she couldn't remember the stage name she'd picked. They all tended to run together in her head, and half the time the girls changed them every other week, anyway. Hell, Diamond herself had been Chardonnay when she first showed up on the 'Pike back in '88. It was a little like starting all over again, even if hardly anybody ever ended up anyplace else.

Of course, it wasn't quite rock bottom, either. As far as Diamond was concerned, there was always someplace even lower than wherever you were, despite how difficult it was to imagine a boss sleazier than Todd Foligno. She was delighted he hadn't bothered to drop by that night, though equally puzzled as to the whereabouts of the doorman, Turk, not to mention Odyssey, who had left the main stage largely unoccupied since she'd vanished at some point earlier on. Ravyn had been milling about around sunset, but even she was nowhere to be seen. It was only Diamond, Sarah, Terry the MC, and a Berlin townie named Joe nodding off at a table between the men's room and the scratched-to-hell pool table nobody ever used. Diamond reckoned she could light Joe's shoes on fire and he wouldn't notice. It was a dull, seemingly endless shift with nothing to do and nobody to talk to.

At least, it was until the entire club seemed to tremble and all the lights flickered for a moment. Diamond nearly lost her balance and held onto the bar to steady herself. Sarah yelped, holding onto the pole in the same way. Joe didn't appear to notice at all.

Sarah said, "The hell was that? An earthquake?"

Diamond laughed. "We don't have earthquakes in Connec—"

The main stage exploded then, every light bulb in its general vicinity shattering at once as the silver pole vaulted through the air like a missile and the floor erupted into a volcano of glass and cement and broken, spewing waterlines. Terry cried, "What the *fuck!*" into the club's speaker system. It was precisely at this moment that the worm's gargantuan head burst through the hole it had made and gnashed its mandibles at the gray water gushing up from the broken main.

"Jesus Christ!" Diamond screamed. "Jesus jumped-up goddamn *Christ!*"

Almost by way of instinct, she seized a bottle of J&B from the shelf behind her by the neck and hurled it at the monster. It shattered against one of the beast's three-mouth parts, but if it noticed Diamond couldn't tell. To her left, Sarah ran shrieking from the second stage, past the bar, and straight out the front door in nothing but her black satin thong and see-through six-inch pumps. To her right, Terry tried to climb over the destroyed DJ booth, but he lost his footing and tumbled head over ass into the gaping hole that used to be the main stage. After that, he was simply gone.

Diamond's mind was threatening to shut down, turn off like a light, or else just break apart like most of Rascal's had done. A part of her longed to just sit down behind the bar and put her head between her knees like she'd always heard they do on airplanes that were crashing. Apart from that, she knew the best possible option would be to get the hell out of there as Sarah had done. But in between those competing noises in her head, what Diamond wanted most was to hurt the thing that had destroyed her club, probably killed the MC, and shouldn't have existed at all. It was disgusting, it was horrifying, and it pissed her off.

She grabbed a damp bar towel monogrammed with the club's name in fading red cursive, soaked it with Wild Turkey 151, joined the bottle and towel to make a Molotov cocktail, and fired it up with the tip of her cigarette.

"Have a drink, you big ugly bitch," she hollered as she hurled the flaming bottle overhand at the worm's wide, cavernous mouth.

The missile bloomed into a colossal ball of fire the moment it struck the inside of the worm's maw, which quickly bloomed into orange and black tendrils that snaked out and around the creature's head as well as straight down its throat, enveloping the monster entirely. Whether or not the brain-shaking noise that came out of the flames was a scream of pain or simply the squeal of the heat melting away flesh and chitin, Diamond couldn't determine, but it was clear that the faster the flaming abomination whipped itself back and forth in a futile effort to escape the conflagration, the more of Rascal's went up, too. The floor was on fire, the walls were on fire, the backstage and even the ceiling were rolling with fire. The bartender reeled with shock and horror, but her survival instinct remained active enough to propel her out of the burning building that mere minutes before had been just another shake joint on the Berlin Turnpike.

Outside, she spied Sarah on the other side of the Rascal's parking lot, where it met with the lot for the Welcome Inn. She stood shivering with only her arms to cover her assets, hugging herself and watching the fire with wide, running eyes. Diamond ran to join her, and they stood together in total silence, watching the club collapse bit by bit as the blaze consumed it. Idly, Diamond wondered if she would be blamed, since she was the one who'd made the Molotov, but considering the rest of the incident's details, she didn't really think it much mattered one way or another. Rascal's was gone. And she was definitely going to stay far, far away from the goddamned 'Pike, no matter where life led her. Maybe even leave Connecticut altogether. She assumed Sarah was thinking much the same, and she was right.

"You know," Diamond said at some length, "I can't remember your stage name, kid."

"I'm Sarah," she said. "Just plain Sarah."

"Don't worry, kid. I've danced in a dozen clubs and bars between here and Bridgeport, and this is the first time I ever saw anything like that."

Diamond gave Sarah a Whalers jersey some dude had left in her backseat and drove her home that morning, and neither of them ever drove or set foot on the Turnpike again.

Kat and Turk pushed out of the front office of the Welcome Inn in time to see Diamond's red tail lights vanish into the distance, heading South. They were so covered in filth and sweat and blood and bile that they looked for all the world like a pair of corpses, freshly risen from their loamy graves, and they felt much the same. It was a difficult and frustrating slog to crawl their way out of the pit, the 90-degree wall face having been transformed into a slope when the worm went after Todd, though they both found stores of energy heretofore unknown to them when the beast dropped, screeching and mysteriously aflame, back down to the depths from the hell it wrought above. Neither of them could imagine exactly what had transpired to result in that ignominious end for the mysterious leviathan, but as soon as they left the motel and caught sight of the burning ruins across the lot, they had a pretty good idea.

The last Kat saw of the creature, it was disappearing into its warren, trailing oily black smoke and pinkish glop from its sundry spouting wounds. She presumed it had gone home to die, or at least deeply and dearly hoped that was the case. As for the pit, much of Rascal's seemed to rain down into it from the opening the worm had made above, all but filling it in with debris as both the club and the cavern underneath it comingled in a smoldering heap. Todd and his monster were done and gone, and along with them the countless murders they committed together in the dark, beneath the world.

Turk extracted himself from the arm Kat had wrapped around him and limped over to the wilting hydrangea bushes to vomit. Kat turned away, afraid she'd soon join him if she looked. Her stomach roiled, but she managed to keep her gorge down.

When he was finished spitting, the former bouncer straightened up, rubbed his sore ribs on the left side, and said, "The girls—Odyssey and Ravyn. Did you see if they . . . ?"

"I don't know," Kat answered honestly. "But if they didn't come up the way we did . . . "

"Yeah," said Turk. "Probably. Good."

"Yeah," Kat agreed tentatively. "Good."

A loud bang echoed out behind them, in the direction of the glowing purple horizon, and they turned in unison to find Brewster Ames, having just slammed the trunk of his shitbox car, hurrying to climb in behind the wheel.

Turk said, "Excuse me a second."

On the short walk from the bushes to Brewster's car, he weighed the pros and cons of outright killing the rotten son of a bitch. Turk had despised the man since the moment he'd met him, had him pegged for the worst kind of male filth and made it his business to warn new dancers at Rascal's to steer clear. Now there was no Rascal's and he knew the fat man was guilty of far worse than he had ever known. An accessory to murder, in legal terms, or in Turk's terms, a guy who had already breathed too much fresh air in his lousy, wasted life.

Ames didn't even notice Turk's approach until the big man was practically on top of him. He flattened himself against the car and put his hands up to protect his face.

"Turk! Look, man—I didn't do this . . . "

Turk didn't say a word. He simply batted both of Brewster's hands away with his left arm and delivered a single, rapid punch to his throat with his right fist. Brewster folded in half before dropping to the oily pavement, clutching at his neck, and gasping for air with wide, red eyes. Turk wasn't certain how hard he'd hit him, nor how badly he was hurt, but he decided he'd done what he came to do and walked away without bothering to see the result. He was pretty damn sick of suffering, anyhow, even in those who most likely deserved it the most.

"What now?" Kat asked him when he returned to her.

"No sense calling nobody," he said. "Ain't anybody would believe any of it."

"Guess not."

"I 'spose you didn't—I mean, your sister. You didn't find her."

"I found enough."

"Oh," Turk said. "I'm real sorry."

"Yeah. Me, too."

They stood side by side for a long while, during which Kat smoked her second-to-last cigarette, and then, finally, her lucky one. Halfway through that, she snorted and said, "Hey, happy birthday."

Turk smiled. "Oh," he said. "Right. Thanks."

Kat knew she'd never tell her mother. She'd never tell anybody because Turk Tolliver was right; they'd never believe her. She would just have to live out the rest of her life knowing what she knew and keeping it hidden, deep inside, like a secret monster in a place only she knew existed at all. Though, unlike Diamond and Sarah—not to mention a number of others—Kat would return to the Turnpike, and to the former site of Rascal's Cabaret in particular, in the months and years to come. She would watch the crew clearing away the debris, and she would witness a few different stages of its regeneration from an empty, overgrown lot, to the wooden frame of a nascent new structure and, ultimately, a dual-purpose check cashing business and convenience store called Lucky's Cash 'N' Snacks. She'd even go inside once, just to stand in a place where Allie once stood, at the sad end of her life, in the moments before Todd and his sycophants dragged her down into the bowels of the earth as sacrifice to the god she helped to kill. She would buy a small coffee and a package of little powdered donuts before leaving and never return again.

The Bloody Merries played a grand total of five more gigs, four in Connecticut and one on Long Island, before splitting up. Kat wept every time she sang "Black Rings." And though she never formed or joined another band thereafter, she still found herself singing her one good song from time to time. She always cried then, too.

Epilogue

The parcel was small, wrapped in plain brown paper and twine, with a small, hand-printed label that originated in the Bayanzurkh district of Ulaanbaatar, Mongolia. The recipient was not entirely sure she could find Mongolia on a map without a few clues first, but that was neither here nor there. The sender, one Arban Gansukh, was no one the recipient knew, no one to whom she had ever spoken or seen. An unknown, faceless resident of a nation about which she knew nothing and cared even less, who found an opportunity to earn a kingly sum by way of a mail order network that stretched across five continents. All Arban Gansukh had to do was to secure a rare and specific object and post it to someplace he had never heard of, some ten thousand kilometers away, to a person he didn't know and would never meet, and he'd be sitting pretty for some time to come.

The object was an egg, approximately the size of a softball, which cost Gansukh 1.7 million tögrög, the vast preponderance of which he'd borrowed at a ludicrous rate of interest from a Russian gangster without so much as batting an eye, because he knew perfectly well he was going to pay it all back and still retain plenty to get himself out of the slum where he lived, maybe even get a secondhand car like his brother's Toyota. All for one opaque casing packed in dry ice and sold officially as a delicacy that would never be eaten by anybody who understood the value, the *power*, of what it really was.

Beth Harbow understood. She paid two grand for the egg— damned near four million tögrög—and if she'd had to, she would have paid double. By the time it arrived on her doorstep, Beth was already completely prepared with an incubator and two bags, one of coconut fibers and the other filled with food scraps consisting mostly of rotting vegetables and fruit. She put down a thick bedding of the coconut fibers inside the incubator, then gently removed the egg casing from the package and laid it on the bedding. Next came the scraps, with which she carefully covered the egg. Once this was done, there was little left to do but keep the substrata moist and wait, though she didn't expect to have to wait for long. Come spring, she would have hatchlings, anywhere from a few to more than a dozen of them, long and thin and translucent, working their way through the food they were given.

Her babies. The new gods. Todd was small-time and he had thought small. He was nothing but a dumb servant to his worm, whereas Beth would be a mother to hers. Her brood. Her impregnable power.

And, once they were old enough, once they were *big* enough, the ritual would begin anew.

Skōlex . . . Minhocão . . . Olgoi-khorkhoi—wake and feast!

The End?

Not if you want to dive into more of the Dark Tide series.

Check out our amazing website and online store
or download our latest catalog here.
https://geni.us/CLPCatalog

Looking for award-winning Dark Fiction?
Download our latest catalog.

Includes our anthologies, novels, novellas, collections,
poetry, non-fiction, and specialty projects.

WHERE STORIES COME ALIVE!

We always have great new projects and content on the website to
dive into, as well as a newsletter, behind the scenes options,
social media platforms, our own dark fiction shared-world series
and our very own webstore. Our webstore even has categories
specifically for KU books, non-fiction, anthologies, and of course
more novels and novellas.

About the Authors

Ryan C. Thomas is an award-winning journalist and editor living in San Diego, California. He is the author of 13 novels (including the cult classic, *The Summer I Died*), numerous novellas and short stories, and can often be found in the bars around Southern California playing rockabilly guitar. When he is not writing or rocking out, he is at home with his wife, son, daughter and menagerie of pets watching really bad B-movies.

Ed Kurtz is the author of *The Rib from Which I Remake the World, Bleed,* and the *Boon* trilogy, among other novels, novellas, and short stories. Ed's work has been honored in *Best American Mystery Stories* and *Best Gay Stories*. He lives in New England.

Cody Goodfellow has written nine novels and five collections of short stories, and was favored with three Wonderland Book Awards. His comics work has been featured in *Mystery Meat, Creepy, Slow Death Zero* and *Skin Crawl*. As an actor, he has appeared in numerous short films, TV shows, music videos by Anthrax and Beck, and a Days Inn commercial. He also wrote, co-produced and scored the Lovecraftian hygiene films *Baby Got Bass* and *Stay At Home Dad*, which can be viewed on YouTube. He lives in San Diego, California.

Anthony Trevino is from San Diego, CA. He's the author of *King Space Void, Hissers 3: Fortress of Flesh* (co-written with Ryan C. Thomas), many short stories, comics, and occasionally dabbles in writing about film. You can find his work in *Hell Fidelity, Tales of Horrorgasm*, and *Walk Hand in Hand Into Extinction*: stories inspired by *True Detective*.

Readers . . .

Thank you for reading *PsychoActive*. We hope you enjoyed this 16th book in our Dark Tide series.

If you have a moment, please review *PsychoActive* at the store where you bought it.

Help other readers by telling them why you enjoyed this book. No need to write an in-depth discussion. Even a single sentence will be greatly appreciated. Reviews go a long way to helping a book sell, and is great for an author's career. It'll also help us to continue publishing quality books.

Thank you again for taking the time to journey with Crystal Lake Publishing.

Visit our Linktree page for a list of our social media platforms. https://linktr.ee/CrystalLakePublishing

Follow us on Amazon:

MISSION STATEMENT:

Since its founding in August 2012, Crystal Lake Publishing has quickly become one of the world's leading publishers of Dark Fiction and Horror books. In 2023, Crystal Lake Publishing formed a part of Crystal Lake Entertainment, joining several other divisions, including Torrid Waters, Crystal Lake Comics, Crystal Lake Kids, and many more.

While we strive to present only the highest quality fiction and entertainment, we also endeavour to support authors along their writing journey. We offer our time and experience in non-fiction projects, as well as author mentoring and services, at competitive prices.

With several Bram Stoker Award wins and many other wins and nominations (including the HWA's Specialty Press Award), Crystal Lake Publishing puts integrity, honor, and respect at the forefront of our publishing operations.

We strive for each book and outreach program we spearhead to not only entertain and touch or comment on issues that affect our readers, but also to strengthen and support the Dark Fiction field and its authors.

Not only do we find and publish authors we believe are destined for greatness, but we strive to work with men and women who endeavour to be decent human beings who care more for others than themselves, while still being hard working, driven, and passionate artists and storytellers.

Crystal Lake Publishing is and will always be a beacon of what passion and dedication, combined with overwhelming teamwork and respect, can accomplish. We endeavour to know each and every one of our readers, while building personal relationships with our authors, reviewers, bloggers, podcasters, bookstores, and libraries.

We will be as trustworthy, forthright, and transparent as any business can be, while also keeping most of the headaches away from our authors, since it's our job to solve the problems so they can stay in a creative mind. Which of course also means paying our authors.

We do not just publish books, we present to you worlds within your world, doors within your mind, from talented authors who sacrifice so much for a moment of your time.

There are some amazing small presses out there, and through collaboration and open forums we will continue to support other presses in the goal of helping authors and showing the world what quality small presses are capable of accomplishing. No one wins when a small press goes down, so we will always be there to support hardworking, legitimate presses and their authors. We don't see Crystal Lake as the best press out there, but we will always strive to be the best, strive to be the most interactive and grateful, and even blessed press around. No matter what happens over time, we will also take our mission very seriously while appreciating where we are and enjoying the journey.

What do we offer our authors that they can't do for themselves through self-publishing?

We are big supporters of self-publishing (especially hybrid publishing), if done with care, patience, and planning. However, not every author has the time or inclination to do market research, advertise, and set up book launch strategies. Although a lot of authors are successful in doing it all, strong small presses will always be there for the authors who just want to do what they do best: write.

What we offer is experience, industry knowledge, contacts and trust built up over years. And due to our strong brand and trusting fanbase, every Crystal Lake Publishing book comes with weight of respect. In time our fans begin to trust our judgment and will try a new author purely based on our support of said author.

With each launch we strive to fine-tune our approach, learn from our mistakes, and increase our reach. We continue to assure our authors that we're here for them and that we'll carry the weight of the launch and dealing with third parties while they focus on their strengths—be it writing, interviews, blogs, signings, etc.

We also offer several mentoring packages to authors that include knowledge and skills they can use in both traditional and self-publishing endeavours.

We look forward to launching many new careers.

This is what we believe in. What we stand for. This will be our legacy.

**Welcome to Crystal Lake Publishing—
Tales from the Darkest Depths.**

9 781964 398082